PROFESSOR *hole*

ANN GRECH

Edited by: Hot Tree Editing
Cover Model: Blaze A
Photographer: Wander Aguiar
Cover design: CT Cover Creations
Paperback ISBN: 978-0-6457813-0-4

Blurb

I play by my rules. My code.

My police handler thinks differently, but little does he know the extent of my hacking skills. I'm a billionaire because of them.

But the case he assigns me tests me in ways I wasn't expecting. The brief was simple—study a university subject on investigative techniques.

Turns out, it's anything but easy.

My professor is an a-hole. I hate him almost on sight. I want to damage his beautiful face, especially because of the lies he's telling about my late mother. My handler believes him, and my oldest friend Flynn is infatuated with him.

I *will* prove my mother's innocence.

I *will* put his accusations to rest once and for all.

But that means working closely with both him and Flynn to prove him wrong.

My professorhole won't know what hit him.

Billionaire Boss Girl is a contemporary why choose/polyamorous series. There is no need for the leading lady (or her men) to choose in order to find their HEA.

Professorhole is book ONE of THREE in this slow-build, high-heat new adult romantic suspense series.

For Dad
We should have had more time with you. But we cherished every moment we had and every memory we made. You'll always be in our hearts.

ACKNOWLEDGEMENTS

These last few months have been some of the hardest that I've been through. But I've learnt so many important lessons, and that's the way Dad would have wanted it. He lived his life to the fullest. He volunteered his time freely for so many good causes and helped his community, friends, and family wherever he could. He would have given you the shirt off his back if you were in need. He loved his family and friends dearly and was blunt to a fault—if he didn't like it, you knew about it! He left behind a gaping void in our world. But it just proves how important he was to all of us. This is the first story I've written without Dad. Even though I didn't tell him about it, I know he knows about it. You were the first man I loved and you were always my superhero. Thank you for looking down on us.

I'm so very grateful for the people in my life who make my stories possible. My family—my gorgeous husband and kids, Mum, my cousin, aunts, my best friend, Robyn (who I count as a sister), Kariss Stone, and Mum's girlfriends—all of you were and still are the rocks that I needed so badly. Words will never be enough.

McKinley Krantz and the team at Hot Tree Editing, thank you for weaving your magic, your encouragement and enthusiasm. I adored working with you and can't wait for the next one!

My beautiful friends who make up the MM DreaMMers authors (Viva Gold, LJ Harris, JJ Harper, Angelique Jurd, Tracy McKay and Megs Pritchard), thank you for always being there. I'm grateful every day for you being in my life.

To Amber, thank you for the work you've done to keep me in line and organized and all the support you give me. I appreciate it, always.

Wander Aguiar, thank you for the gorgeous photographs of your guys. A massive thank you also goes to Clarise Tan from CT Cover Creations. You worked your magic and both the photographic and discreet covers are stunning. Absolutely gorgeous. Your talent is incredible.

Linda Russell from Foreword PR, my friend, you are amazing. I love working with you. Thank you for all the work you've done and always do behind the scenes for every one of my releases. It's truly appreciated.

To my A-Teamers, I love you guys and girls. You're my safe space to fall and you've been there for me every time I hit rock bottom.

Last and most certainly not least, thank you to you, the readers and bloggers, for your unending love and support. Sharing, reviews, general shout outs and, importantly, reading our words means the world to every author. I never dreamed it would be possible to make a career out of my childhood dream, but you've made it a reality. I'll forever be grateful.

Ann xx

Mum, this book is all levels of spicy. For the love of all things holy, please stop reading now!

ONE

Zali

The ocean was crystal clear, shafts of late-spring sunlight filtering through to me even a few metres below the surface. The aquamarine of the water against the sandy bottom morphed into a deeper royal blue as the current carried me over the rocky reef.

The Broadwater was busy, engine noise from the hundreds of boats traversing the waterway a constant hum in my ears against the rush of the outgoing tide. A familiar rumble started overhead, the inboard motors of my yacht—the Noble Steed—turning over as Ryder moved my baby down current from me.

It was a rare day that there were no divers at the rocky reef, leaving me alone in the water. Conditions weren't ideal, despite the pristine clarity of the water and the picture-perfect day. A king tide, care of the full moon the night before, had reached its crescendo half an hour earlier. The outgoing tide was now rushing from the nineteen-kilometre estuary through a two-hundred-and-fifty-metre-wide bottleneck, sucking everything except the strongest of swimmers out with it.

I liked to live on the edge.

Being alone out here, the rush of the water surrounding me as I kicked, descending ever deeper, was my kind of freedom. I rarely got to swim like this so close to the main hub of the Gold Coast. Apparently, there were some rules even I had to follow.

Like not being naked in public.

Clothes were overrated.

But now, blessedly alone, I was free.

I loved the ocean. The serenity of it, despite its constant motion. It was the place where my personalities converged. Where the multiple personas I had to maintain fell away, leaving me at my most honest.

I'd never leave if I had the chance. Just me, my scuba gear, and speargun were the only things I needed. There was a sense of freedom in being surrounded by salt water, a detachment from the real world. Sometimes I needed that. Sometimes I needed to pretend that the pressure and the memories weren't waiting to catch me off-guard and drown me. Sometimes I needed to forget the shitty people I came across online too.

There were very few people who ever got close enough to see any kind of vulnerability from me. I had a reputation to maintain. Professionally, I was known as Queen. To the handful of people who knew me personally, I was Zali. My personas had been an uncomfortable fit for far too many years. As a kid, I'd been sweet and always smiling. My preteen and teenage years were almost the complete opposite. I'd rather forget my past, but it was imprinted on my very soul.

Queen had become my shield, but she'd also trapped me too. I'd become hardened. A loner too, except for the handful of people who wouldn't let me walk away from them.

I was the infamous hacker. A queen by name and status. I was untouchable. Uncatchable. Unstoppable. I'd taken down Australia's largest internet service provider when I was thirteen because they were mean to my dad.

I'd done far worse since.

I could get into anything, do anything with a computer.

Boundaries didn't contain me the way they corralled the rest of the world.

Like the chess piece, I went anywhere I desired. It wasn't that I didn't respect boundaries and security measures others set. They were just meaningless to me. I lived by my own rules, my own moral code. If I wanted something, I took it. Data was the most important currency to me. Knowing how to access it and use it for what I determined was a good cause had served me well thus far. I had no intentions of changing any of that.

Clearing my mind, I concentrated on the task at hand—dinner. Ryder probably already had a feast planned like he always did, but I was in the mood for freshly caught fish.

My legs were burning, already tired from the exertion of swift-water swimming. I inhaled slowly, preserving my short supply of oxygen in my mini scuba tank. I only had a twenty-minute window, but it was all I needed. I swam deeper, the blue landscape enveloping me as I neared the bottom of the plunging hole.

The rocky reef was a shelter from the current, providing cover for the palm-sized baitfish that called it home. They were still prey though, a school of jewfish, each half as long as my arm, darting between the rocks to gorge on them until their bellies were full.

A nylon net was hooked around my wrist—easy enough for me to detach if I had to fight a shark for the fish I was about to catch. In my other hand, I gripped my speargun, aiming it at the largest of the nearby fish.

Depressing the trigger caused an instantaneous chain reaction. The spear launched, whizzing through the depths before piercing the fish straight through its gills. Baitfish scattered, zipping into crevices between rocks while the school shot away from the impaled jew, then regathered outside of my range.

I bagged the fish. It was a good size, plenty big enough for me to eat. But I was in the mood for company tonight. Having a second fish for Ryder would at least encourage him to stay on deck after he'd cooked for me.

My oxygen was getting low, and I was now holding a ticking timebomb. Bull sharks frequented this spot almost as much as divers, and the smell of fish blood in the water would make them curious. A curious, hungry bull shark was a dangerous one.

But I wasn't a quitter.

Reloading my spear as smoothly as possible, I tried to avoid startling the school again. Keeping an eye on my surroundings was easier in the slower currents but more difficult in the lower light.

Two jewfish were edging closer, choosing food over the apparent safety of the seagrass. I aimed, lining up the shot.

Held my breath.

Fired.

The arrow whizzed through the water, fast as a bullet, but unlike with my last shot, the fish were already spooked. They scattered.

But the spear was faster.

Another hit.

It was holding on by the skin of its teeth. The spear was lodged precariously at the point where the fish's body met its tail. Any jerky movements reeling it in, and the delicate membrane would tear. The fish would be lost to the sweeping tide, even in the sheltered waters of the hole.

Scooping it into the bag, I steeled myself to fight through the current to get to the yacht. My body was screaming for rest, my muscles burning and lungs on fire. I was low on oxygen, cutting it far too close.

Rising toward the surface, I kicked in long, even strokes, catching the tide and letting it do most of the work to take me there.

A flicker caught my eye.

I spun.

Searched the waters.

A propellor churned the surface at the edge of my visibility. I tried to block out the distraction.

My heart thudded in my chest, banging around at a frenetic pace.

My breathing shallowed out. My breaths were more gasps than inhales. My pulse skyrocketed.

There. To the left.

A shadow.

Moving silently toward me.

A bull shark.

A big one.

My breath lodged in my throat. Where the fuck was I? I tore my eyes away from the predator. Still at least a metre from the surface. The hull of my Noble Steed was just out of reach. A few metres away.

The shark wanted lunch.

I wasn't about to be it.

A piercing whistle broke through the muted sounds underwater. It was like a jolt of electricity to my system. It broke the stalemate.

I kicked hard, crashing through the surface.

Sunlight assaulted my eyes even through my mask. My arms above my head, I reached for Ry. He stood on the diving platform, waiting for me with a scowl on his face.

Strong hands hauled me out of the water, lifting me like I was weightless. Ry might be pissed, but he deposited me gently on the deck. I didn't look back at the water—it was easier to feign indifference than show any weakness.

I'd learned the hard way never to let my guard down, to never reveal the truth of my feelings. Had I come too close this time? I didn't want to know.

Ry was safe—I could trust him with my life—but it didn't matter. I wouldn't let him see that I was rattled.

To Ryder, I was his unflappable boss. The queen my knight loyally served, catering to almost every one of my whims. I was low maintenance most of the time, but, well... sometimes I wasn't.

He was my navigator, my pilot, and my chef. To me, he was my big brother's best friend, left behind like me when Asher was lost at sea. My mum and Ryder's dad had been the very best of friends. It was never a question that Asher and Ryder would be inseparable from the moment they could crawl until that fateful day.

He and I had gravitated to each other after that, united in our loss. Ry became my shadow, his loyalty never wavering as I made something of myself. A silent sentinel as my wealth grew. I'd isolated myself after Asher died, shutting everyone except for Flynn out.

He'd been my childhood best friend, and we'd never give each other up.

School hadn't been the dream for us that everyone makes it out to be. The only reason I'd survived high school was Mr Vella, my maths teacher. There was no fucking Pink Ladies and "Grease Lightnin'" for me. It had been vicious—mean girls, and boys who wanted one thing only.

They got what they wanted most of the time.

Not because I wanted anything delusional like their love, but to feel something. To wield a power over them with my body. I wanted them brought to their knees because of me, even if it took me being on mine.

I'd tried to conform, to become the good girl the school expected, all the while servicing half the male population of the school. But the whole time I'd tried fitting into someone else's skin, I'd been quietly dying inside. The bullying turned into slut-shaming, and I'd snapped. Queen reared her head and shouted from the rooftops.

Fuck them and their small-minded views.

Fuck their righteousness and their judgement.

The pieces then started falling into place. I didn't need them. I didn't need their toxicity or their jealousy.

I started living as Queen.

Flynn had stood beside me, his chin up, defiantly ignoring the haters. Ryder had flanked my other side, beating to a pulp anyone who side-eyed me.

I'd made my first million while they were still hanging pictures of boy bands on their walls, my first half-billion before I was even an adult.

Mr Vella was the only reason I'd stayed. The only reason I hadn't chucked school. He'd given me the chance to reinvent myself in front of their eyes. He'd demanded that I accept nothing less than their respect.

I added the requirement for awe.

When I'd graduated, I flipped those fuckers the bird before getting into the silver Ferrari I'd bought for Flynn as a graduation present and leaving them in our dust.

Neither of us had ever looked back.

Now I had control. I chose who got near to me. I chose who I spoke to and when. My inner circle were the only people who had free access.

On a planet of eight billion people, I could count on one hand the number of people I trusted. Ry and Flynn had pride of place at the top, second only to Dad.

"Jesus, Zali. Cutting it a bit fine," Ry scolded as I took off my mask, and then he relieved me of it and my speargun before wrapping a thick white towel around my shoulders. He slipped the bag off my wrist while I remained silent, lifting my chin defiantly and narrowing my eyes at him. He liked to act as if he was in charge, but we both knew the truth.

Ryder locked my weapon in the storage cupboard and called, "Flynn, catch," as he tossed the fish to the deck above. His words took me aback. I hadn't even realized we had company. Flicking my gaze to the stern, I spied my runabout moored to the yacht. That little boat was one of my best investments.

With it, I got to see my oldest friend whenever he could make it between his non-stop schedule of classes and two part-time jobs. I was rarely docked at a marina, so Flynn just puttered out to us.

I looked up at his angel-like form leaning against the railing of the deck above us. His mop of blond hair was haloed by the sun while his shirt flapped in the breeze. I smiled my first genuine smile in days. I loved that boy so hard.

I could have done without the company he'd brought though. But at least Ezra, my police handler, was fun to torment. Giving them a two-finger wave, I tugged off my fins and rolled my eyes when Ezra looked away. He cleared his throat and discreetly stepped behind one of the lounge chairs while Flynn reached into the bag he'd caught and fumbled the fish, dropping it on the deck as soon as he'd lifted it out.

"Let's get you dry," Ryder muttered, shaking his head, still unimpressed with my close encounter of the shark kind. He knew I took calculated risks, but every time I did it, he was furious.

He tugged the towel across my naked body, covering me up. It was sweet, in a way, like he actually wanted to protect my virtue. I didn't give a shit about artificial shame-driven concepts like that, but it was cute that he tried.

Ry rubbed my arms in quick, rough strokes with the towel, warming me up as well. Moving his big hands to my back and drying so he could dry me there, he pulled me against his chest, and I relaxed into his hold.

Standing this close, his heat radiated into me. My nipples pebbled at his proximity, gooseflesh prickling my skin. He looked down at me, his hazel eyes flashing with satisfaction when I met his stare. Wearing a smirk and nothing but his usual uniform of boardies, he was beautiful. Taller than me by a full head and a half, he had that broody and handsome vibe down pat. Broad shoulders that tapered to a narrow waist with a perfect six-pack from being active all day, he was utterly lickable. But even though I was easy, our relationship had never taken that turn. He probably thought of me as his little sister—he certainly treated me like one, getting all pissy and admonishing me as you would a child. I rarely let him get away with it, but this time I knew it would frustrate him more if I acted unaffected.

"Get dressed, Zali. We have company," he chided as he gripped my arms and stepped back, holding me away from him.

This time he was pushing his luck.

I smiled sweetly—the same sort of smile a wolf gives to a lamb—and slid the towel off my shoulders. Getting grim satisfaction from the way his jaw ticked despite eying me with cool detachment, I took my time scrunching my waist-length hair dry. Sauntering up the steps, I dragged the towel along the deck in my wake. I greeted my sweet friend with a genuine, bone-crushing hug before turning my attention to Detective Fraser. If Flynn was light and laughter, and Ryder was dark and stormy, Ezra oozed sex. Golden skin and hair the colour of caramel with bedroom eyes in the darkest of browns, Ezra Fraser was gorgeous. Even though he was thirty-seven, he didn't look a day over twenty-five. The man should have been a model, not a detective with the Australian Federal Police.

"Detective, what do I owe the pleasure to today?"

"You're naked," he deadpanned, subtly adjusting himself as he looked up to the sky and clenched his jaw.

I huffed out a laugh. "Yes, I know that."

"Why?" he grated out.

"I always swim naked. The feel of the rushing water against my skin turns me on. So sensual and sexy." I lowered my lashes and tucked my elbows into my sides, pressing my tits together. They were my best assets by far—a perky double D that never failed to draw attention.

"Zali," Ryder snapped, swinging his gaze around to me and narrowing his eyes in a challenge. He snatched the fish from Flynn and stomped forward, heading toward the bow to clean and fillet them. *Damn him.* I sighed, hating that he'd put me in this position. Covering up would look like he was winning, something I wasn't prepared to allow him. Not when I was the boss, and it was my body on display. But up on this deck, the breeze coming off the Pacific was strong enough—and brisk enough—that my nipples were about to snap off. The only compromise I was prepared to make was the micro bikini laid out over the very seat Ezra was hiding behind.

Plucking the tiny black G-string up first, I slowly stepped into it, inching it up my legs and over my hips, letting the elastic waist snap into place when I was finished. The micro triangles of my bikini top didn't come close to covering my tits, but that was how I liked it.

And maybe we'd be able to move on from men acting awkward around a woman secure enough in her body to be unafraid to bare it all.

At least if Detective Fraser got to talking, I'd be able to go bask in the sun and keep building up my tan for summer. It'd be worth temporarily succumbing to societal clothing expectations for that.

"Sexy," Flynn commented as he reclined on the two-seater lounge.

It didn't take long for the detective to eye me over again and move woodenly to the couch, strategically white knuckling a manilla folder in front of his groin. I waited until he was comfortable and had shifted in his seat a few times before I adjusted the tiny triangles, revealing a little more underboob and the edge of my areola.

I slipped onto the couch next to Flynn and stretched my legs over his lap. He leaned over, wrapping me in his slim frame and squeezing tight. "Missed you," he murmured.

"The job I just wrapped up took me longer than expected," I explained with a sigh of contentment. Flynn's touch was gentle yet firm, and he understood my need for human contact—for sensual touch, even though it was entirely platonic. He also knew when I needed alone time to achieve the outcomes I wanted. The compulsion to get to the bottom of every dirty crevice and clean out every skeleton in my target's digital closet was so strong, it was overwhelming sometimes.

"Was it a good outcome?" he hummed against my hair as he glided his hands over my shoulders, massaging my tight muscles.

"Yes. The guy was a dirty fucker. If the prosecutor can secure a conviction, he'll be eating quite a few meals from jail."

"It was worth it, then." He kissed my cheek, brushing my hair off my shoulder. His eyes were the colour of the ocean on a clear day, a bright blue to match his sunny personality.

He was a few months younger than I was—he hadn't yet turned twenty-three—but we may as well have been light years apart. He was innocent, untouched by the grubbiness I associated with. Kind-hearted and loyal to a fault too, the only thing more beautiful than his personality was his angelic face. He had the ideal trio—a perfectly smooth jawline, a straight nose, and pouty lips absolutely made for kissing. Add to that his eyes and hair, and he was prettier than any man had a right to be.

He wasn't oblivious to the attention, but he didn't get a high from it either. I'd also never known him to have a crush on anyone. He was proudly and openly bisexual; he said he enjoyed sex, but he'd never once told me about a hook-up either. The ideal kind of man in my books.

"If you need to talk about what you found, I'm here." I knew what he was implying. I'd found enough kiddy porn online to last a lifetime. But this guy, Denyer, was a white-collar criminal, and although he'd done horrible things to good people, he didn't seem to be that kind of monster.

"He handed out bribes, used secrets to extort people, that sort of thing. There wasn't anything more disturbing than that," I assured him, patting his knee.

Now that I'd wrapped up my search on Denyer, I had some free time. I'd planned on kicking back and enjoying the scenery at my favourite spot to drop anchor. But instead, maybe I could convince Flynn to stay. We could drop Detective Fraser back to where he'd boarded, and I could spend some time cuddled up with my best friend.

Either way, I was ready to get the show on the road. "Detective?" I inquired.

"Right." His voice held a distinct rasp, deeper than normal, and he cleared his throat. "I have an assignment for you."

I absently played with my hair, curling a piece of it around my finger before letting it fall between my breasts. Running my fingertips along the same path, I waited for him to continue, but his words had stalled, his gaze fixated on my pebbled nipples and the goosebumps that had appeared over my body.

My baiting was unintentional, but a perverse part of me loved the detective's discomfort. It was the biggest reaction I'd ever witnessed. Mr Cool, Calm, and Professional had finally revealed a chink in his armour. In all the years we'd known each other—ten to be precise—I'd never seen him do anything more than look away.

I was a kid when the overzealous rookie had come knocking on my father's door, ready to arrest him. My first big, successful hack, and I'd made a beginner mistake, forgetting to hide my tracks well enough that I couldn't be traced. When he realized I was the mastermind, not my father, the officers' tones changed. Instead of charging me, they set about conscripting me, figuring I was young and impressionable enough to convert to the light side.

It left me moonlighting as a good girl, helping out Australia's equivalent to the criminal investigative arm of the FBI. The irony that I was guilty of enough criminal behaviour to put me in the same jails as my targets wasn't lost on me.

"So, this assignment?" I asked, resting my head on Flynn's shoulder.

"Yes." He clasped his hands and looked at my friend.

The hairs on the back of my neck pricked and I knew whatever he said wouldn't be go—

"Flynn has already signed up."

Mother fucker.

"No." I held my hand up in a stopping gesture. Shaking my head, I dropped my feet on the deck and pulled myself out of Flynn's arms. If the detective thought for one second that I wouldn't fling him off my yacht for such a stupid-arse suggestion, he was kidding himself. Maybe he and Jaws could get better acquainted.

"Abso-fuckin'-lutely not. Stop right there," I ordered, my tone leaving no room for dispute. "Flynn doesn't get involved in your investigations. He stays out of whatever you have going on. It's not negotiable."

Flynn's warm hands landed on my hips, pulling me back and onto his lap with a gentle squeeze. The move sent an involuntary shiver of desire through me, but Flynn misread my reaction. He slipped off the pale blue cotton shirt he'd worn unbuttoned over his tee and slid it over my bare shoulders. "It isn't what you think, Zee," he assured me, his voice as calming as the ocean.

"It'd better not be," I warned, my eyes fixed firmly on the detective. "Spit it out, detective, and make it good."

"I want you to enrol in a summer school subject at university. Go to class, learn, do the assessment."

"Why? Who's the target?"

"There is no target in the traditional sense. It's a chance for you to experience university life and study something relevant to our field—investigative techniques. The professor teaching it is an old friend of mine." Ezra held his hands up in supplication and waited for my answer. "That's it."

"Why are you doing it?" I asked Flynn.

"It's an extra credit elective that I can do over summer. I liked the look of it. The assessment is totally practical, hands-on stuff. We work with the professor to design how we present the findings of our research for the podcast."

Ezra licked his lips, hesitated, then spoke again. His voice held a note of pleading in it. "I want you to do this, Zali. It's big."

"If I say no?"

It took him a moment to answer. "I'll be disappointed. But more than that, you'll have cheated yourself out of doing something important."

Low blow, but luckily I decided what was important enough for me to work on it, not him.

"What's the podcast? I'm not being part of some hack job." The detective's responding smile stopped me in my tracks. It had been a while since I'd seen him genuinely happy like this, and it made me pause. If Ezra had oozed sex before, now he was panty melting.

"I can assure you that he's no hack. He's intimately familiar with the criminal justice system and is just as particular as you are about getting his facts straight."

"Fine." I sighed. "Send me the paperwork, and I'll have a look."

"No need," Flynn responded brightly, snatching the manilla folder off the table before us. "I already filled out the application for you. All you have to do is sign it." He handed me a pen and flipped it open to the signing page.

"You knew I'd procrastinate until the cut off date passed, didn't you," I accused him with a grumble.

"I did. Or you'd blame a faulty internet connection." He pointed at the helpful "Sign here" stickers and grinned unashamedly. I loved putting that smile on his face. The way it lit him up from inside was enough for me to give him anything, and he knew it. "We're gonna be study buddies."

"Looks like we are," I groused, signing on the dotted line.

Two

Zali

I pushed through the doors of a room that made me pause. It wasn't the lecture theatre I was expecting. There was no tiered seating, no tiny pivot tables. Instead, there were desks at different heights, some slightly higher than a coffee table and others that chairs would slip straight under. One was even at standing height. A colourful mix of typist chairs, padded cubes, a two-seater couch, and a few floor cushions were arranged around them. Each table had a television-sized screen mounted to the wall nearby, and a projector beamed an image onto the white screen at the front of the room. It looked like it would make for great collaborative work, especially if the screens were interconnected so people could freely share their progress.

Conversation ceased, but I ignored the stares of the dozen other students who'd spun to face me when the doors whooshed closed again. I spotted Flynn at the front of the room, sitting at the table closest to the lectern. I grinned, affection warming me. He was such a teacher's pet; only he'd pick the table that close to where the professor would be.

He flashed me a smile over his shoulder, and I sauntered up the aisle between the tables and slid onto the stool next to his. He greeted, "Way to make an entrance. Going for what? Cute sea captain?"

"You like?" I showed him my sparkly red Louboutin peep toes with a pencil thin heel. They matched my cherry-red '67 fastback perfectly too. My Mustang was just as gorgeous as she was powerful. A little like me. But I drew the line at driving in these shoes. They were too pretty to scuff up the heel.

I'd paired my heels with matching red lipstick, denim cutoffs, and a blue-and-white striped crop top with three-quarter-length sleeves. Cute, sexy and playful.

The doors slid open and closed again, but I didn't bother turning around. "Welcome to Investigative Techniques. I'm Professor Tristan Reid." The man's voice... holy fuck. It was like warm honey. Velvet sliding over silk. Deep and sexy. A shiver lit up my insides. When he turned and faced us, still holding onto his brown leather satchel, I swallowed.

Hard.

His eyes were... wow. The most piercing green I'd ever seen, light enough that they practically glowed under the artificial lighting in the room. Those beautiful eyes were framed by long dark lashes that only seemed to enhance his intensity. Serious, intelligent, and assessing, the professor's gaze travelled over us, acknowledging each student with a pause. Some got a nod, as if he recognized them.

Professor Reid met my stare unflinchingly. I pulled my shoulders back and sat up straighter. Would he drop his gaze to my tits like so many other men did? I'd gone braless today, upping the challenge. Being naked was empowering for me. Those people who suggest pretending everyone else is naked while you're giving a speech? Not me. I imagined myself naked, the object of everyone's desire. I'd let them look, some I'd let touch. Others I'd let take me, spreading my legs or opening my mouth to them, allowing them to fill me in every possible way. I shivered, my nipples peaking as much from the cool wash of the air-conditioning as the desire spiralling through me. Would he focus on my nipples? Would he stare at my legs, imagining how tight my cunt would be around his cock? How wet?

He moved on like it was no hardship, his expression unreadable as he met my best friend's smiling gaze. With a quirk of his lips and a tilt of his chin upward, the gorgeous professor clicked a button on the remote he was holding, and a slide appeared on the screen.

He spoke, and I listened raptly but didn't hear a word he said. I was too focussed on his cheekbones, his skin. It was a glorious olive, hinting at an exotic heritage. His beard was clipped short, styled but not manicured, and his jet-black hair was shiny. Cropped short on the sides and back with a wave in the quiff.

Professor Reid. I rolled his name around on my tongue. It was sexy. *He* was sexy. Older, almost my dad's age, but that just made him hotter.

His voice was like warm honey, silk against naked skin. None of that skin was on display though, and I wanted it to be. His suit pants fitted him like a glove. Muscular thighs shifted with each confident step he took. He commanded the room, his voice, his presence taking over in a way that pulled me into his orbit.

He lifted his arm, pointing out one of the steps on his slide—investigation of the case study—and his charcoal shirt, which looked like it was tailor-made to show off all his best assets, pulled tight around his bicep. With every deep inhale, that fitted shirt highlighted just how fucking sexy his chest was too.

Professor Reid leaned over the other front row desk, switching on the screen, and I about swallowed my tongue. His arse was a work of art. A sculpture that belonged in the Louvre, or naked and sweaty on my bed. His broad shoulders tapered to a narrow waist, and that butt... it was like a perfect meaty bubble. I imagined sinking my teeth into it. Mmm-mmm.

Flynn sighed, the sound more like a whimper. Tearing my eyes away from the appetizing morsel before me, I turned to check him out. He was leaning forward, his lips slightly parted and his heavy-lidded gaze locked on the professor as he strutted back to the podium like he owned the room. I smirked. I finally knew Flynn's type. I had to give him props because he had damn good taste. My mouth watered. Horny looked good on Flynn too. His angelic appearance looked dirtied up, downright lustful.

I rubbed my legs together, needing the pressure against my cunt. My juices slicked up my labia, my clit throbbing as my imagination ran wild. I was soaked and not wearing any panties.

Visions of their hands on me, stripping me naked, bending me over so I could take both the professor and Flynn, slammed into me. Would they be into having an audience, or would they get all possessive and growly, demanding only they see me sans clothing? Would they touch each other? I nearly came on the spot, imagining the professor's big hand splayed on Flynn's back as he bent my best friend over and sank into his tight little hole.

Damn, the combination of the two men was potent. I couldn't help but wonder what they'd be like together.

I wanted to watch.

Then I wanted to get between them and have them do everything and more to me.

"Any questions?" Professor Reid asked, jolting me out of my lascivious thoughts.

"What did he say?" I whispered to Flynn, alarm in my voice. Had I spoken my thoughts out loud?

Flynn furrowed his eyebrows in response, confused. "He asked if anyone had any questions. You okay? You're flushed."

I nodded, licked my lips, and pretended to read the notes he'd typed on his tablet.

When no responses came, Professor Reid turned his lips up in the ghost of a smile. Self-satisfaction looked even better on him than competence did. "Right, let's get into it, then."

He moved to our table and my breath caught. I wanted him to strip me naked—mentally and physically—but inexplicably, I also wanted him to see me as more than a sex object. Would he underestimate me like the others always did? I held my breath, waiting. Watching. Wanting.

The hint of a smirk on his lips was dangerous. Far too tempting for decent company—not that it would ever stop me. He handed out a single page, his eyes flicking down to it. I took the hint and flicked my gaze down. The sheet was blank except for a heading that read Assessment Proposal. He moved on, and it was as if the air had been sucked out of the room. Fuck me. My reaction to the man was visceral.

He continued explaining, "The assessment for this subject is completely hands-on, and it's designed between us in collaboration. You pick how many pieces you do, within reason. You also decide the weighting." He paused, taking us in and giving us the opportunity to ask questions.

"What are the grade cut-offs?" someone piped up from behind me.

"Normal." He delineated the cut-offs and described how the assessment would work. "Jot down some notes, then make two appointments with me, one for your own assessment and another for both you and your partner to talk about the group element. My available times for this week are online, together with my office location."

Flynn nudged me, and I rolled my eyes, aiming a grin at him. As if we weren't going to be working together.

"Right, let's look at our subject. A local businessperson who was the sole director and shareholder of a multi-million-dollar company that collapsed in 2008 during the global financial crisis."

"Why such an old case study?" a man behind me asked.

"Because I believe that there's more to the story than the investigation unearthed. The company was regarded as a victim of the times, and the inquiry was shelved as a result. But I've had my own specialists look at the financial data, and I'm convinced there was more to it."

He put the logo up on the screen.

I knew it. I'd seen it before.

ReimagINC: Redefining the Future of Investments

I closed my eyes, the white text on a cerulean background so familiar that I could pick it out anywhere. I reached for Flynn, threading our fingers together and breathing through the shock. I held onto him for dear life.

"What's wrong?" he whispered.

I couldn't answer. My throat had closed, my voice fleeing. My heart beat harder, the desire to leave, to hide, overwhelming.

He let go and wrapped an arm around my shoulders, pulling me to his side. I sheltered against him, needing his strength.

"Do you need to leave?" His voice rumbled against my temple, its familiar cadence soothing.

I took in a slow breath, trying to ground myself. But my legs were like jelly. My hands shook. I clutched him, gripping his shirt tight. Needing him.

"Zee?"

I shook my head, my eyes burning. Why was this happening?

"ReimagINC was established in early 2007 as a financial investment firm. It was operated for over six months with no licences in place, its director staying under the radar from regulators." He paced, reciting the information from memory.

His words kicked the stuffing out of me. Winded me. My chest was cleaved open.

Memories.

Pain.

Loss.

They hit me all at once, like a giant tsunami. Engulfed me. Lifted all the nice, neat pieces of my life and swept them away, leaving me in the rubble.

I tried to swallow past the lump in my throat. I failed.

I tried to breathe, but my chest was too tight.

The professor pointed at the screen where an image of an egg cracking open was displayed. Fitting. With a few sentences, he'd just done that to my carefully constructed world. Shattered me. Hacked open my chest.

"It began with investments from associated entities—friends and family of the director. Then it expanded operations, seeking direct investment from high-net-worth individuals through word-of-mouth referrals."

He flicked over to the next slide, and I pulled Flynn closer. He rubbed my back, his warm hand the only thing stopping me from crumbling. The wound where my heart once was stole my breath, the pain overwhelming. Why this? Why now? Why at all?

"The company had quite a few early wins, investing in solid growth companies. Investments flourished, and the company got the attention of the financial media." The slide displayed headlines of various shapes and sizes showing just how much media attention it had gained.

"It was billed as 'up and coming' and a 'mover and shaker' in the financial world, its director an 'investment queen.' It was living up to its promise to reimagine investments and capital for everyday Australians. The director promised to redefine the future—hence the corporate slogan—and there was a resulting surge of investment."

I knew those catch phrases; I'd heard them repeated so many times. Excited ramblings with big smiles. Passion. So much passion and determination. A fierce will to make it.

A flicker burned in me, that same determination sparking.

The why didn't matter. Not really. That was the question of someone who wouldn't act. Who was afraid. I was no wallflower. I wouldn't be beaten down. Not before. Not now. Not ever.

I fanned those embers. Let the spark ignite. Felt the fire burn inside me, build me up into a raging inferno.

The professor would get his dues. I'd make sure of it.

Graphs filled the board at the front of the room, lighting up the screens next to us too. I focussed on them. Channelled my cool. Built my walls. Reinforced them with steel.

I let the anger grow. Imagined the scorched earth as I let it all out. As I directed it toward the professor.

"But things were happening behind the scenes as well. The director was facing questions about whether the company was licenced. Within weeks, advertising materials reflected the addition of a licence number in compliance with legislation. Searches revealed that a new licence was granted, the director noting herself as the qualified financial advisor." He spoke as if he didn't believe the information he'd found. His tone warned us to take his words with a grain of salt.

Fuck that. I remembered. I knew the truth.

"What went wrong?" a student asked.

Professor Reid nodded, and I resisted the urge to smack the smarmy smirk from his face. Barely.

That self-satisfied smirk faltered when he cast his gaze over the room and saw the hatred in my eyes. Reading the tension between us, Flynn tightened his embrace. He was no longer rubbing my back in soothing strokes. He'd sensed the shift in me. The shock morphing into blind fury. He clutched me, anchoring me to the seat. He pinned me in place, stopping me from climbing over it and removing the professor limb from limb.

Professor Reid cleared his throat and looked away before boldly meeting my stare once more.

"Good question, because this is where things get complicated." He changed the slide to show a list of organizations with amounts of money next to each one. "This is an overview of the company's investments disclosed—twelve months late, I should add—to the regulator when Reimag-INC first started trading."

I gnashed my teeth, my hands balling into fists as I gripped Flynn's shirt. *Twelve months late, I should add.* As if he was a fucking saint and dotted every i and crossed every t. He hadn't been there. He hadn't seen her. That fire, that passion, the desire to help everyone. She was overwhelmed.

He pressed a button on the remote, and each line was highlighted in one of three colours. A pie chart appeared at the bottom of the screen. He looked so fucking proud of himself, so impressed by his own excellence. Woop-de-fucking-do, he could generate a pie chart in PowerPoint. Cue the screaming crowds and adoring fans. *We must bow down to the professor's talent.* Fucking idiot.

"This reflects the industry each investment operated in. The pie chart shows the percentage of investment in each industry overall."

Another screen with additional colour coding. Oh, fuck me, he'd managed to figure out how to add another colour. The man was a genius. Give him a round of applause ladies and gentlefuckers.

"Six months after it was established, its customer base had doubled. You can see that the industries ReimagINC was investing in were the same, with a similar breakdown across the total portfolio."

A third slide appeared, and a fourth colour was added. Oh, look at that, he deserved a fucking Nobel Prize.

"Six months after that, you can see a fourth investment portfolio was added—the US mortgage market. But by September 2008, Wall Street and much of the rest of the world had abandoned investments into that sector. Yet Reimag-INC persisted. Rosa Weatherall was singing its praises."

Flynn froze. Went rigid.

Hearing her name on his lips… my blood boiled. I would fucking kill this bastard. Rip his throat out with my bare hands. Cut his dick off with a rusty knife and watch him bleed. Watch the life fade out of those green eyes.

No one, and I meant fucking no one, was going to disrespect her.

Over my cold dead body.

I raised my gaze, radiating as much hatred his way as I could. My fists went to the table, readying to push myself up.

Flynn clamped his arms around my waist, locking me to his side.

That fucking professor….

Fantasizing driving the spike of my Louboutin's heel into his eye wasn't an overreaction.

But my blood ran cold.

There on the screen. An image of her.

She was wearing headphones and speaking into what looked like an old-school radio mic. The headline read "Investment queen touts market recovery."

My anger fled. My heart shattered once more, broken and bloody pieces of it falling into the hollow in my chest.

God, she was beautiful. I'd always thought she looked just like Jennifer Garner.

A lump lodged in my throat, my chest squeezing tight again.

My eyes burned, tears springing to them.

I blinked, frantically clearing them. I would not let them see me cry—no one in this room. Not the professor, not the students. I would never show them. Never in a million years would I let this fucking motherfucker see me vulnerable.

An anvil sat heavy in my gut. Queasiness stole over me, bile creeping up my throat.

Queen. I needed Queen. To channel her strength and her sass.

I mentally detached myself. Took a step back. The young girl sitting on the floor by the woman's feet wasn't me. It wasn't my golden hair tied up in cute pigtails. It wasn't me in a pink pair of shorts and a white T-shirt with a rainbow on it.

"I need that photo," I ground out. He couldn't have it. Not that memory. Not any. "I need that photo," I demanded louder this time, pulling out of Flynn's arms and disrupting the professor's flow. He paused, regarding me with a lift of his eyebrow.

Fuck you very much, arsehole. That was my photo, not his. It was my memories, my family.

He nodded. "The slides are available online. You can get a copy of the picture from it. May I continue?"

"No," I spat back, gritting my teeth. I shook my head, my lips turned up in a snarl. I wanted to take him down. I wanted to hurt him and punish him. But first I needed him to say the words. No beating around the bush. No implications. Cold, hard words so I could get the most satisfaction from exacting whatever painful end on him I could. "Rosa Weatherall is the person behind ReimagiINC? You're saying she was responsible for the investments?" They were framed as questions, but I already knew the answers.

"Yes." His single-word reply was like a punch to the gut, but Queen was in charge now, and she wouldn't dare give him the satisfaction of seeing her flinch.

I sat up straighter. Looked directly at him, never shying away. Never hiding for a moment. "You're doing a podcast on her. On Rosa?"

A murmur ran through the room, a soft snicker. I was proving my classmates right—*the dumb blonde can't even keep up in the introductory lesson*—but little did they know that I was more powerful than any person in this room. I could make every one of them beg me for mercy.

The professor was a bold one though. He regarded me, shifting his stance to widen his legs. He was bracing for a fight. But he was running scared too. His arms crossed over his chest was a shield. A defensive stance—a reaction to the wrath I was directing at him.

"Yes," he dragged out, trying to throw out all the big dick energy. I bit back a caustic laugh. "The podcast, Tarnished Crown, is an investigation into Rosa Weatherall's actions as company director and her subsequent disappearance in late 2008."

Her name on his lips again. I snarled, narrowing my eyes at him.

His mouth twitched. He was biting back a laugh. *Stupid emotional little girl.* I could practically hear the words going through his mind like he was beaming them onto a jumbotron. If he wanted to play that way, fine. I cracked my neck, tilting my head from side to side while I buried my fury deeper than the Mariana Trench.

"She died," I stated, my voice cold. Utterly devoid of emotion.

Surprise registered momentarily before he buried it under a mask of professional indifference. "Yes, in a boating accident."

I pressed on, still needing more. I was going to delight in hurting this man. In making him wish he'd never even come across Rosa Weatherall's name. "What do you suspect she was guilty of?"

"At best, gross negligence." Silence greeted us as we went head-to-head. Every other person in the room sensed danger. But he barrelled on, his bravado overruling any sense. I almost felt sorry for him.

I was a wolf. He was the oblivious grandma, opening the door to the harbinger of his death.

"Right." I plastered a saccharine smile on my face while my insides boiled. It was as if my skin was as paper thin as Earth's crust, bubbling pools of super-heated lava flexing the membrane in the moments before it blasted through, turning him to ash and dust. "Thank you. Please, continue."

I waved my hand as if shooing him away. Professor Reid narrowed his eyes, his glare a spark to my tinder dry temper.

"Zee," Flynn cautioned. When I turned to him, ready to flay him for telling me not to disrespect the professor, I only saw concern in his eyes. Worry for me. He cupped my face, brushing his thumb against my cheek, and the move nearly undid me. I slid my fingers through his, gently taking his hand off my face.

Queen's walls slammed into place again, that cold bitch ready to scorch the earth for me.

"Talk to me," he begged.

"I'm gonna fucking kill him," I gritted out, a hatred as pure and evil as the devil himself surging through me with the ferocity of Mt Vesuvius exploding over Pompeii.

THREE

Flynn

A lick of desire coiled low in my belly, jitters travelling through my body and raising gooseflesh. I could blame the air-conditioning, but it was the combination of Zee and the professor that was really doing a number on me. He was... heck, he was dark and mysterious. Sensual. The way he moved, the way he spoke, even the way he thought were all such a turn-on. And those muscles and that serious expression he wore throughout the introductory lecture were sexy as hell.

Combine his dark good looks with Zee's blonde beauty, and sparks erupted. He tried hard not to notice Zee, but I saw him. I saw the bulge in his perfectly tailored pants—one I would absolutely volunteer to get my mouth around. I saw the way his eyes lingered on her, not breaking her stare until I'd been as hard as a fence paling. When he looked at me, it sent a ripple of awareness through me, one I was still feeling the aftereffects of. I saw what she'd done to him. I'd seen his blown pupils and the tight set of his jaw as he fought his body's instinct to prime for sex. He was far better at controlling himself than I was. My dick was standing at attention, begging me for relief within a few minutes of class starting.

But now, I wasn't sure whether to run and hide or stick like glue to Zee's side. Actually, that wasn't true. I would always stick by her, no matter what. It didn't matter that I hated confrontation. She needed me, so I'd be there.

After her outburst, Zee had sat still as a statue for the rest of the session, glaring daggers at Professor Reid. I didn't blame her. I could only imagine how she was feeling after the topic of the podcast was announced. The question I'd been mulling over in my head was whether Ezra knew, and if he'd known, why hadn't he said anything to forewarn her.

Ezra was in deep, deep trouble.

Zee had suffered more loss than anyone our age was supposed to—losing both her mother and brother at once changed her in ways she doesn't even realize. Then the bullying started, and she'd become harder, more cautious about letting people in. She let anyone use and abuse her body, but all the sex in the world hadn't made her feel any better.

On top of all that, she was delving into the online world. Sinking into her online persona. Her computer was a shield. Her weapon was Queen. She interacted with people on her terms, dictated the conversations they had and how they spoke. She never let her guard down.

Part of it was necessary. She couldn't be too careful in her line of work—no one could know anything about her—but it made for a lonely existence.

She was an island personally too. She wouldn't admit it, but she hid away on her multi-million-dollar yacht, only speaking with a very select group of people and meeting even fewer in person. Ezra had been one of those privileged few, but he never gave her much of a choice either. First Ezra made her dad take him out to the yacht, then I was roped into it whenever he needed to talk. I didn't push back much because she'd never asked me to. But going forward, it might be a different story.

I'd be beyond annoyed if her circle got smaller because he'd screwed up.

And if it affected my relationship with Zee, he'd have even bigger problems.

I was one of the few people she let her guard down with completely. I didn't know of a single other person—apart from Ryder and her dad—who'd ever stayed the night on the Noble Steed. But unlike those two, I shared her bed. I got to hold her whenever she was lonely. We'd never done anything more than cuddle—her trust in me was worth more than pushing for any of my fantasies to come true. I'd give the world to kiss her and make love to her. Except our friendship. I would never risk losing her, so my fantasies had remained just that—dreams. Wishes.

Instead, I kept her close. I restricted myself. I forced myself to stay in the friend zone, never touching her the way I wanted to. I'd live with it if it meant keeping her in my life.

She trusted Ryder too, but their relationship was different. Zee always complained that he acted like her big brother, but I saw the truth. She needed him around, and he wanted her as much as I did. Even though Zee and I had one of those touchy-feely friendships, in his mind, I wasn't a threat. He made a good point—if Zee hadn't cottoned on yet that I was in love with her, she probably never would.

Zee hadn't lost it in class, but I could see it coming. She was like a star about to go supernova. She would obliterate everything in her orbit if she did.

But I wasn't worried about being burned.

I'd gladly walk the fires of hell if it meant keeping her safe.

I just didn't know whether I could. She'd directed her rage inward, being consumed by it. I could see the flames burning behind her eyes, the cold desires she needed to ex-cise.

I wanted her to scream and shout, to rage against the unfairness of it all. But this would never be about what I wanted myself.

♟ ♟ ♟

The doors to the building containing Professor Reid's office creaked closed after us and we silently followed the signs along the red-grey-and-white-carpet-lined corridors to his office.

The professor's name was etched onto a stainless steel plate mounted on the door. Zee knocked, never hesitating, and "Enter," sounded from within. I opened the door, holding it for my girl as she strode in, her chin up and her shoulders back. There was no cowering, no timid girl as she owned the room. No, Zee was spoiling for a fight, and she wouldn't back down from it either. I admired her strength and resilience among so many other parts of her.

The door clicked closed after me, the sound carrying like a gunshot in the silence that enveloped us.

Staring at the two most beautiful people I'd ever seen would make me hard again. This was neither the time nor the place. So I blatantly ignored them, taking in my surroundings. The office was bigger than I'd imagined, with a floor-to-ceiling window behind the professor's desk overlooking the grassy quad. A gauzy blind pulled part way down shaded him from the midday sun. On the left in front of his desk was a bench seat against the wall, a square table, and six chairs surrounding it. An armchair was perched in the corner, the professor's satchel and jacket tossed haphazardly on it. On the wall to my right, a whiteboard ran halfway down the length of the office, filled with notes for what looked like a publication schedule. Beyond that, A1 sheets of paper were tacked to the wall with a hand drawn timeline and bubbles of indecipherable scrawl written at different points in time.

The weighted silence was pressing in on me, tension ratcheting up. My gaze finally came to rest on Professor Reid. He sat behind his desk, sexy black-framed glasses perched on his nose. His fingers were steepled in front of his mouth—a mouth that I wanted to taste. He took his glasses off, finally breaking the tension as he stood up and gestured to the table.

"I didn't catch your names in class." He held out his hand to shake, and Zee looked down at it with contempt, her chin rising defiantly once more as she kept up her stare down.

I was a terrible friend, but I couldn't resist the chance to touch him, albeit innocently. My fingers closed around his, and I practically purred. The strength of his warm grip was a dream. My traitorous dick thickened like a cat unfurling and stretching out as it basked in the sunshine.

Squeezing his hand a little, just so I'd know what it was like to have him apply some pressure, I introduced myself. "Flynn Kennedy and Zali Stephens. Thank you for meeting with us."

"You're Ezra's colleagues. Please take a seat." He gestured again, slipping onto the chair closest to him. I accepted his invitation, sitting kitty-corner and strategically placing myself between him and Zee. Separating them was the most nonconfrontational way of ensuring my beautiful but lethal friend didn't beat the gorgeous professor to death with her bare hands.

The ghost of his touch lingered, and when Zee crossed her arms over her chest, pushing up her gorgeous breasts, my self-control crumbled to dust. My mouth went as dry as the Sahara too. There was no way she was wearing a bra, given the way her perky nipples were showing straight through the stretchy material.

So much for not getting hard.

I spun, hooking my hands under her butt and spreading her legs so I could nestle my hips between them, rubbing my shaft against her mound. Propping her up on the table, I laid her back, nudging her top up and feasting on her skin as I uncovered her breasts. Lapping at the tight peaks I'd seen but never had the privilege of touching before, I turned her into a quivering mess. When I finally made my way back down her body, pausing to slip off her tiny shorts and whatever scrap of material she called underwear—if she was wearing any—I licked her, tasting her essence and taking her to heaven. After she came on my tongue, I plunged inside her in one long stroke, working her until she came screaming my name, her core tightening around my length.

Then I did the same to the good professor.

Focus, Flynn. Focus.

Mentally slapping myself upside the head, I pulled my thoughts back on the straight and narrow. My best friend needed me, not my erection.

"Did you have questions about today's session?" Professor Reid prompted, his light green eyes bouncing between us.

"Yes," Zee hissed. "What. The. Fuck?"

I flinched.

"I'm sorry?" he huffed, leaning back in the seat, his elbows resting casually on the arm rests. Only his hiked-up eyebrows gave away his surprise. "I'm going to need you to clarify."

"Who the fuck do you think you are?" she shouted, pointing at him before moving around my seat. Getting up in his personal space, her tightly held control spiralled. Zee's face turned a deep red, her eyes flashing and her body vibrating with anger as she pointed at the timeline. "You think this is funny? That doing a podcast on a dead woman is, what, going to make your career? You think you're some hot shit, chasing ghosts where they don't exist? You're a joke. It's a witch hunt, nothing more. There's nothing to find." Zee gripped the arm rest of his chair and pushed, the castors carrying Professor Reid back a step.

The professor didn't react. In fact, he looked bored. Completely unaffected by her tirade. He tilted his head, regarding Zee.

When he spoke, his words were quiet and precise. He'd carefully picked them. "I beg to differ. Independent evidence backs up my suspicions. If it didn't, I would have abandoned my research, and I certainly wouldn't have run this course." He paused, seemingly waiting to see if Zee would interrupt him. But she remained still, breathing through her nose, her mouth pursed tight and her blue eyes the colour of flint. He added, "I believe she's guilty of gross negligence, but I'm interested in hearing your take on Ms Weatherall."

Zee pointed at him, her jaw tightly clenched as she grated out, "She's. Dead. Let it go."

"Zee," I murmured, looking at her, pleading with her not to go down this path. Threatening the professor couldn't be a good idea.

"No, Flynn. I'm not backing down on this." She shook her head, her eyes hard, but underlying that armour-plated strength, I could see the heartbroken little girl, lost and missing two of the three most important people in her life. The fight seeped from my body. I couldn't dispute why she was doing this, and I wouldn't. Not when it was someone so important to her whose memory was being tarnished. Zee turned to the professor. "I'm warning you now. Let her rest in peace."

"Why does it matter so much to you, Ms Stephens?" he asked, leaning back in his chair further as he threaded his fingers together, resting his hands in his lap as he crossed his ankles. The move was deceptive. It looked like he was relaxing, but I could see that he was trying to put some space between them.

The professor was smart.

He was aware of his body language, but it was as if he was trying to provoke a reaction from Zee. Perhaps he wanted to get her kicked out. Maybe it was a perverse curiosity to see just how far he could push before she snapped. Who knew?

Zee reacted instantaneously. She lifted her hand, fingers outstretched. Holy heck, she was going to slap him.

I jumped up. Put myself between them again. "Zee, we should go."

"Ms Stephens?"

"Shut up, would you," I barked, my raised voice surprising even myself. Turning back to Zee, I gently gripped her hand and brought it to my lips, brushing a kiss over her knuckles. Wrapping my free arm around her waist, I hauled her curvy frame against my own. My voice was barely a whisper when I added, "Let me take you home."

"I am going to fucking kill them both," she gritted out, struggling against me. "Him and Ezra. They're both going down."

"The professor's just doing his job," I soothed in a murmur, rubbing her back. "He doesn't know who she is. Maybe he'll stop if you tell him."

Zee pulled out of my embrace and spun away from me, pacing toward the window. She paused, resting her hands against on the glass.

"Rosa Weatherall was my mother." She balled her fist and slammed it against the glass. The whole window shook, bending and flexing under the blow. "She wasn't incompetent, and she wasn't negligent. There was a reason why she was recommending those investments."

The colour drained from Professor Reid's face, his lips parting as the breath whooshed out of his lungs. "I... I'm so sorry." He shook his head. "I...." He clasped his hands in front of his face again, his pale green eyes troubled. "I can't change the podcast. It's too late. I've spent months researching this, and I can't pick someone else on the fly to do this class on. I've got funders—"

She whirled around, her finger pointed at him and her lips curled back in a feral snarl. She shouted, "I don't care!" She stalked forward again, her eyes narrowed on him. Venomous hatred radiated off her. She added in an eerily calm voice, "All of that is your problem, not mine. But it's a problem that you're going to fix. You're not doing this podcast. You're not publishing anything that will destroy my mother's reputation. Got it?"

He shook his head. His words were quiet but had an underlying core of steel. "I can't. Not in the way you want me to. But give me a second to think." He stood slowly, moving over to the whiteboard. His hands in his pockets were deceptive. He looked relaxed, but I could see the tension coiling his shoulders tight.

"I'll change the content. I've set it up as a deep dive into Ms Weatherall's behaviour with background information—financial data, the reality of the economic troubles, that sort of thing, to fill in the gaps. There is no doubt Ms Weatherall managed to set up her company and get investments without complying with basic legislative requirements. Then the company started floundering after she passed away, and a lot of people lost a lot of money. Yet, the investigation was sloppy. Everything was glossed over, then wrapped up in a neat bow and filed away as bad luck."

"And?" she asked, her tone full of expectation and short on patience.

"I can focus on the shortcomings of the investigation, the way we can do things better in the future. The company failed. Why? It's still going to be an investigation on your mother, Ms Stephens. I still want justice for the people who invested their funds. But perhaps we can achieve a better balance."

"What are you saying?" I asked.

"If Ms Stephens is as good as Ez said she is—"

"I'm better."

His lips tilted up in the barest of smiles at Zee's interruption. The confidence in her tone was unquestionable. She set the bar high and exceeded expectations every time.

"Then find me something to say that your mother made those investments with the benefit of her shareholders in mind. Show me that her boating accident was exactly that—an accident—not her suicide to dodge responsibility for mismanagement of investor funds."

She stood before him, her arms crossed, tapping her foot quietly on the carpet. "What will you do with the evidence I find? Because I will find it. Are you planning on just dismissing it, burying it under the rug, or will you actually present it?"

"I haven't recorded any of the podcast episodes yet, only a few teasers. Teaching this subject is a prelude to recording. The research needs to be solid. Some sensationalism is part of the appeal of the podcast, but I will expose the truth, even if it's not the truth I expected to reveal."

"I'll hold you to that promise of the truth. I'm sure you'll change your mind about the sensationalism soon enough." She stepped forward to stand chest to chest with him. He was a good head taller than Zee, his shoulders twice as wide, but she wasn't intimidated. She didn't back down or even give him a hint of vulnerability. When she spoke again, her voice was low and cold. She was utterly terrifying. "Because know this, if you aren't very careful about what you publish, I'll ruin you personally and professionally. You have no idea who you're dealing with, professor. I *will* break you."

She brushed past him, her shoulder connecting with his chest, and I rushed to the door to hold it open for her.

"Flynn, wait," Professor Reid uttered as Zee stalked out.

"Yes?" I asked with my hand still on the doorknob and facing the door.

"You're right, I didn't know." His voice was sincere. I believed him, but I didn't trust him. Not yet. He had one heck of an incentive to stick to the truth rather than embellishments; Zee would destroy him. But did he realize just how serious she was? And more importantly, what would this podcast cost her?

"Make sure you keep your end of the bargain," I warned. "Zee wasn't kidding. She's dangerous in ways you can't even comprehend."

"She's brilliant. Beautiful too. The perfect kitten." At his words, I turned and narrowed my eyes. The effect was probably lost. No one took me seriously when it came to being threatening. I was the dress-up-as-cupid-for-Halloween kind of guy. I couldn't pull off scary. He stepped forward, closer to me than he was before, and his voice dropped an octave deeper. The professor's gaze dipped down to my lips before meeting my eyes again. "And you're the perfect angel," he breathed, his voice barely a whisper.

I opened my mouth to respond, but no words came.

Clearing his throat, he added, "I'm guessing Ms Stephens doesn't like to be kept waiting." When he reached around me to take the weight of the door from my grip, I inhaled slowly, breathing in his scent. It was complex, something woodsy and spicy, and want curled low in my belly. I shook my head dumbly, incapable of anything else in that moment. I wanted to be loyal to Zee, I wanted to hate him, but good lord, he was potent. It took everything in me not to reach for him, curl my hand around his nape, and crash my lips to his.

FOUR

Ezra

My phone was propped between my shoulder and ear as I spoke to Roe. He was one of my closest friends; a decade of sport, beer and being mutual sounding boards would do that. "Sure," I agreed. "Tonight works. I'll be home by 7:00 p.m, so I can swing by after I get changed."

"Pizza or Chinese?"

"Either. Surprise me. I'll bring the beer." The catch-up to watch the cricket would either be a welcome chance to unwind after a shitty afternoon, or the exhale after spending the day on edge. Whiskey would have been better than beer, but I needed to be able to drive home.

"A'right, mate. See you then," he agreed. We said our goodbyes, and I went back to waiting on tenterhooks.

I'd been on edge all day. It was Tris's first class, and Zali and Flynn would figure out why I was so insistent on them enrolling. It was a good thing that he'd opened the subject to non-university students, or I would have had a harder time nudging them together. A perverse part of me wished

I were a fly on the wall during the class. The rest of me wished I could have protected Zali from ever having to go.

But her participation was necessary. If that podcast ever went to air—and Tris had some seriously monied-up backers pushing for it to be recorded—it would destroy Zali and her dad. But of all the contacts I had at my disposal, there wasn't a single cyber investigator who I could trust with this assignment. None of them were as good as Zali, and this needed to be handled once and for all.

The only way I could protect her was to throw her in the lion's den.

I should have prepared her. I should have given her the brief I'd compiled on her mother years ago. But it was all speculation. There were even fewer facts supporting my theory than there were in Tristan's research. My gut told me there was more to the way she'd died than an accident. It had to have been suicide, but the marine safety officers disagreed, advising the coroner that the fire was likely accidental.

Then there was Tris's research grant application. Funding had been refused, but the project had been picked up by a private investor. I couldn't see who'd signed off on the approval or who'd donated the funding, not by using official channels, and Tris was largely in the dark too. The only contact he'd had was with the investor's attorney who was acting strictly per their principal's instructions. There was no way of accessing who that principal was. That was why I needed Zali involved.

She was only eight at the time of her mother's death. She either didn't remember the bad press and the angry investors demanding their money be refunded, or her parents had shielded her from it well enough that she genuinely didn't know. I'd met her a few years after the accident, and by that stage, she was an adult in a thirteen-year-old's body who had a chip on her shoulder, a talent behind a keyboard that most people would give their left nut for, and a ton of sass.

Bringing all that up now and making her live through it was tough, but it would do more harm than good if I kept shielding her from Tris's research.

Putting her in his class at least meant that I had a fighting chance of Zali proving Tris was barking up the wrong tree.

As much as I wanted to tell her about his research, doing so would have backfired. She would have found a way into the university's system and shut it down, deleting every record of it on her way.

I turned a blind eye to most of her work—most of her targets were international criminals outside my jurisdiction. I chose to ignore the fact that she was well within it.

Zali had an effective, if not wholly legal, way of neutralizing the threat from them. The targets who were Australian or committing crimes in Australia were served to us on a platter. She'd dig up just enough evidence from public sources to allow a judge to issue a warrant. Then she'd tear their digital histories to pieces and find everything. She made cyber investigation look easy and had put away more people than every other investigator combined.

But by giving her the heads-up, I would have caused her to break every privacy and anti-hacking law in the country. She would have launched an attack on an Australian institution and targeted an Australian citizen. Those would have been crimes I couldn't ignore.

It also would have been motivation for Tris. I knew him well enough to know that research disappearing from the university servers would push him to look deeper. A death threat hadn't dissuaded him. If anything, he'd be even more doggedly determined to find the truth. The stubborn man didn't scare easily.

Not even a decade of pushing him away had worked.

The gay bar was small and dark, but the beer was cheap, albeit watered down. Music thundered from the speakers, and the queue at the bar was four people deep. Men from every walk of life and in every state of undress were there, grinding on each other, making out and drinking and laughing. Being with my people was a necessity tonight. I needed to get out of my head.

I had no idea what I was signing up for when I volunteered for the High Tech Crime Centre. I'd thought it was all international identity-theft crime rings and hacking of government servers, and it was, but there was also a much seedier side. A more evil side. The side I'd been exposed to today.

Countless videos of human-trafficking victims—young men, women, and children, skinny and dirty, naked and bruised, some bleeding and all with blank looks on their faces. I wasn't sure if it was the drugs they'd been plied with or a coping mechanism. Detaching themselves from the horrors of their reality to protect themselves didn't seem like a stretch.

The images were burned into my memory. I was desperate for something—anything—to make me forget. It probably wasn't healthy coming to a club, but I needed to be reminded of what a normal twenty-something's life looked like. I needed to lose myself in the pulse of flesh pressed together on the dance floor and the high of an orgasm.

I pushed my way through to the front of the line, flagging down the bartender as soon as he lifted his eyes. "Beer," I shouted, instantly wishing I'd asked for something a hell of a lot stronger, and quite a few more than I'd ordered.

"Make it two, and add four shots of whiskey," the man next to me tagged on in a deep, smoky voice. Awareness pricked over me. A shiver. A certainty.

I tossed a look over my shoulder, feigning casual, but my breath caught.

Hypnotic green eyes stared back at me. They were captivating.

The man was dressed in a tight black tee. A tattoo peeked out from under his sleeve. His dark hair shone in the dim light, and stubble that was only just longer than a five o'clock shadow dotted his jaw. He screamed sex.

"My shout," he murmur-growled, leaning in closer. "You look like you need it."

"Is that your way of telling me I look like shit? Because I gotta say, you're shit outta luck with a pick-up line like that."

He laughed, his grin shameless. It transformed his face into something a whole lot more wicked. If he was sexy before, it was danger he screamed now. "Nah, you look pretty fuckin' edible to me." His smile slipped, and he became more serious, adding, "But you also look like you're carrying the weight of the world on those shoulders."

"Shitty day at work." My eyes slipped closed, but the memories of those videos lit up my mind's eye, and I shook my head to rid them.

He clasped my chin, bringing his lips close to mine. "Good thing I'm here, then."

"Yeah, why's that?" I asked, nudging his nose with mine, getting close enough to breathe in his air.

"Because I can make you forget."

Our drinks were placed on the bar before us, and the sexy man before me handed over a few bills. I picked up two of the shot glasses before I could second-guess myself and downed both, the burn of the liquor leaving a trail of warmth down my throat.

Sexy smirked and threw back a shot. Watching the way his Adam's apple dipped as he swallowed was hotter than hell. I wanted to lick him there.

Fuck it.

"Do that again," I ordered hoarsely, handing him the final shot glass. He repeated the action, and I grasped his hips, pulling them to mine before leaning in and licking a

first come across her trail of destruction online, she'd been angry, trying to control a world that was uncontrollable. Much to my supervisors' dismay, I'd recruited her. I'd tried to channel her talent, pull her onto a road that wasn't as destructive as the one she'd been heading down.

As a teen, she had either been used for her body or targeted for it. She'd grown into a woman who had an even more polarizing effect—people were either envious or they despised her. But I admired her. I'd watched her grow up and mature. I'd watched her become successful and rich in her own right. I'd watched her take on the haters and overcome them. She made no apologies for who she was and what she'd achieved. She knew she was brilliant too, and she apologized even less for that.

She gave as good as she got; her blunt honesty was a trait I'd come to value. She was strong and beautiful and didn't give a fuck what the world around her thought. She did her own thing, never bowing to pressure.

Queen's moral compass might not quite point true north, but I'd always known where I stood and what to expect. Stay on her good side, and she'd move mountains for you. Fuck her over, and she'd bury you.

I'd betrayed her.

I might be a police officer, but I was powerless against her.

"How could you play us both like that?" Flynn asked, his lips turned down and his normally vibrant blue eyes a stormy grey. Disappointing him was like a punch to the gut.

For as long as I'd known Zali, he'd been her sidekick, her dose of happy.

When he was younger, he'd been like a cherub. Blond curls that haloed his face, chubby cheeks even though he was as skinny as a runt, and a smile that always lit up the room. He still had the blond curls, was now more lean than slim, and still wore the smile.

Except right now it was a frown.

I'd done that. I'd hurt him.

I never wanted to do it again.

These two people—my queen and her angel—would be the death of me.

"He's studying my mother, Detective Fraser," Zali spat with venom in her voice and a derisive shake of her head. "Like a bloody lab rat. He's going to pull apart every business decision she made and put her under a microscope. Then he's going to talk shit about her. He'll twist and turn the facts around to suit his agenda." Her hand curled into a fist, and she thumped my chest hard. Her blow was nothing compared to the crack in my heart from knowing how much she was hurting.

Zali was like a cornered animal about to attack. Her hands shook and her eyes flashed, a mix of anger and fear invading her expression. "We all know how these things go, detective. He admitted that sensationalism is part of the appeal. And what, you thought I'd help him? You thought I'd break my father's heart like that? You thought I'd dishonour my mother's and brother's memories? For what? What do you get out of it?"

"Nothing," I mumbled. "I don't get anything. I wasn't trying to hurt you, Zali."

"Well, you did," she shouted, that fine thread of control she was holding onto with an iron fist finally snapping. Her face reddened, and she shoved me again, pressing me against the wall once more. "I had to sit through a lecture while Professor Arsehole there accused my mother of being a con artist. He said she stole nearly a hundred million dollars. He painted the picture of families losing everything just because they trusted her. He called her a thief, for fuck's sake." She threw her hands up in the air before spearing her fingers into her hair and gripping it hard. Zali tugged at the long tresses, letting out a growl and spinning away from me, kicking at the closest seat.

"Prove him wrong, Zali," I murmured. Gripping her arms gently from behind, I squeezed them encouragingly. "Pull apart every one of his arguments. Find the evidence to prove that she didn't do what he said. Learn about what your mum did, about the company she ran. None of us are perfect, and the GFC turned amazing companies into steaming piles of dogshit. She made mistakes just like all of us did and still do. Get to know your mum, Zali. Prove him wrong."

"She's innocent until proven guilty," Flynn encouraged, coming to stand in front of her. He stepped in close, resting his hands on her hips and pressing their foreheads together. "Do what Ezra is saying—prove to Professor Reid that he's wrong."

I rubbed her arms as she gripped Flynn's shirt and held him to her. The moment was intimate, one I knew I'd replay over and over with every possible ending. I ached to watch Flynn kiss her, to see his tongue slide into her mouth. I wanted to watch as he pulled down her top, baring her beautiful breasts, and licked them, sucking on her nipples until they were just like I remembered from her yacht. Then I wanted to watch him make love to her. I wanted to watch her come apart in his arms, to let him care for her in the way I knew he wanted to.

Then I wanted to do it. I'd fantasized about sliding into Zali, feeling the tight clench of her pussy around my cock. I'd show her just how amazing she was, just how much I adored her. But even if our relationship wasn't complicated enough, it was made harder by my attraction to Flynn. They were like chalk and cheese, personality-wise, but they fit to-gether perfectly, and I was as gone for him as I was for her. Yes, my queen and her angel would almost certainly be the death of me.

But it would never happen. I was the last person who could get involved with Zali or Flynn, never mind both of them. There were more complications there than in plan-ning a mission to Mars. I had to think with my head, not my dick, and especially not my heart. Zali needed to be my fo-cus, and she needed me to fix this hurt I'd caused. The only way I could even begin to do that was by being honest with her.

"If there were another way of doing this, I would have taken it. I never wanted you in this position, Zali." I closed my eyes, unable to meet Flynn's accusing stare. While shame over my actions and my desires attacked me like piranhas on a carcass I had to explain why I'd done it, why I'd thrown her in the deep end. "But you're the best at what you do, and your mother's legacy is too important to trust to anyone else. I should have told you what Tris was doing, but I didn't want you hacking into the university servers. I was trying to protect you. But I know I hurt you. For that, I'll always be sorry."

I slid my hands down, curling them over hers and the handfuls of Flynn's shirt she was still clutching. The move brought me closer to her, the warmth from her body radiating against my own. I wanted to hold her tight, to let her know I was there for her, that I wanted her. Instead, I tried to act with a modicum of professionalism. "Find the evidence to prove Tris wrong. If anyone can do it, it's you."

"We'll get it, Zee. We'll shut it down."

"Don't let Tris give your mum a trial by media. Search the evidence. Find the information to prove him wrong. Take the wind out of his sails and disprove every piece of content for his podcast," I encouraged, hoping to whatever god was listening that she could do it.

"What if he's right?" Zali asked, dread lacing her voice. It was my greatest fear too. Her father had worshipped his wife. He still loved her as much today as he did when they were married. It would break his heart, but he'd survive. I was more worried about Zali.

"He's not," Flynn responded, his voice firm. "It's up to us to prove our professorhole wrong, and we *will* do it."

FIVE

Tristan

'd turned back into a fucking teenager in the space of mere days. There I was, happily going about my business, when I'd been sideswiped by the duo who'd signed up for my class.

I had one rule—no sex on my desk. I'd broken it twice after our meeting, taking my cock in hand and coming all over myself in the space of thirty seconds after they'd walked out the door. I hadn't even locked it that first time—anyone could have walked in on me. Not that it was likely given how quick I'd finished myself off. I was back at it again a couple of hours later when I couldn't get either Zali or Flynn out of my head. The fantasy of seeing her legs spread wide and Flynn licking her until she was screaming while I plunged my dick into his arse was as tempting as the one where I was sinking into her pussy while she sucked Flynn dry.

Or was the one where I was buried in her arse while Flynn fucked her pussy the best?

I couldn't decide. My imagination was running wild, and my cock was rubbed raw, but I was still perpetually at half-mast.

The whole situation was a fucking disaster waiting to happen. I couldn't sleep with one of my students. I'd lose my job. My entire career would be over in a heartbeat because no matter how good my research was and how many successes I'd had, it was still a battle getting a foot in the door with my criminal record. Adding a fundamental breach of ethics to the list of my indiscretions would make me unemployable. Multiply that by two students, and it was a hole even I couldn't dig myself out of.

But my dick didn't seem to get the message.

Flicking my gaze to the clock on my computer, I groaned, palming my hardening cock once more. Flynn and Zali were due in my office in less than ten minutes, together with two other students. I couldn't sit there hard as nails for the duration of this meeting. Unzipping my pants, I slid my hand down, shuddering at the touch against my sensitive skin. As tempted as I was to bring myself to a hard and fast orgasm, I couldn't. My office would smell of sex, and I wasn't prepared to deal with questions if they arose. Brushing my forefinger over my slit, I spread the bead of precum pooling there and gave myself a hard stroke. Fuck, it wouldn't take much. I clamped my fingers around the base of my dick and squeezed hard, pulling my balls away from my body with my free hand. Fuck, I wanted a plug in my arse and a tight hole to bury myself in. My hips thrust forward, my body overriding my mind's feeble attempt at stopping the freight train that was already out of control.

Fuck it.

I shoved my pants down my hips, the warm leather of my chair hitting my arse as I sat back down. Licking my fingers, I spread my cheeks and pushed in, groaning at the burn of my hole stretching around two of my digits. With my other hand, I worked my cock, rough strokes up and down until I was ready to explode.

Shoving my fingers deeper and finding that spongey pad that was guaranteed to make me erupt, I pressed down. Gasped. *Oh fuck. Yes, right there.* Another stroke.

A knock.

Seeing stars, I groaned long and low, my orgasm rushing at me. I was nearly there. Nearly at the precipice. One more stroke, and I'd be coming.

I needed it.

A knock and "Professor, are you okay?" in that sexy voice of Flynn's. I'd know it anywhere. It had haunted my dreams as well as my waking moments. Zali's voice too, that raspy, seductive tone reminding me of sex and trouble.

My eyes popped open. I looked down. My legs were spread, my slacks around my ankles and my fingers buried in my hole, my other hand strangling my dick. Never mind losing my job—this could involve me facing criminal charges if they'd walked in. Fuck me, I needed to get my head read. What was I doing?

"Ah, yes," I mumbled, panic infusing my tone. I cleared my throat. "Give me a second." Pulling my hands free, I cleaned up as best I could, fixed my clothes, and squeezed my shaft hard, willing it down.

It didn't work.

I opened the door, still having the erection from hell, gesturing for the students to enter and praying they didn't notice. "Apologies, come in."

"Are you okay?" Flynn asked, concern drawing his brows together. My breath caught. He was beautiful.

"Yes, ah, lower back issue. I was stretching." Zali rolled her eyes, looking wholly unimpressed, and I swallowed hard. Damn, she was gorgeous. "Please take a seat. I'll just go wash my hands and join you in a minute."

Walking out of there without my erection saluting every passerby was a challenge, but I managed it.

Barely.

Fuck, I was in for a world of trouble if I didn't get a grip, and quick. After washing my hands and splashing water on my face, I stared at my reflection in the mirror. Disgusted with myself, I shook my head and huffed out a sigh. It was time to face my students.

Nudging the door closed with my foot, I nodded hellos at the two other students joining us—Samantha and James. "Thank you for coming. You all know each other, yes?" At their nods, I clapped my hands and added, "Right, let's get started. I'm sure everyone's busy."

I snagged the envelopes of USB sticks off my desk and distributed a stick to each of them before sitting down opposite Zali and Flynn. "Each of the drives I'm giving you is labelled. One is a record of my research, together with a few papers some colleagues of mine have written on the GFC. None of you would likely remember it, but the financial landscape at that time was changing quickly. There was a lot of uncertainty."

"You said it was pretty bad, and Mum and Dad said they lost a bit of their retirement savings," James interrupted. "But was it really that much of a disaster?"

I nodded, trying to figure out a way to explain what went down to someone who clearly had no background knowledge of it and would have been too young to remember. Scrubbing my hand down my face, I groaned. Fuck, I was getting old, and teaching never failed to remind me of just how far away from college age I was getting.

"Australia was spared from the worst of the global impact due of two reasons." I counted them off on my fingers. "First, our banking sector is highly regulated by reasonably good laws. Unlike in other countries, we didn't have any banks becoming insolvent. But there were a lot of non-bank lenders who went under, as well as a lot of investment firms. If your parents only lost part of their retirement savings, that's good. Others weren't so lucky."

Counting out the second reason on my finger, I added, "The other reason Australia kept its head above water was the mining industry. We had a booming resources sector while the rest of the economy was stalled. It allowed for a shift in the workforce from construction and other industries into mining, keeping a lot of people employed."

James nodded, and Samantha turned the USB stick over in her hand before smiling sweetly at me.

"Samantha and James, you wanted to look at how the GFC impacted the economy. Start with that information, and expand your research out from there."

I handed another USB out. "This one is a complete copy of ReimagINC's financial records. You can plot the growth of deposits being made into the company and the turnover of those deposits when investors wanted to withdraw them. In the early days, most of the requests were complied with soon after receipt. You can also see where the company invested its clients' funds."

Pointing to the stick that Zali had left sitting on the table, I added, "You can verify all the data I spoke about in the lecture from this stick. Ms Weatherall was known as the investment queen for a reason. The company was going well enough for its first six months that it failed to raise a single red flag. It's why ReimagINC was able to operate with no licences in place for so long. I want to do a breakdown of these figures. I want names of every investor, how much they put, in and what, if anything, was paid back to them. I also want the same information compiled for the investments made."

"This is bullshit," Zali grated out, her eyes flashing. "You want us to prepare lists of data that you've already put together? So you can build a few pie charts and spend thirty seconds speaking on it—"

"Ah," Samantha interrupted, looking uncomfortably back and forth between Zali and me.

"Samantha, why don't you and James get started, and you can check in with me in a couple of days." My dismissal was blatant, but they didn't need to be a part of this conversation.

The soft click of the door after the whirlwind of activity as they packed up seemed to prompt Zali into action. She rose gracefully from her chair and stalked around the table. I couldn't resist letting my gaze sweep down her body, lingering on each part of her as she came to stand beside me. She was wearing a top that was barely more than a scrap of frilly yellow material wrapped under her arms. Loose at the bottom, it barely covered those generous breasts of hers. Her black leather miniskirt wasn't any better. She had no room to bend over before her pert little butt would be showing. The desire to push her onto the table, spread her legs, and lift that tiny top to see what she had on underneath was far too tempting. Compound that with the black heels that added half a head to her height, and my dick was back to heat-seeking-missile status.

"You took the first opportunity you got to fuck with our agreement."

"Tell me what you want to do, then," I challenged, pushing my chair out and resting my hands in my lap. I didn't give a fuck that the move was framing my hard cock. I had a feeling that Zali used sex as a weapon—certainly she used her body was one—and I was like any other horny-as-fuck man. I had no shame in letting her know she affected me, despite the fine line I was walking between proprietary and getting myself off.

She crossed her arms under her breasts, pushing them together. My dick twitched, my balls drawing up closer to my body. Fuck me, I was ready to combust, and being interrupted earlier was coming back to haunt me.

"Drop the podcast."

I stood, crowding her against the table and getting way up in her personal space. "I told you I can't do that."

Flynn was next to me in a split second, his hand snaking out and pressing firmly against my chest, halting my movement forward.

Zali lifted her chin defiantly, pushing her breasts against my chest and trapping Flynn's hand between us. "I'll do your shitty review, and then I'll find the truth."

Damn right she would. I'd make sure of it.

I wanted Zali on my team. But she was so much like me, so stubborn and determined to do things her way. If I gave an inch, she'd take a mile, and demanding that the podcast be dropped would only be the start of it. But persuading her to stick it out could be fun.

And I was definitely up for the challenge.

I pressed my body against hers so she was leaning back, her spine arched. Flynn moved his hand, his fingertips brushing the tight bud of my nipple, and I bit back a groan at the shot of sensation that zapped through me like lightning. My voice was a rough rasp, filled with desire and anger at the way this woman pushed my buttons.

"What truth is that?" I goaded. "Is that like the man—a friend of your mother's—who invested his family's life savings? She promised him that his funds were safe, that they were as good as cash. Completely liquid. He could retrieve them at any time. Hmm?"

I didn't let her answer before I continued. She needed to know the truth. Her mother wasn't an investment prodigy like she held herself out to be. At best, she was incompetent. Negligent. "Dear old Mum's friend lost everything. Is that the truth you'll find? What about the truth that he couldn't face his family anymore? He committed suicide, Zali. That family wakes up every day without their husband and father because of your mother. Is it that truth?"

"Fuck you," she spat, her knee pressing between my legs as she tried to take out my nuts.

Flynn twisted, quickly shifting to stand behind me. He hauled me against him, pulling me off balance for a moment. One step back into his embrace, and it pulled me out of reach of her knee. My brain scrambled, every cell evaporating on a puff of sex-scented air. I bit back a groan. Talk about a fucking fantasy come to life.

"That's enough," he ground out, gripping me harder, his bulge nestling between my cheeks. "Who the hell do you think you are?"

I ignored Flynn's question and stepped forward, hooking a hand under Zali's knee and hitching it over my hip. The heat emanating from her core was like a siren's call, and I reacted on instinct, closing my other hand around the beautiful woman's throat. I didn't squeeze, and it wasn't hard enough to hurt, but it was firm enough to remind her of the pecking order in this office.

She was my student.

My kitten.

I was her professor.

I was the one who decided how this assignment would be done, not her.

She fought in my hold, gripping my shirt at my waist with both hands and pressing her gorgeous tits into my chest, yet she pulled her face away. It was as if her mind and body were at war. Her eyes flashed, her lips a thin line as she pressed them together, but her body undulated against mine, rubbing herself like a cat on me. Her nipples were pebbled under the soft-as-silk excuse for a top, and I was sure there would be a wet patch on the front of my suit pants when we finished this little discussion.

My dick bucked as I thought about delving inside her. I wanted deep in her with a desperation that bordered on obsession.

Zali's breathy moan snapped the last thread of my control. I ground my hard dick against her pussy, a possessive growl bubbling up my throat. When Flynn did the same to me, one hand gripping my hip hard enough to bruise and the other still firmly wrapped around my chest, thrusting his hips and grinding the bulge in his sexy white pants against my arse, I couldn't help the clench of my hole. Fuck, I wanted them both.

Zali twisted again, trying to pull free while also tugging me closer. Her eyes narrowed and lips twisted into a sneer. I wanted to wipe the attitude from her face.

I was way beyond any form of reasonable decision-making, so far beyond behaving appropriately, it wasn't funny, but I wouldn't take what I really wanted. Not yet anyway. "Angel," I rasped, "Kiss our kitten."

Six

Zali

I wanted to kill him. No, I wanted to hate fuck him, then kill him. Angel? I was no fucking angel. But Flynn's sharp intake of breath had me pausing, and I knew. I just knew.

Professorhole wasn't talking to me.

Flynn zeroed in on my lips. He bit down on his, teeth scraping over the plump flesh. It was a shock to my system. Desire flooded me once again. But this time it was for Flynn.

The professor was talking to Flynn, telling him to kiss me.

A shiver ripped through me. I wanted it. I wanted him.

He was my best friend, the boy who needed as much of an escape from his shitty childhood as I'd needed from my shitty teenage years.

He'd grown up the odd kid out, the baby of a dirt-stained gaggle of kids who was terrified of the rats that called their squalid hoarder dump of a house home. I was the girl who had everything and lost nearly all of it. The one who was so destroyed by grief that she did ever more daring things just to feel something. Whether it was letting men use me like my cunt was a revolving door or hacking into whatever top secret records I could get my hands on, I didn't care.

But Flynn never judged me, never criticized me for the way I lived. He never called me names or treated me like I was an object like so many others did. His eyes on me felt good, but he'd never once taken advantage. In my darkest days, I wouldn't have hesitated to spread my legs for him, but he'd always been kind. Respectful. That meant more than anything to me.

He was gorgeous too, beautiful. The light to my dark, the soothing balm to my raging inferno.

I couldn't live without him.

I loved him. I always would. He was my best friend.

I'd never crossed that line before, and now I didn't know whether I should.

But I needed it too. I rubbed my clit against the professor's body, trying to get off, despite the hatred thrumming through me. Logic told me I wasn't quite right in the head for wanting it. For needing the professor's cock like it was a life preserver and I was drowning in shark-infested waters. I knew it was wrong. Even though it had been a long time since I'd craved dick like this, I knew what society would label me as. I just couldn't muster up the fucks to give. Other people's rules could take a flying leap off the nearest cliff for all I cared.

But I didn't want to hurt Flynn. I let go of the professor, tapped the hand holding my leg, and he stepped back, moving out of my peripheral vision.

"Zee," Flynn whispered. I saw it in his eyes. I finally understood the way he looked at me. It was love. It was adoration. It was home. We were each other's safe harbour. But instead of my breakwaters holding steady, keeping the calm inside, a crack appeared in mine. My walls were crumbling, giving Flynn this part of me I'd never given him before.

I reached for him, lifting my hands to his face. Brushing my thumbs over his smooth cheeks, I finally saw the man he'd become standing before me. "Hi," I whispered, revelling in the strength he exuded. He reminded me of a gymnast. Compact muscles, lean and firm everywhere. His warmth seeped into me, lighting up the darkest of corners of my cobweb-filled, cracked heart. When he wrapped his arm around my waist and pulled me closer, his other hand cupping my cheek gently, I sighed.

"You finally understand, don't you?" he asked. When I nodded, he smiled one of those joyful light-up-the-room smiles that radiated outward from his very soul. "And you aren't running?"

"I'll never run from you, Flynn. I… I can't—"

"Shh," he whispered, his lips hovering only a hair's breadth away from mine as he nudged my nose with his. "Do you want me?"

"Hell, yes," I huffed with a smile. "I really do."

"Stay," Flynn demanded, breaking the trance he'd lulled me into. I'd forgotten about the professor even being there, forgotten where we were standing and what we'd been doing only a moment earlier. I ground my teeth together, a sudden flare of anger sparking in me. But that rage immediately morphed into heat. It pooled in my cunt, leaking down and wetting my thighs until they were slippery. "Lock the door," Flynn growled like a man on a mission.

I turned to the professor then and shivered. He screamed sex. Dark, dirty, hard fucking. His eyes were like molten emeralds, intense and hypnotic. His hand flexed, white knuckling the doorknob. His jaw tensed as he ground his teeth together. I broke his stare, my eyes wandering down his body. He was big all over, but the bulge in his pants that he was gripping with his free hand was one I wanted my mouth around. Or my cunt. My arse. Whatever, I didn't care as long as he made me come long and loud.

My clit pulsed and my cunt clenched tight. Fuck me, I was going to have sex with both Flynn and the professor in his office. I whimpered, needing them, wanting them.

"Your kitten needs you, angel," Professor Reid rasped.

"So clear the table for me," Flynn challenged, lifting his chin defiantly. I saw the quirk of the professor's lips, a smirk like he'd seen the move before. He had. It was one I'd practically patented for use on him.

Flynn gripped my chin gently but surely, staring into my eyes as he spoke. "We're gonna take her apart." A gush of wetness soaked my cunt again as it practically rolled out the welcome mat and begged to be stuffed full.

The flick of the lock was loud in the quiet of the office. The only other noise was my laboured breathing. Needing them, wanting them, desperation crawled over my skin.

Breaking Flynn's fierce stare, I watched as Professor Reid stalked to the table like a predator, swiping the contents off in one fluid stroke of his arm. Why was the bastard so hot?

"I'm still waiting for you to kiss her, angel," he challenged.

Flynn moaned, a deep gravelly sound in the back of his throat, and it turned my insides to a shivery mass of want. My nipples peaked and my cunt clenched hard as I tunnelled my fingers into the baby-soft strands of Flynn's golden locks and dragged his body closer to mine. He came willingly, running his hands down my back, over my butt, and clasping them under my thighs. He lifted me effortlessly, positioning me on the table as he pressed his lips to mine.

Electricity.

Fire.

Calm waters.

Serenity and bliss.

I inhaled his scent, taking it into my lungs and holding it there. He was all my favourite things—the ocean, blue skies, and a light breeze on a spring day. That perfect lie-naked-in-the-sun-and-let-warmth-infuse-your-bones kind of scent. I wanted him inside me forever. With me forever.

He pressed a kiss to my mouth again before he flicked his tongue against my lip. I opened for him, our mouths connecting for the first ever time. Our tongues touched, and he sipped from my lips, gently and reverently. I couldn't help the moan that travelled through me like a ripple in a pond. Slow but purposeful, Flynn took me apart at the seams, flaying away every mark every man before him had left on me. He cherished me, worshipped me in his kiss.

His hands travelled the length of my body from hip to shoulder, raising gooseflesh in their wake. A third hand landed on my back, squeezing my nape as Professorhole's lips nuzzled my hair.

"I can't stay away," he admitted against my temple as he pressed his erection into my thigh. "I don't even want to."

"Undress me," I begged. "Need to feel you." I wasn't even sure who I was speaking to. All I knew was that I needed them to own every part of my body, to use me, to take everything they wanted in order to give me everything in return.

Four hands were on me at once. The professor lifted my top, exposing my tits to the men before me.

I loved bras. I loved the feel of silk against my skin and the way my boobs sat when they were locked in tight with underwire and fitted cups. But there was nothing better than watching a man's gaze at the moment he figured out there was no bra, that my girls were hanging loose, and with the slightest movement the wrong way, with the slightest catch of my top, they'd go tumbling out. I fucking loved being watched and the jiggle that my double Ds gave me was enough to turn even me on.

It was even better when I didn't wear panties.

Like today.

Flynn unzipped my skirt, and the professor laid me back, his warm hands easing me onto the white tabletop. Canting my hips, I moaned as leather skated down my thighs, leaving me exposed to these men. Dressed only in my pencil-thin black heels, the cool wash of air from the air conditioning soothed my overheated skin.

"Dirty kitten," the professor murmured as he bent to capture my nipple in his mouth and slid his fingers over my mound. My legs fell open as he ran his fingers over my cunt, swiping at my juices while he sucked and nibbled on my nipple. "No panties."

I pushed up onto my elbows, needing to see them both. The visual was just as hot as the sensation.

The professor was a sight to behold. He and that talented mouth of his were determined to turn me inside out. But it was Flynn who I couldn't tear my eyes away from. His eyes were filled with something indescribable as his gaze ping-ponged between the places where the professor was touching me.

"Flynn?" I asked, wanting to know whether he was okay with this.

"Yeah," he replied, his eyes meeting mine. The something that I'd seen was unbridled desire. He didn't say the words, but it was clear as day—both from the rigid tenting of his pants and the heat in his gaze—that he wanted this as much as I did. I couldn't even be upset that it was the professor with us. The teasing touches he was granting me told me he knew how to fuck, and he and Flynn were like matches to kindling, ready to ignite the flames burning deep inside me.

"My turn," Flynn murmured as he trailed his lips down my belly, his tongue dipping into my navel before nipping the sensitive skin at the crease of my inner thigh. My cunt was quivering, and my juices were leaking freely from me—there was probably a puddle on the floor—but it only seemed to ramp up Flynn's heated stare.

Professor Reid moved his fingers as Flynn's lips connected with my clit. I whimpered, loving and hating that I only had one of them touching my cunt. Flynn's eyes never left mine, and whatever he read in my gaze prompted him into action. He shifted the professor's fingers back, and my breath hitched. When Flynn licked around those talented digits that unerringly found my clit, a shock of ecstasy ripped through me. I moaned long and low.

"Take her to heaven, angel," the professor ordered, his voice a rough rasp.

"I want your cock," I gasped, reaching for his belt.

"No." He shook his head, his lips tilting up in a wicked smirk. "Let's save that."

My frustrated grumble was cut off when he slid his fingers lower, spearing me with what had to be three digits. The stretch was intense, the burn instantly satisfying my need to be filled. "Oh, fuck. Yes," I moaned, letting my head fall back. My back arched, pushing my tits out, and the professor was there, his wicked tongue doing devilish things to my nipples.

Flynn's approving hum was the only warning he gave me before hooking my legs over his elbows and spreading me wider. He lashed his tongue over my clit. I saw stars. Gasping, I gripped the edge of the table and rode Flynn's face, desperate for more. Flynn nipped me, licking my cunt as the professor thrust his fingers deeper.

My orgasm hit me like a freight train, every nerve ending exploding simultaneously. I shouted out, but the sound was muffled by the professor's hand clamping over my mouth. The action sent me straight into orbit. Wave after wave of sensation hit me, my cunt clenching tighter around the professor's fingers as Flynn shifted to nipping my clit and prolonging the ride.

When the contracting finally slowed and my body stopped spasming, Flynn shifted lower, leaving my clit. I sobbed, not ready for this to end, but he didn't go far. He travelled further south, lapping up my leaking juices from my skin. All I could see was his blond mane, messy curls framing his closed eyes. But even I could see the serene ecstasy in his expression. I clenched my star, and Flynn shivered, swiping his tongue over it.

"How does she taste, angel?" the professor murmured against my skin, his gaze locked on Flynn's too.

"Like fucking heaven," Flynn groaned, the vibration sending a skitter of sensation through my body beginning at my hole and travelling through me until my skin was a mass of gooseflesh.

"Mmm," Professor Reid hummed against my nipple. "Get your dick out, angel. Fuck her until she's screaming."

Flynn stilled, his eyes popping open and silently asking me for permission. I bit my lip, nodding. I loved the contrast between them—that take-charge attitude was hot as hell, yet Flynn's gentleness was one of the many reasons I craved his presence.

His shoulders suddenly fell, the glint of excitement fading from his eyes. "I don't have protection," he uttered, disappointed.

I didn't care. I just wanted him. Needed him to be the one filling me. I needed to be connected with him in that way. "Doesn't matter," I reassured him, shifting my hips so the professor would move his fingers again. He rewarded me with a finger at my arse, rubbing my hole and pushing in just deep enough to stretch me.

"How many people have you been with since you last got tested?" Professor Reid asked.

Flynn shook his head, his cheeks pinking up, a rosy-red flush travelling over his skin down to the collar of his polo shirt. "No one."

"Me neither." I shifted my hips again, and cried out when the professor pushed in harder, pressing against my G-spot as he fingerfucked me and breached my arse. I was on the edge again, another orgasm building inside me.

"Strip, angel. I want to see that body of yours against kitten's while you fuck her."

I gasped, arching into him again. Fuck. The picture he painted, the way I was open and completely at their mercy, and the rough way he took my cunt and arse together was enough to toss me over again. I cried out, and this time

Flynn's hand clamped over my mouth as I rode wave after wave of bliss.

"That's it, kitten," the professor encouraged. "Come for me again."

When it was over, and I was slumped back on the table like a starfish, I finally opened my eyes. The professor was there, licking his fingers, a lascivious look in his eyes. I flicked my gaze to where he was looking between my legs, and the sight before me took my breath away.

Every one of my fantasies were ramped up from zero to one hundred in a split second. I'd seen Flynn shirtless before, even seen him in boxers when we slept, But I'd never seen him naked. And fuck me, naked was a sight to behold.

All that compact muscle was tensed as if ready to pounce. His jaw was clenched tight, and his biceps bulged as he moved his hand. His abs jumped as if he was struggling to stand still.

Then there was his dick.

His cock stood proudly erect. Long and thick. So long and thick, it deserved its own damn postcode. He was slim and lithe, his skin pale. But his cock had nothing in common with the rest of him. He was so well hung that his cock rose well above his belly button. I'd be lucky to be able to fit that thing between my lips.

My mouth watered, and a gush of wetness slicked up my cunt again. Oh, hell yeah.

His fingers trailed over the head of his dick, teasing me as he smeared the drop of precum leaking from his slit. Shifting his fingers down his length, he traced the silver bars that ran all the way down the underside of his shaft and along his sac. "Oh yeah," the professor groaned as I whimpered.

I didn't think I could move—my limbs were still tingling—but somehow, I did. Gripping my knees, I lifted my legs, opening myself once more for him. I wanted him inside me. But not because I wanted to make that pierced monster my new favourite plaything. I wanted Flynn, the man. My best friend.

He lined his dick up with my opening, and my cunt fluttered around him. But the professor gave a slight headshake. Flynn froze, cocking his head and waiting for the other man's permission. Not good enough. I wanted him now, not when our professorhole said I could have him.

Professor Reid walked over to his desk and plucked out a travel-sized bottle. With a wicked grin, he squeezed out a generous pool of it into his hand and reached for Flynn, slicking him up. My man's eyes rolled back in his head, and the whimper he let loose was filled with pure need. But he pulled away, canting his hips and stepping back to break the professor's hold on him. "Too close," he breathed with a blush and an embarrassed smile.

The professor turned his attention to me, slicking up my arsehole with the lube. He didn't falter plunging a finger back into my depths. I moaned, my ring of muscle tightening around his finger as he pumped. "Now, angel. You're both ready."

Flynn didn't hesitate again. He shifted forward and pressed his cockhead against my opening, rubbing the lube around. He didn't need it. I was soaked.

I noticed the additional piercing at the base of his cock, right where it would hit my clit, and I moaned, opening my legs further, willing him to come inside me.

With his bottom lip held between his teeth in concentration, Flynn's gaze met mine. The heat and adoration in his eyes were enough to set me on fire. When he slowly pushed in, carefully letting me adjust to his girth, that fire exploded into an inferno raging out of control.

The stretch, the burn, was everything I needed and more.

His hips met mine, his balls pressed against the fingers the professor had buried in my arse, and he stuttered out a breath. He bent and rested his elbows at my shoulders, pressing our bodies together. He nuzzled my nose with his gently, his body covering mine. All I could see was Flynn. He surrounded me, enveloped me in his hold, and I arched up, needing the connection. Wrapping my legs around his waist and bringing my hands to his back, I pressed my lips to his and breathed in his air. He moved then, a slow backward glide of his hips until only his cockhead was inside me before he surged forward once more. He lit me up like a fireworks display, and I knew it wouldn't be long until I was screaming through another orgasm. The professor timed his thrusts with Flynn's, each of them taking me higher.

Flynn moved his lips, kissing down my throat and burying his face in the crook of my neck. His hot breath washed against my sweat-soaked skin, the intimacy of it driving me wild. His movements were sharp, hard thrusts and slow retreats, exactly the way I loved it, but unlike every other man who I'd screamed out "harder" to, Flynn wasn't using my body just to get off. He whispered, "I love you."

The gentle brush of his fingers through my hair, the way his lips trailed reverently along my skin, and the tight squeeze of his arms was nothing like I'd ever experienced.

With every deep thrust, the ball pierced into the base of Flynn's cock hit my clit. It was as if the warm metal was charged, each connection firing off a lightning bolt, ratcheting up the ecstasy zinging through me.

Flynn's thrusts quickened, his control wavering as his breathing sped up. He shifted then, stretching one arm out to hold his weight up as he brought his other hand to my tit, brushing his thumb over my erect nipple. Another burst of electricity spiked through me, my cunt clenching tight. He did it again and again, each time edging me closer to an orgasm I wasn't sure I'd ever recover from.

The professor shifted, his finger slipping out of my arse. I whined, but Flynn circled his hips, punching forward and coming into direct contact with my G-spot. I gasped, arching into his hold again, and he used those talented fingers to flick my nipple, short-circuiting my brain with his tongue in my mouth.

Professor Reid's hand slide along my belly, his thumb finding my clit and pressing down whenever Flynn retreated. My man's eyes rolled back in his head when the professor closed his hand over Flynn's throat and kissed a line across his shoulders. Professor Reid ground his hips against Flynn's arse, pushing him deeper into me with his movement. Flynn swelled, stretching me impossibly tighter around his thick length.

"You're going to pump your cum into our pretty kitten," he murmured against Flynn's ear, his voice hypnotic and his eyes locked on mine. They flashed, desire radiating from him as he licked the shell of Flynn's ear. "Then when you're done, I'm going to flip her over, put my cock in her arse and empty my load in her. My beautiful students. All fucking mine for the taking."

Flynn slammed forward, and quick as a flash, the professor clamped his hand over my man's mouth. His muscles strained, every tendon going taut, and a roar ripped from deep within him. Pulse after pulse of his hot cum shot deep within me, soaking me. Like a trigger being squeezed, it set off the orgasm that had been building deep within me. I screamed into the crook of my elbow as my body shattered into a million pieces.

Fireworks lit up behind my eyelids and every nerve ending detonated, each one seemingly connected to my clit. Like it had a mind of its own, my cunt squeezed Flynn's monster cock tight. It set off another wave in him, emptying more cum from his balls into my channel.

Flynn slumped forward, dropping his weight onto me. Exhaustion claimed me, my arm falling beside my head and my legs slipping down to dangle off the edge of the table. Flynn huffed out a laugh and pressed a kiss to my throat before working his way across my cheek to my lips. I groaned as his cock slipped free of my cunt, and he took my lips in a kiss almost as hot as the midday fuck we'd just had.

He broke away, gasping for breath, and nuzzled his way back down to my ear. "I want to watch you and the prof fuck," he murmured, lifting off me and slumping into the closest chair.

The professor was there, squeezing the outline of his cock through his suit pants. Eyes locked on my leaking cunt, his gaze was like a heated caress. He unbuckled and unzipped, not even bothering to pull his belt free before shoving both his pants and tight boxer briefs down to his knees. Without a single word, he spread my legs and angled his impressively thick cock toward my cunt. But before he could plunge in, Flynn was scrambling up, his arms against the professor's chest, pushing him back.

"Not so fast. Condom."

I groaned, and the professor smirked before running his thumb along Flynn's bottom lip. "You're her knight in shining armour, aren't you, angel? I've been tested too. All negative." He gestured at me with his chin. "Can I fuck our woman now?"

Without waiting for an answer to the question, he thrust hard, getting balls deep inside me. I gasped, my sensitive walls contracting hard around his girth. He wasn't as long as Flynn, but he was fucking thick. Two sharp thrusts, and his hands closed over my tits, pinching my nipples hard between his fingers. The bite of pain was electric, and I arched into his touch, loving the contrast between the two men who'd fucked me.

Another slam of his hips against mine, and he was pulling away. I growled, clawing at him to come back. But he ignored me. Turning on his heels, he faced Flynn and pointed that beautiful cock at his lips. "Lick me clean, angel."

Flynn hesitated only a moment before the professor's hand was on his head, pushing him down. He leaned forward, tentatively licking the professor's cockhead. Flynn closed his hand around his own dick, the thick meat plumping up again as he licked the professor like a lollipop. Fuck me, it was sexy watching my bestie take cock. I slid my hand down, finding my clit and working myself while watching them together.

"Suck on the head," he ordered, and Flynn complied, closing his lips over his glans. He sucked the professor deeper, taking him as far into his mouth as he could before gagging. Gripping his hair, the professor ground out, "Take a breath, angel. I'm gonna fuck your throat." He thrust forward, burying himself deep. Flynn gagged and gagged again, his eyes watering before the professor pulled completely free and turned back to me.

Roughly, he flipped me over, the surface of the table biting into my hips as he manoeuvred me until I was bent in half and gripping the other end of the table. My arse up in the air, my legs spread, the professor thrust into my soaked cunt once more. Deep, hard thrusts, and I was on the edge again, my cunt tightening around him.

But he pulled out once more.

I was going to murder the fuck.

"Get your dick back inside my cunt, and fuck me like you mean it," I grated out, lifting my arse into the air.

He slapped me, his hand connecting hard against my cunt and my arsehole. I reared back and swore, "Motherfucker." The burn was instantaneous, but it morphed into a tingling fire that amped me up more.

The professor chuckled and rubbed his dick over my cunt once more before pressing his cockhead against my star. He pushed forward, stretching me at the same time as he jacked off, my combined juices and Flynn's cum all the lube he needed. "Fuck, I'm nearly there," he grated out. "You ready for my cum, kitten?"

It was a rhetorical question I didn't have time to answer even if I wanted to. He pushed forward, breaching my arse with his glans. I gasped, rearing up again, the burn more intense than I could have imagined. I'd been fucked in the arse before, but never like this. Never without insisting on a shit-ton of preparation and copious amounts of lube.

But my body fucking loved his rough touch. He wasn't even in contact with my cunt, but it didn't matter. As if his cock was magical, the stretch and burn it imparted was enough to set off my orgasm. It rocketed through me, obliterating my thoughts. I sobbed against the table, ashamed of how much I fucking loved the pleasure/pain.

The professor gripped my hips. His fingers would no doubt leave bruises where he held me. He shoved in deeper, making me cry out, before withdrawing to his cockhead and slamming forward again, burying himself to the hilt in my arse. I screamed, pain ricocheting through me as he tore me in half.

But I shattered again, my orgasm renewing itself. The professor's cock swelled, his grip tightening even more, and he shot inside my arse. He growled as he withdrew slowly and punched his hips forward again.

"You're my beautiful little slut, aren't you." He pulled back and thrust hard again, his jizz lubricating the way. Pressing his forehead against my spine, he rumbled, "So fucking sexy bent over my table, your arse strangling my cock." He shifted his hand down, cupping my cunt and sliding his fingers through my juices mingled with the remnants of Flynn's cum leaking out of me.

I shivered, my overworked clit sensitive to the touch. He was softening, but it didn't seem to matter. He kept moving, kept thrusting in and out of my arse.

"You wanted me from the moment you saw me, didn't you? Practically fucking begged me for it. Those slutty little tops that show off your tits with no bra and panties are hot as hell."

He hummed and thrust forward again, pinching my clit. I gasped, widening my legs so he could keep playing me like a fucking instrument.

"I want to see your cunt in our next lecture. Show my how much you want my cock again. Wear another skirt and spread those thighs wide so I can see my property."

I groaned, shaking my head. I didn't want to love it, but he was pushing every one of my buttons. He gripped the base of his cock as he pulled out to the tip and guided himself back in, his stroke gentler this time.

Flynn cried out, and I strained to see him. He was working his cock, his stare locked on the professor's dick stretching my hole. He was breathing hard as cum shot from his slit, hitting his chest with every spurt.

"No cleaning yourself up before you leave, kitten. I want you to carry my cum around all fucking day, like a good little slut." He pinched my clit again, and another shudder passed through me. "Come for me again, and I'll let you lick up Flynn's spunk."

"Need your fingers," I gasped, on edge again. He hitched my knee up on the table and shoved his fingers deep. I cried out again, sobbing as he pressed a finger into my arse alongside his cock.

Another orgasm rushed through me. Still stretched with his dick and now with his fingers, I was completely at his mercy. And he took advantage, wringing every pulse and contraction from my overused cunt.

I loved it.

I never wanted to stop.

Shame crept in at the edges of my consciousness, but I pushed that fucker aside. I knew I shouldn't love it. I knew I shouldn't be spread out on this tabletop while my professor had his cock buried in my arse and called me a slut. I'd just been fucked by my best friend, I had two men's cum inside of me. I shouldn't have loved it. But I did. And I wouldn't apologize for wanting them to do it again.

And again.

The professor pulled out slowly, and I winced at the burn. I probably wouldn't be able to walk straight, but I would wear that badge of honour proudly.

He helped me up, guiding me to my knees before Flynn. He murmured, just loud enough for Flynn to hear too, "Clench that hole tight, kitten. I don't want any of my cum wasted on the carpet. Keep it inside you while you eat him up. Clean up our angel before I get back."

SEVEN

Flynn

Zee was spaced out, loopy after so many orgasms and happy hormones flooding her system. She rested her head in my lap, burying her nose in my sac and breathing deep. I ran my fingers through her sweaty hair, and she darted her tongue out, licking me.

I couldn't help the shudder that ran through me when she nuzzled me again, sweeping her tongue over the line of barbells that ran along the seam of my sac. I was pierced from my frenulum right down the length of my cock and all the way over my sac to my perineum. I didn't know why I'd wanted them so badly a few years ago until I was speaking with the piercer. She'd said something that resonated with me. She'd nailed my reasons when I hadn't even been able to make sense of them myself, but making my outer shell look the way I pictured myself on the inside was important to me. I wanted authenticity. I wanted to live true to myself.

So I'd gotten the piercings for me, though they were apparently just as good for other people too. The one I'd added for Zee was at the base of my cock, a ball to touch her clit every time I moved inside her. Call that decision blind hope because it certainly wasn't confidence.

My feelings for her had been buried as deep as the floor beneath the ceiling-high stacks of hoarded garbage that took up every inch of floor space in my parents' house. She never could have wanted someone like me. It was impossible.

Until it wasn't.

I was still kicking myself. Spinning like an out-of-control top.

This woman, the one I'd been in love with for most of my life, had let me touch her, kiss her, make love to her. And better yet, she'd seemed to enjoy it as much as I did.

At least I thought she had.

Had she?

Zee's eyes were closed, a serene smile tilting her lips up. At the very least, she'd loved what the professor had done.

She was on the floor, resting one butt cheek on the carpet, her legs curled underneath her. She still wore only her pointy-toed shoes. Zee was beautiful. A vision. An absolute dream. Curves for miles, hair as golden as sunshine, and a heart as big as big as her brain was smart.

She blinked, and it took a moment for her glassy-eyed gaze to sharpen and focus on me. "Is this going to change us?" she wondered, her voice a rough rasp.

"I hope so and I hope not at the same time. I want us to be together, Zee, but I still want my best friend. I need her too," I admitted, heat creeping down my throat and over my chest.

Zee raised her hand, her pointed red nails tracing the line of heat down my chest as it flushed my skin pink. Her fingertips met a splatter of my cum, and she scooped it up, bringing her fingers to her lips. With a satisfied hum, Zee sucked her digits clean before she spread my legs open further, lifted herself onto her knees, and continued cleaning me with her tongue, teasing my abs as she went. I sucked in a breath, my muscles jumping as she dipped into my navel. With every swipe, she cleaned more of my cum off my belly. It was breathtaking, watching her do that, seeing her take care of me the way a lover does.

I needed her closer than that though. I tugged Zee onto my lap and wrapped my arms around her waist, drawing her in close. She cupped my face with delicate hands, her touch gentle. When she tentatively pressed her lips to mine, I moaned. This was a dream come true. I needed to show her just how much I adored her. She was my heart, the sun I orbited around, the lifeforce to my being.

Kissing her long and slow, I tangled my tongue with hers and tried to communicate what was in my heart. It was overflowing, bursting at the seams with love and possibility and hope. I loved her. I'd been in love with her for years. Now we'd finally—finally—taken a step forward.

Zee had hinted at the question that had always plagued me—what if our friendship didn't survive us sleeping together? I'd never wanted to risk it, but after what happened today, I knew we were perfect together. I could give her what she needed. Whether it was just the two of us or more, it didn't matter to me.

"Was that okay for a first time?" I whispered, wiling my voice not to hitch. "I mean, it wasn't yours, but—"

"It was beautiful," she murmured, nuzzling my shoulder. Her muscles went lax. Exhaustion was overtaking her, and she'd need to sleep the afternoon off very soon. Heck, I did too.

"We should get you back to the yacht," I murmured, rubbing her back.

"Mmm," she sighed and snuggled in closer. "In a minute."

The door to the office swung open, and the professor slipped in, moving like a spy. He closed and locked it quickly behind him. He scanned the room, his gaze falling on our clothes still tossed all over the floor before darting to our naked bodies. He pursed his lips, frustration radiating off him.

"You need to go," he muttered, picking up Zali's top and skirt and shoving them into her hands. "Or this is going to get very awkward."

Every one of Zee's muscles went rigid. She sat up and glared daggers at the professor. "Maybe you shouldn't have fucked your students then," she shot back.

"No shit," he growled. "Get dressed and get out."

"Fuck you," she snapped, slipping on her top before bending over and making a show of shimmying into the tight-as-sin skirt. There was no hiding the wetness between her legs—mine and the professor's cum sliding out of her—and she let the professor know without words exactly what he had on the line.

"Zali, don't push your luck," the professor grated through clenched teeth, his eyes flashing dangerously.

"Or what, professor?" She stalked over to him and poked him in the chest. "You aren't in any position to be making demands." She stood before him, staring at him. Their gazes clashed, and a thousand-word conversation passed between them as I scrambled to get dressed. The sooner we got out of there, the less likely it was that the heel of her shoe would make contact with his head.

"What do you want?" he asked, his eyes narrowed and those gorgeous green eyes cold and hard.

She huffed out a sad laugh and shook her head. "For you to do what's right. You fairly present my research proving you wrong and keep the sensationalism to a minimum."

He sucked in a breath, a flare of warmth lighting up his eyes. He nodded and clasped Zee's elbows gently, leaning forward to press a kiss on her forehead. "You have my word."

She pulled out of his grasp and stood up straighter, her chin lifting defiantly. "Good. Let's go Flynn."

She was lying in my arms, both of us curled up on her plush sofa. I was in heaven. Nirvana. This was even better than the sex. More meaningful. Zee drew circles on my chest with her fingertips, playing with the collar of my shirt. I ran my fingers through her still-wet hair, massaging her scalp. We were quiet, comfortable in each other's presence. This was how we'd always been, but now that I knew what it was like to have more, I never wanted to give it up.

Zee sighed and nuzzled into me. "I like it here, but I want to be on the water, not moored."

We were at Marina Mirage, just outside of Surfers Paradise. It was the nearest marina to my apartment but also Zee's least favourite. She hated the hustle and bustle of the waterway there, never mind the traffic on the roads and people everywhere. It was right along the tourist strip, and whenever she was moored there, people always came out in droves to look at her yacht. It was why all the privacy blinds were drawn and the sliding doors closed.

"I can ask Ry to take us out."

"He's not here." She pouted before rolling her eyes. "He's gone grocery shopping."

"Oh, poor baby," I teased, giving her my own pout. She didn't hesitate, snagging the cushion I was resting my head on and yanking it out from under me. She playfully pushed it down on my face—pressing more against my forehead than my mouth and nose—and laughed one of those mwuh-ha-ha laughs. I snorted, giggling until my cheeks were hurting and lungs burning. I'd had a smile plastered on my face all afternoon, and this was icing on the cake. When she added a twist to my nipple, I gasped and cried out, "Mercy!"

Zee relented and lifted the pillow, waiting until I was sitting up in a crunch before stuffing it behind my head. "I like this couch," I mumbled and sighed happily.

The whole yacht was amazing. It should be for thirty-odd-million dollars. Zee had fallen in love with it the moment she'd seen plans for it on Insta. Within weeks, she'd travelled to Italy and bought it. Somehow she'd roped Ryder and another boatie mate of his to navigate the yacht home, and she'd rarely spent a night off it since.

The man loved this yacht as much as Zee did. Ry insisted that he maintain everything, keeping it sleek, spotless, and in perfect working order. He wasn't even as possessive about Zee's plane, and it was his idea to buy that.

I was just happy with the couch. I'd proven over and over again that I could fall asleep on it at any time of day or night. Everything inside me was quiet and calm when I was here. I always unclenched. Maybe it was the neutral tones—timber floors, cream furniture, white walls, and a couple of white orchids on the buffet. It was more likely the uncluttered surfaces and minimalist decorating Zee had gone with. The apartment I lived in, also courtesy of Zee, was a lot like that too, but darker and more masculine.

"I got you something," Zee said excitedly. She was bouncing in her chair with one foot underneath her butt, while I sat on her bed. It was how we studied together—or pretended we were studying. I used any excuse I could not to go home. It was worse than it had ever been there, and tonight I wanted to be as far away as possible.

"Oooh, what?" I asked.

"Close your eyes."

I did, holding my hands out. She placed a small box in my hands about the size of a cigarette packet. It was light too.

"Okay, open them."

The box was wrapped in blue paper the colour of the sky. It was my favourite colour, the one Zee said matched my eyes. She was always so kind to me, so unlike the others. I'd been picked on for as long as I could remember for being the kid who lived in the junk house. You could smell the funk from two blocks away when the wind caught it—a mix of rat piss, decaying paper, and dead animals. No matter how much I scrubbed myself, I couldn't get the smell out of my nose and off my skin and clothes.

The wrapping had "happy birthday sweet 16" written on it in marker.

"Dad has another present for you, but this one is from me."

I bit back the flood of emotion that threatened to bring tears to my eyes. Zee had never once forgotten my birthday. I wish I could say the same thing about my own parents. But I was used to it by now.

One day.... I couldn't wait to move out and get away from them.

"Open it," she squealed, bouncing so high in her chair that I was surprised it didn't tip over.

I tore away the paper and lifted the lid on the box. Inside was a key and a black fob of some sort. "What is it?"

"An apartment."

I was waiting for the punchline. The "gotcha" moment.

But she was serious. Her smile was gone, her eyes wide as she waited for me to say something.

An apartment.

I blinked. Opened my mouth and snapped it shut again. An apartment? Was she serious?

"I bought it. For you. So you could move out."

"I'm sixteen," I mumbled. I wasn't allowed to move out. Was I?

"Da-ad," Zee shouted.

I picked up the key, flipping it over in my hand. I was speechless. Hope was cruel, and I was too beaten down by my parents and older sisters and brother to dare let it rear its head.

His head popped in the door a few moments later. "What's up?"

"Flynn needs your present."

He smiled. "Okay." He ducked out of the room, coming back a moment later with a manilla folder. "This isn't exactly a present, but when Zali told me what she wanted to do for you, I wanted to help make it official."

"She... what?" I asked, my brow furrowing. Completely confused, I turned over the key in my hand again, waiting for reality to step in and slap me upside the head.

"Yes, she told me, and I support her 100 percent." He reached out, gripping my shoulder. "I've done what I could do to get the authorities involved, but they just don't want to hear it. No matter how many calls I make, they just don't follow through. You know you can stay here as long and as often as you like. I'm happy for you to move in completely, but you keep saying no. We thought it might be because you wanted your own space."

"*I don't want to take advantage,*" I mumbled, ashamed that I hadn't been able to hide how bad it was from Monroe. It was my problem to deal with, my issues.

"*I know that, buddy. I don't agree with you, but I refuse to continue to be part of the problem. Zali wanted to help you, and so do I. So, I spoke with a friend of mine, a police officer.*"

My head snapped up, and I squeezed the key tight. My jaw cracked, a shooting pain rocketing through my tooth as I clenched them together as hard as I could. I hated living there, I hated Mum and Dad, but they were my parents. They weren't right, and it wasn't their fault. I didn't want them to get in trouble. Not the way they would if the police went there.

"*It's not what you think,*" he responded, taking my hand in his and uncurling my fingers. "*I asked about whether you could move out. Kids won't get sent back to live with their parents once they're sixteen if they've got somewhere safe to go and can support themselves. You can move out, Flynn.*"

"*I don't have a job. I can't pay for anything.*"

"*You won't be paying rent,*" Zee stated matter-of-factly. She was stubborn as a... whatever was the most stubborn creature, and with that set of her jaw and the glint in her eye, I knew it was pointless arguing the point. I'd never won an argument with her anyway.

"*I bought this for you. I've been saving up my pay from the jobs I've done—*"

"*But—*"

"*No, Flynn. I've had a million bucks sitting in my bank account set aside for this for ages. Dad told me I had to wait until I was sixteen to buy anything big, so now I'm doing it.*"

A million bucks.

A. Million. Bucks!

"*How do you have a million dollars?*" I practically shouted. "*How is that even possible?*"

"*This job, the contract work, it pays sooo much money.*" She laughed, circling her hand around the room. "*I'm going to buy a boat, Flynn. Just for me. I'm gonna get one of those big yachts.*"

"*Flynn,*" Monroe said, shaking his head affectionately at Zee. "*These forms are an application to the children's court to emancipate yourself. You don't have to go through with it, but if you do, you'll be considered an adult, and your parents won't have any control over you.*"

"*I'll pay for it all,*" Zee offered. "*And because you need a job, I'll hire you too.*"

"*Doing what?*"

"*I dunno. Does it matter? You won't be doing anything.*"

"*No.*" I shook my head. "*This is too much. I can't....*"

"*You can, buddy.*"

"*No. I'll get a job. I promise you, I'll pay you back. Every cent of it.*"

"*Should we go check out your new digs?*" Monroe asked, and Zee rolled her eyes. Her dad was cool, the absolute greatest, but he was such a dad too. A complete dork.

"*I chose furniture for it,*" Zee babbled but hurried to add, "*but if you don't like it, we can change it all.*"

If I didn't already love her, that would have clinched the deal. It would have been the moment I fell for her. She'd given me a chance to pull myself out of the hellhole that had been my life.

Resting her chin on the hand Zee had laid across my chest, she gave me a small smile and asked, "Can I ask you something?" I nodded and she went on. "What did you mean before when you asked if it was okay for a first time?"

My heart flip-flopped in my chest, my stomach bottoming out. I'd never shared what I was about to tell her with anyone. I wanted her to know, but Zee was so sex positive that I was kind of embarrassed to admit the whys. Then again, Zee didn't care about other people's expectations. Maybe she would understand. Either way, I trusted her.

I sucked in a breath and borrowed some of her I-don't-give-a-hoot courage. "I'll get better with practice, you know? It was our first time. My first time." I swallowed hard. My voice was tight, and I was sure I was the colour of a beetroot. "You were my first. Today... was my first time."

"I'm your first?" she whispered, a mix of confusion and awe in her voice. When I nodded, she shuffled up, pressing her lips to mine with infinite gentleness. "Why?"

I rolled my eyes. The answer was obvious. "Because I've been in love with you for years, Zee. How could I be with anyone else? I wanted to wait. Call me an eternal optimist, but I kinda hoped that one day you'd want me like that too." I shrugged, trying to play down how big a deal it had been when I was a teenager and everyone except me was experimenting.

"Oh, Flynn," she murmured. But it wasn't pity in her voice. It was reverence. "The professor—"

"Yeah, him too. He was my first too. Is that ridiculous?"

She shook her head. "Are you kidding me? No, it's incredible. I feel privileged that you chose me to be your first. But I also wish we could scrub Professorhole out of the equation."

I grinned and shrugged again. "I don't know. He is pretty hot."

Zee sighed and agreed. "I still hate him and his perfect body."

"Urgh, he's smart too." Zee snapped her gaze to mine, shock and anger flaring in her eyes like bright sparks, but I continued, explaining my reasoning to her. "Totally misguided, but intelligent."

"I'll need to start my research soon. Want to come with me to Dad's house for dinner?. Then if you're not busy, we can get stuck into it."

Nodding with a grin, I replied, "I'd love to. I haven't seen Monroe in ages." While we were speaking about the research…. "Did you, ah, get a copy of the photo that the prof put up on the slides?"

"I did. It's funny, I don't think I've ever seen that photo before. Or maybe I have, but it didn't stick in my head. Seeing it, though, made everything come back. It was like it was yesterday."

"You remembered that day?" I asked softly.

"Yeah." She sat up, pulling away from me. But when she twined her fingers through mine and held tight, I knew she was okay. Sitting up, I pressed a kiss to her temple and waited, giving her the space to share it if she wanted to.

"I remember Mum telling me how you couldn't come over that day because we were going to her work. I was sad but so excited to go with her." She huffed out a laugh, her smile soft and eyes misty. "I loved that office; it was so big and bright, and hers overlooked the canal so I could see the boats outside. But that's not where we went." She furrowed her brow and tilted her head, her gaze far away. Grinning again, her lips tilted up in a huff of laugher, her eyes sparkling.

"I was sitting on the floor, listening to music on Mum's iPod. She used to listen to this European DJ who was, like, hardcore happy techno. I loved it. I'd dance around every time she put it on, and I knew all the words to the songs. But whenever I started singing, Mum nudged me with her foot. I'd stop for a few minutes, then do the same thing again. Mum promised to take me out for sushi if I stayed as quiet as a mouse—"

"You love sushi. Did she still get it for you?" I smiled and squeezed her hand, encouraging her to keep speaking.

Zee shook her head as if clearing the cobwebs. "I don't know. I can remember sitting there. The carpet was scratchy, but I didn't care. I was at work like a big girl. Mum had taken me with her. She never even did that with Asher. I don't remember why I was off school and Ash wasn't...." Her smile turned sad. "I haven't thought about that day in years."

"I know it hurts." I hooked my finger under her chin and turned her to face me, pressing our foreheads together. The happy memories were the ones we treasured. There were too many bad ones that came to her when she closed her eyes.

Watching them drown again and again. Even though she hadn't witnessed the accident, she'd lived the fallout, and her mind was a powerful thing, filling in the blanks based on circumstantial evidence.

Zee would wake up, breathing hard and reaching for her mother and Asher, trying to save them but never succeeding.

Her phone dinged, and Zee reached for it. Her smile was warm, and she shook off her sadness with a slow breath out. "Dad's home from work. Want to head there now?"

"Sure."

EIGHT

Zali

Dad lived in a cute little town home in Hope Island. I'd shown him houses of every style and price range, but he'd said no to every one of them. It wasn't that he was attached to the shitty fibro cottage that his landlord refused to fix. It was that he didn't want to take advantage of me. No matter how many times I'd said, he still insisted that me buying something for him was wrong—apparently parents needed to provide for their kids, not the other way around. As if a million bucks was a bother.

He'd shot me down for this one too, but it was hard to miss how he'd gazed wistfully out the double sliding doors to the patio that had its own private beach along the tidal river. His eyes had lit up as he watched the boats sail by. He was meant to be on the water—like me—so I'd bought it for him.

We pulled up in my Range Rover, and I parked in my usual spot under the awning. Dad met us at the door, waving us in. "Hey, beautiful girl," he murmured into my hair as he wrapped his arms around me and held tight. I sank into his embrace, holding on for a moment longer than I usually did. "I missed you."

"Missed you too, Dad." With his arm still around me, he ruffled Flynn's hair and pulled him in for a hug too.

"How are you kids doing?"

"Good, Dad," Flynn uttered, a smile in his voice. "Really good."

"Come on in." Dad's beaming smile was welcoming. It warmed me from inside out. Thinking about Mum and Asher always got me off-kilter. Knowing they were gone was still like a knife to my heart even years later. But Dad made it better. He was my rock, the kind of guy who would do anything for anyone. Nothing was ever too difficult or too much to ask.

My smile was genuine even though my insides were still held together with sticky tape.

Dad led us outside to the covered patio, and I sighed happily. We were cut from the same cloth, Mum, Dad, Asher, and me. We all loved the water.

Flynn sat on the couch, patting the spot next to him, and I curled into him. Kicking off my thongs, I popped my feet up on the sofa and rested my head on his shoulder. Dad watched us with an indulgent smile and gestured toward the kitchen.

"How about a pot of green tea?"

"That sounds great," Flynn replied, and I nodded, my eyes closing contentedly.

A few minutes later, Dad returned carrying a tray with a teapot and three traditional yunomi teacups. He poured them and sat down, leaning back in the chair and crossing one leg over the other. "So what's new?" he asked, the suggestion in his voice holding a teasing note as he gestured between the two of us.

Flynn always held my hand, and he was always affectionate with me, but the grin that stretched across Flynn's lips at Dad's question was like a flashing neon sign.

It wasn't that I didn't want to tell him, I just wasn't ready. I wanted to savour what was building for just a moment longer, so I redirected.

"Detective Shithead had Flynn and me enrol in a university course. We're doing research for a criminal investigation podcast."

He blinked. Clearly, he hadn't expected me to say that. "That sounds interesting. You enjoying it?"

My mind flashed to that afternoon's session in the professor's office, and I bit back a Cheshire cat grin. "Yeah," I replied, my voice husky until I cleared my throat.

I needed to tell him what we were researching, but I didn't have the heart to do it then. I didn't want to hurt him, and knowing Mum was the subject of the podcast would destroy him. But there were things I wanted to know for myself personally as well as professionally.

"Dad, can you tell me about Mum? I saw a newspaper clipping the other day and remembered going somewhere with her for her work. I was listening to music while she was talking. I remembered headphones, but I'm hazy on the other details. I think I missed school."

He dropped his gaze, and Flynn's arm around me tightened. Dad blew out a breath and dropped his ankle from his knee, leaning forward and resting his elbows on his knees. He hummed and put the teacup down on the coffee table before clasping his hands together. "I remember that day. You didn't miss school. It was a drive home segment on the radio. Asher had football practice, so you went with Mum to the interview and picked up Ash afterward. The interview was a big deal. It was one of the national radio stations. Her advice was all over the news the next day. Photos of the two of you were plastered on all the major newspapers. She was calling for calm when everyone was going crazy, selling off all their stocks. The media thought she was nuts."

"When was this?" I asked, taking a sip of my cooling tea.

"A month or two before the accident. September 2008, maybe." He wiped his hands down his shorts and huffed. "Your mum was really stressed. The business had been expanding faster than she could keep up with for over a year by that stage."

He shook his head, his eyes glassy as he blinked back tears, and my heart shattered. "Rosa was working eighty- and ninety-hour weeks for months. We fought non-stop about how much time she was spending at the office. She hired staff, but the media coverage she was getting had money flowing in faster than she could invest it. Everyone was trying to recoup the losses they'd already suffered and stave off certain future losses."

He stood up and paced over to the edge of the patio. Hands on hips, he inhaled deeply then exhaled, his shoulders curling in on him like he was carrying the weight of the world. With his head hung low, he wiped his face and turned back to us, gesturing past the short lawn to the beach that ran the length of the townhouse complex and beyond. "Let's walk."

Flynn kicked off his thongs while I went to Dad and wrapped an arm around his waist. Flynn took my hand, and I stepped off the grass onto the beach, dodging sticks and pebbles until we got to the wet sand.

Closer to the water, the sand was sticky between my toes, the tide lapping at our ankles as we walked. Dad's words were quiet, almost haunted as he spoke. "We were always so happy together. She was my first and only love. We were high school sweethearts, you know? When she said she'd go to senior formal with me, it was the best day of my life. It was the beginning of the best years of my life. I loved her. I still do." He sighed, the sound filled with the pain of regret. "I'd do anything to turn back time and stop her and your brother from stepping foot on that yacht."

Dad's voice wobbled, and he blew out a harsh breath. I held him tighter, needing him as much as he needed the comfort. Tears tracked down his face, and he wiped them away with the back of his hand. I left mine to fall.

"She was desperate for a break. We were all supposed to be on the yacht for the weekend. We were about to head to the marina when I got a call from work. They were short-staffed after an injury and needed me there. I agreed to go in, and your mum started yelling at me. I asked her to wait until after my shift—twelve hours, and we'd be able to head off." He shook his head, his self-loathing written all over the downward curve of his lips and the dullness in his eyes. He continued, his voice breaking as he pushed through the painful memory. "But she was barely holding on to her sanity. She needed to escape." He sucked in a breath. "I saw the desperation in her eyes. It'll haunt me forever."

"Why did I stay home?"

"I was worried about her. Asher was only a touch older but more mature. He helped out on the yacht. But you were a handful." He managed a watery smile, and I bumped my shoulder into him. I was still a handful, and he knew it. So did Flynn, if the snort of laughter was anything to go by.

"You were so active and fearless. When I'd taken you out a few weeks earlier, you'd jumped off the back of the yacht in the middle of the seaway. Boats everywhere and a swell a couple of metres high, and there you were, diving into the water so you could swim with a pod of dolphins. I was worried you'd pull a stunt like that, and no one would be watching you."

I swallowed. Our not being on that yacht had been a near miss. Such a close shave that if the circumstances were different, I'd have suggested buying a lottery ticket.

"I'm sorry I'm bringing it up." More than anything, I wanted to be able to share happy memories with Dad, but it still hurt so much. I wanted to be able to talk to him about funny things they did—the good memories—and laugh about them. But our conversations always ended in tears, both of us missing them so desperately. We held on to our memories like a lifeline, but they were all tainted with a grief so deep, it could envelop us whole, and we'd never be seen again.

"I'm glad you did. That was a happy memory. It's the stuff that came after that was awful. That whole time was a living nightmare. I blamed myself for the longest time. The should-haves and what-ifs still consume me. If I'd suggested we go to the beach house instead, maybe they'd still be here. If I'd been on the yacht, maybe I could have saved them. But if we were, I might have lost you too."

"It wasn't your fault, Dad. It was an accident. No one saw it coming."

"You're right, and logically I know that, but it doesn't make it any easier to accept. I'll always live with my regrets."

"Mum knew how much you loved her."

"I hope so." He stopped walking and stood, quietly watching the water for the longest time. When he finally began walking again, it was back toward his townhouse. "I didn't get to say what I needed to. I didn't apologize for being so inconsiderate and self-absorbed. I should have been there for her that day, not for work. They could have called someone else, but she only had me."

He swallowed, his breath catching as he sniffed back a sob. "I didn't even tell her that I loved her when she left that morning. I was angry that she couldn't understand why I needed to go to work. And now, I don't even remember why it was so important. I was so stupid."

We walked quietly for a while, the sand cool against my toes. With every step, I sank down to my ankles, the water acting like a suction device on my feet.

"What happened with the business when she died?"

"The economy was already on rocky ground. News report after news report showed companies going bankrupt. People were abandoning their houses in the US, just walking away from them. The whole world was heading to a crash, and Rosa's investors were panicking. It was a complete one-eighty from only a few months earlier. They wanted their money out, but without your mum there leading it, the whole thing fell to pieces. Within weeks the investments were worthless, and the company had nothing. It became a victim of the economic times."

"Why did we move?" I asked, a lump in my throat.

"The company had debts. I sold everything that had your mum's name on it and handed it over. I don't know amounts; I didn't want to know either. I was in a dark place. The solicitors did what they needed to do to make it all go away."

Flynn squeezed my hand so hard, my bones were cracking, but it was the only thing keeping me upright. I remembered those dark days all too well. Dad was barely holding on. He wasn't eating, wasn't sleeping. He was like a zombie. I thought I might lose him too.

Until Ry's mum intervened. His dad had died around the same time. They helped each other. They leaned on each other to pull themselves up. Slowly Dad started to see light again. Slowly he came back to me. He and Ry's mum were like sister and brother nowadays. There was a deep platonic love between them. They'd saved each other, and that gave them an unbreakable bond.

I hadn't realized that I'd detached myself too. I was alone by choice. I had Flynn and Ryder there with me, but I couldn't connect with them. It was like a brick wall had gone up between us. The gaping wound in my heart was like the Grand Canyon. I was trapped on one side, and Flynn and Ryder were on the other—close but yet somehow so far away too.

Flynn was there now though. So was Ry. Dad too. I concentrated on their touch—Dad's arm around my waist and Flynn's hand in mine—and I slowly put one foot in front of the other.

"Did they ever salvage the yacht?" I asked quietly. I knew it was painful to answer, but this was the most openly we'd spoken about this stuff in years, and I couldn't let it go. Not yet, not while I needed to know this to protect both Mum and Dad.

Dad stopped walking right where grass met sand in his backyard. He sank down onto his butt, like the bones in his legs had suddenly disintegrated. I collapsed next to him, hugging him as Flynn moved around to Dad's other side and wrapped an arm around him. We bracketed Dad as he shook his head, and whispered, "No." Tears tracked down his face once more. Dropping his face into his hands, he cried harder, his quiet sobs like a knife to my heart.

It took a long time for him to start talking again, and when he did, his voice was hoarse, scrubbed raw by the pain that had a chokehold on him. "They think it broke apart. We don't know if there was an explosion or just a fire, but the wreckage that washed up suggested an explosion. The water was too deep for what was left to be salvaged, especially because they didn't know exactly where the accident happened."

He sucked in a breath, seeming to force distance between himself and his emotions. It was as if he was recounting someone else's loss, his voice turning monotone. "The Coast Guard did an air and sea search when Rosa didn't check back in and couldn't be reached on the radio. But it was too late." His voice cracked on the last sentence, his battle to keep his heartbreak at bay a lost cause.

The despair in his voice, the sheer desolation shattered me. The love of his life and his little boy had died. He was left with a kid who couldn't fathom a loss like that, who was angry and confused and retaliated by hating the world. Add the survivor's guilt and money woes, and my respect for the man who raised me skyrocketed. He was a survivor. Even while he was holding on by the skin of his teeth, he was still there. Still putting in the hard yards.

"When nothing except the few pieces of floating debris and your brother's foot had been found after five days, Rosa and Asher were presumed dead, and the search was called off." I remembered their funeral. I remembered two white caskets with the brightest-coloured flowers on them. I remembered walking with Dad behind them, wondering what had happened. I remembered the pink frilly dress my aunt had chosen for me that was so itchy, I scratched until

I bled. I remembered being confused about why we were saying goodbye to them. I remembered Dad being a shell of himself.

"Your mum loved the ocean. She would have spent every day out on the water if she could have. That yacht was her pride and joy, much like yours is to you." His smile was brittle, and tears still tracked down his face. "I feel closer to them out here. Connected somehow."

I got it. Subconsciously I think I did the same, trying to keep a part of them close. "Me too. I wish I could remember them better," I whispered.

"Maybe it's time," Dad wondered aloud, and I stilled, tilting my head in question. "Come with me."

Flynn helped him up and gestured for me to go first, his hand on the small of my back, as we followed him inside and into the spare bedroom. It was where he kept all of Mum's and Asher's things that he couldn't face giving away even after all these years—Mum's wedding dress and her favourite robe, Asher's school uniform, the football he'd scored his first try with, letters and artwork, baby photos and toys, CD mixed tapes they'd given each other, and the Lego set Asher was building. He opened the cupboard and retrieved two archive boxes from the back. After putting them down with a thud, he opened one of the lids and ran his fingers reverently along the leatherbound books. "These are some of your mum's diaries. She wrote in them every night before bed. They were a comfort for her."

"Have you read them?" I asked, touching the aging binding.

"No, I could never bring myself to. I couldn't face it if I saw her frustration and anger with me in writing."

"Dad—"

"Read them, Zali. Remember who your mum was."

NINE

Zali

I woke up still groggy from the emotional toll that the evening before had taken. It had been a day of highs and lows, and I was zapped. But I was in a good place. Being the little spoon to Flynn's warm body was heavenly. He held me tight, his arms cocooning me safely. His warm puffs of breath on my throat were long and slow. Peace radiated through me. It was this quiet moment and so many others like it—the times when Flynn didn't even try to tell me that he loved me—that were the most meaningful. He was always there, always cherishing me. I was never in any doubt about how much he loved me. Now I knew it was as more than a friend too.

The knowledge warmed me inside, a tiny spark igniting in my heart and lighting the shadows. I knew I was damaged, a little dysfunctional—or a lot. But Flynn had always treated me like a queen. And I loved it.

Flynn shifted and nuzzled my neck, his semi nestled between my cheeks throbbing as it hardened.

I shivered in delight as his cock flexed, and Flynn hummed.

He dropped a kiss on my nape, and I gasped, desire awakening in my body and humming in my veins.

Like the noises I made had a direct line to his cock, it bucked, prodding my hole when Flynn slowly rocked his hips forward. I probably still had some lube inside me, and the temptation for him to thrust into my arse was delicious, but I really wanted those piercings to kiss the walls of my cunt again.

I needed him to take me, to make me come so hard, my bones liquefied. After the emotional rollercoaster of the night before, I needed to feel alive.

And I couldn't wait any longer. I needed him inside me.

Kicking off the sheet, I canted my hips and lifted my leg, leaving no room for misinterpretation. "Oh yeah," he rasped, guiding his cock up and down my lips, teasing both my openings with barely-there nudges.

"Flynn," I begged, my voice a rasp filled with longing. He hummed and moved his hand up to my tit, flicking my nipple sharply like I loved.

"I love waking up to this. My perfect woman spread open for me."

"Need you," I gasped, my cunt throbbing with a desperation to be filled.

Flynn let me go, reaching down to guide his cock into me. He notched his head at my opening, and I whimpered. His teasing was driving me wild with want, and my cunt juices were already leaking freely onto my thighs.

Movement in the corner of my eye caught my attention. Ry stood there, his hazel eyes a molten gold in the light. His jaw was clenched tight as he ground his teeth together. I moaned, loving that his gaze was riveted on us.

Flynn stilled.

"Don't you dare stop," I threatened, arching my back and lifting my leg higher. If Ry wanted a show, I was going to give him the best fucking live spectacular he'd ever see.

Flynn huffed out a laugh and rocked forward, impaling me in one hard thrust. I cried out, my body breaking out in gooseflesh as a wave of heat rushed over me. His cock was splitting me open, my cunt struggling to adjust to the sheer girth of it. But fuck, I loved how big he was.

His fingers found my clit, and I held on to my knee, keeping myself open. I wanted Ry to see everything, for him to watch Flynn's cock tunnelling in and out of my cunt. I wanted him to know how wet I got and how much him watching me turned me on.

Ry had seen me naked more times than I could count. But he'd never seen me fuck—not that Flynn was some throwaway hook-up. He'd never seen me writhing on a cock, never seen me come. Never seen me make another man come. I wanted him to see everything. I wanted him as desperate to fuck as I was.

Maybe one day he'd even see me as a woman rather than the little girl who used to tag along when her big brother played with his friends.

The outline of Ry's cock tenting his shorts and the knowledge that he was as turned on from watching us as I was set me on edge. Flynn's deep, hard thrusts, the way he ploughed into me without hesitation, knowing I loved it rough, had my walls tightening. The quickening in my cunt started. Those gorgeous piercings and the perfect angle that Flynn was hitting my G-spot were to blame. I wanted their hands everywhere. I wanted their hard cocks in my cunt and hands and mouth. I wanted them in my arse. I wanted to be filled until I was overflowing with cum, my whole body tingling from orgasm after orgasm.

Then when I was exhausted and sated, I wanted to watch my guys fuck each other. I wanted to watch their cocks disappear down throats and into arses. I wanted double penetration and rough kisses. I wanted it all.

I wanted Ry right there with us. I wanted him to know what he was missing out on by not bending me over one of my Noble Steed's surfaces and plunging deep inside me. I'd let him anytime he chose. I just needed to tempt him enough to drop the rigid self-control he always possessed.

I reached up, pinching my nipples and crying out at the rush of sensation shooting straight down to my clit.

"So fucking tight," Flynn gasped.

He propped himself up on an elbow and gripped my hips with both hands, changing the angle of penetration. He must have given himself some leverage too, because the way he slammed his tree-trunk-thick-cock and those beautiful piercings into my cunt was worthy of an award for best performance.

His cock lit up every nerve ending in my body, and my orgasm closed in on me, just out of reach.

My gaze didn't leave Ryder's. He hadn't blinked. Hadn't moved. His body vibrated. Fists clenched, every muscle was primed, ready to lunge forward and fuck.

My mouth watered. I wanted that beast in my mouth. I wanted to choke on it.

But before I could beg him for it, Flynn shifted and hit my G-spot dead-on once more.

I shattered. My cunt clenched hard, a tsunami of sensation bursting through my body like fireworks on New Year's Eve. I cried out, my nerve endings electrified. The orgasm was never-ending. It radiated from my cunt through every molecule of my body, simultaneously shattering and remaking me.

I squeezed my nipples like Professor Reid had, and I choked out another cry, my orgasm renewing itself. Oh hell, if the prof were here, he could take my arse again, he and Flynn double-teaming me. Ry could pour his cum down my throat as the others fucked me until I couldn't walk.

My cunt strangled Flynn's cock with its contractions. But my man kept shuttling in and out, prolonging the ecstasy flooding my veins.

I wanted more hands on me. Needed more. But I was beyond words. Unable to form a sentence and ask the man hovering like a sentinel to cross the threshold to give me his dick.

My frustrated cry sounded like a sob, and Flynn reacted immediately. He crashed his lips down on mine. Thrusting his tongue deep, he pillaged my mouth. His cock was getting thicker, becoming even harder. He was close, and I needed to feel his cum shooting into my depths almost as much as I needed him to keep fucking me hard and fast.

Flynn bellowed, his teeth closing over the muscle at my neck as I shot my gaze back to Ry's. The man looked winded, his breath coming hard and fast. His lips were wet—he'd clearly licked them—and the wet patch blooming on the front of his boardies gave away just how close he was to coming himself.

Fuck. One lick, one suck. If only.

The heat of Flynn's cum flooded me, triggering more aftershocks from my orgasm. Out of breath, he panted as he nuzzled my cheek and his fingers delved to my clit, pinching and flicking me until my cunt tightened again. Oh fuck, he was going to make me come again. This time, though, he leaned down, sucking hard on my nipple as his cock twitched in my cunt and he worked my clit.

I shattered again, moaning incoherently as he kept up the slow thrusts of his softening cock. I was ready to throw my legs open and lay out the welcome mat just so that feeling would never end. I loved cock. I loved Flynn's cock. I loved the orgasms he gave me.

He waited until I was shying away from his fingers, the aftershocks turning into too much as my overworked clit begged for a break. Lifting his digits to his mouth, Flynn sucked them. I watched as Ry diverted his gaze, shifting it to Flynn. With an I-got-the-girl smirk, Flynn caressed me from hip to throat and down again.

"Morning, beautiful," he murmured.

I hissed as Flynn pulled his cock free of my depths, the shock of the air-conditioning on my overheated cunt soothing. His featherlight caress of my nipples had them hardening again, and I sighed happily. "Mmm, morning."

"Breakfast's ready," Ry grated out through clenched teeth, still standing in the doorway. "Dish yourselves up. I've got somewhere to be." He stomped away in the direction of his cabin, his heavy footfalls following him down the hall.

Flynn snorted out a laugh. "I feel like I've skipped all the intro sex classes and jumped right into the advanced ones. Two different audiences in two days."

I couldn't help my chuckle. "I'm a good, pure influence like that."

He shrugged and smirked, a twinkle of mischief in his eyes. "Eh, society's puritanical expectations are overrated."

"And this is why you're my best friend... and boyfriend?" My cheeks heated, and I huffed out an embarrassed laugh. "Maybe? I mean—" My voice came out as a squeak. Thank fuck he interrupted me.

"Yes. If my 'I love you' declaration and saving myself for you didn't make it obvious already, yes, I wanna be your guy."

Wrapping my arm around his shoulders, I pulled him tighter against me and smile-kissed him until we were breathless.

My stomach chose that moment to rumble. Loudly.

Flynn chuckled and kissed me again. "Let's feed you."

TEN

Zali

The awkwardness had persisted after Flynn and I dished up breakfast for ourselves and Ry had returned from his suite with a fresh pair of boardies on. We'd heard his groan of relief, then his shout barely a minute later. He hadn't even gotten his door closed before he'd come.

The first time. The second took a little longer, but not much.

But now I needed to stop fucking around and get down to business. Except this shit was personal, and I... wasn't sure if I was strong enough. I was scared—both of what I'd find and what I wouldn't.

Flynn held my hand, stroking my knuckles in a soothing rhythm. It centred me, gave me something to focus on besides the responsibility sitting on my shoulders. It was easy to bear when it was someone else's life. But the people I loved were in the firing line here, and I was the only one who could protect them.

Right now, I needed my friends. My boyfriend—I couldn't help the cat-that-got-the-cream grin at the thought—and the only other person, excluding Dad, who'd lost as much as we had. I swallowed hard. Had I fucked up? Would he forgive the way I'd behaved? He'd always been professional, and I'd crossed lines. Actually, I'd completely blown them out of the water, leaving no trace of their existence. I liked the sound of it, but it wasn't fair to Ry to put him in that position. I was his boss, and he was my employee.

"Ry," I asked. "Can you sit with us?" My voice was a thready whisper, fear and panic stealing through me and twisting my stomach into knots.

Wholly aside from the question of whether I'd still have my most loyal employee by my side was the research before me. Mum's diaries lay organized in chronological order on the coffee table. I was out of excuses too. I'd been procrastinating, trying to delay reading them. Now I knew why Dad hadn't read them. I couldn't turn back after I'd cracked open the first cover.

But I needed to dive into them. I'd promised myself that I would leave no stone unturned. I was going to hunt down every shred of evidence and prove her innocence.

Fear was a bitch though. What if my memories of Mum were completely wrong? I remembered her as being fun and full of life. She would laugh with Asher and me, take us to the beach and build sandcastles. She'd sing to me at night and read stories until my eyes slipped closed. What if these diaries changed those memories? What if the thoughts she put on paper showed her to be a completely different woman to the one I'd known?

What if I didn't know her at all?

"Sure," he answered stiffly, sitting down on the sofa opposite us and clasping his hands on his lap. "Look, about this morning—"

"I'm sorry," I cut him off. "I screwed up in more ways than one. I should have had the door closed. I hope this doesn't change our professional relationship. You're the most loyal employee I've ever had, and I'd hate for that to change."

He nodded with one sharp dip of his chin, but I got the unmistakeable impression that he was disappointed. He pursed his lips and averted his gaze, looking down at the spotless deck as if it held the secrets of the world. "Yeah." His smile was brittle, not even close to stretching across his face like it did when he was having fun. "What can I do for you, boss?"

"These are some of Mum's diaries. Could you sit with me while I read them?"

"Of course. Is Flynn leaving?" He looked between us expectantly.

"No, but—"

"Let me get my laptop. I've got some maintenance reports to fill out." He eased off the couch, slipping away toward his office.

Flynn elbowed me gently. "Told you he'd be here for you. He loves you too, Zee."

My only response was a squeeze of his hand and the small smile I shot him.

"Nervous about what you'll read?"

"Like you wouldn't know." I huffed out a breath. "I've been trying to psych myself up for fifteen minutes just to ask Ry to sit with us."

"I don't think your apology was necessary, but I'm sure he appreciated it." Flynn opened his laptop and inserted two USBs.

"What are you working on?" I asked.

"These are the USBs Professor Reid gave us. I'm doing the tasks he set for us. I figure I'll do the analysis while you make your way through the diaries."

Ryder returned and sat next to me when I patted the couch cushion. The three of us sat side by side, the two guys working on their laptops as I leafed through page after page of Mum's diaries.

The further I read, though, the more I smiled. In among the business talk that permeated every post, there were funny anecdotes, snippets of conversations, and cute things that Asher and I were doing. Warmth seeped through every line. Mum was fun and vivacious and wickedly smart. Every page showed just what kind of juggling act my parents had managed, Mum starting ReimagINC from nothing and building it into something spectacular while Dad held down a full-time job and was constantly running around with us kids. Mum's level of excitement when she could see good things happening was through the roof, and her fears were written into every page. What if work took her away from us? What if she didn't work hard enough for people? What if she made bad choices and lost money? What if she succeeded and it changed her?

She bounced around, as if her mind was travelling at a million miles a minute. One sentence she was talking about something Asher or I had done, and in the next, she'd be discussing how this stock or that stock was going to make them money. Throughout each diary and often when she was struggling, she'd stick printed images of tropical reefs, white sandy beaches, and towering forests. It was a tropical paradise. Knowing that she never got to see it in person, my smile turned sad.

I brushed aside the melancholy and focussed on details. I could go back and read the personal parts of the entries again when time wasn't tight.

Another name jumped out at me—one I'd read before.

"Flynn, can we cross-reference the investments the company had against what's in here? Take a look." I showed him the highlighted names and Mum's comments. From the dates in the diary, I could set out a timeline for investment targets she was impressed with. Whenever investments were mentioned, she was precise, setting out arguments for choosing one stock over another, predictions for increases in value in certain markets, and so on.

We went back to it, Flynn flipping from page to computer and back to the diary as he searched down each investment against the ones Mum talked about. Pausing to watch him, I leaned my head on his shoulder and waited.

"This could be big," I murmured, trying to fit the puzzle pieces together in my mind.

"Talk me through it," Ryder offered congenially.

"Ignoring the personal parts of the diaries, the rest is almost a rambling investor's report. She explained exactly why she made certain investments."

"Is it time to call Professor Reid?" Flynn asked. "Because I'm thinking that if these diary entries match up to the investments, we've got detailed justification for so many of the moves your mum made."

I hesitated. I wanted to rub the dickhead's face in it. I wanted to shout from the rooftops that his careful research meant fucking squat. Mum knew exactly what she was doing. She had a good reason for making the investments, and maybe, just maybe, the whole company fell apart after her death because she was the lynchpin holding the whole fucking thing together. Maybe it was everyone else's incompetence that made all those people lose their money.

But I wasn't sure we were there yet. Flynn needed to check the transactions, matching up the dates in the diary with investment funds coming in or going out. We also needed to verify the information in her entries. Were the companies performing as well as she thought they were? We needed more eyes checking them out, or it was going to take too long to get through everything.

I bit down on my lip and made the decision. I needed to act. "Call Professor Reid. Let's see if we can send him some company names. Maybe he can get some of the other students to check their performances over the relevant years.

If we can verify that they were doing as well as Mum said they were, that's pretty concrete evidence they were good investments."

"Agreed." Flynn dialled the professor's number, and after a few short rings, he answered. I only heard half the conversation, but I gathered from Flynn's surprised "Oh" and stuttered explanation of where the Noble Steed was docked that the hot professor had invited himself over. Flynn hung up. "Ah, he's coming here. Is that okay? I should have asked."

"It's fine," I reassured him, waving off his concern. "I don't mind."

"Aye aye, Cap'n," Flynn teased, and I snorted out a laugh, rolling my eyes at him.

Less than forty minutes later, Professor Reid was standing on the dock, messaging Flynn. *Am I in the right spot? The Noble Steed?*

Flynn showed me his phone, and I smirked. Of course he'd underestimated me. I peeled myself off the couch, stepped over Flynn's outstretched legs, and padded out to the deck. I met him at the gangway and opened the security gate for him to walk across.

I put on my sweetest voice. "Morning, professor. Come aboard. Watch your step as you cross."

"This is some yacht," he called, still gazing at its sleek lines. It was beautiful; I'd fallen for her the moment I saw her plans. The hull, platinum in colour, came to a point at the bow, high enough out of the water that when the engines were fully open and it was cruising, it looked like a bullet skimming on the surface. The floor-to-ceiling glass that ran along the sides of the boat, partially hidden from view by the walkways up the side of each deck, were tinted black. There were no straight lines along the hull. From the point at the bow, it sloped up and over, meeting the water-line at the stern in an elongated arc.

"I think you'll be interested in what we've found." I led him inside and introduced him to Ryder. "Ry was my brother's best friend."

"I'm sorry for your loss."

"Yeah, me too." Ryder had his laptop packed and the paperwork he'd been flipping through neatly clipped to a board. With a tight smile directed my way, Ry added, "I'll make myself scarce."

He slipped out, the professor's gaze following him as he turned in the opposite direction to where we'd come from only moments earlier. "Is he leaving?" he asked.

"No, he'll be down in the engine room for a bit." It didn't take a genius to understand what the professor was trying to get at while attempting not to sound nosy.

"Does he live aboard?"

"Yes. He looks after the yacht, my cars, plane, and—" I shrugged. "—me. He cooks, cleans, basically anything I need."

The professor huffed out a derisive laugh. "Spoilt kitten."

I crossed my arms over my chest and narrowed my eyes. I probably didn't look very intimidating in thigh-length white stockings with lace embroidered around their scalloped edges, white jean shorts, and a cropped grey jumper that was hanging off one shoulder. But what the fuck? Spoilt? He didn't know me. Underestimating me was one thing—assuming I was some trust fund baby was quite another. "Excuse me?"

"You're spoilt. This yacht has got to be worth at least a few million."

"Thirty, actually. What are you getting at, professor? Come right out and say it."

"Okay." He nodded again slowly. "You've got a generous sugar daddy."

I huffed out a laugh, but it held no humour. "The Noble Steed is mine."

His eyes widened for a fraction of a second before he buried his surprise under a wall of indifferent disbelief.

Patting the professor on his cheek like a dog, I smirked when his eyes flashed molten emerald. Leaning forward as if telling him a secret, I mock-whispered, "I stole it."

Technically I had taken the money to buy it, but I didn't look at what I did like that. It was merely a reallocation of resources. I rendered my services, found my target, and got paid for doing so. I had the pleasure of exacting punishment on those I deemed irretrievable, but ultimately, I worked and got paid. It was as simple as that. I'd put down some big names—international scammers that had stolen billions of dollars, owners of child pornography sites, organizations that specialized in identity theft, and so many more that I'd lost count. Then there were the smaller-worth individuals like my most recent put-down.

I did my bit, returning whatever sum I chose to identifiable victims, but I was no Robin Hood. I wouldn't ask for forgiveness for that either. I was Queen, and like any noble, I didn't give a fuck if people approved of me or not.

"No, I don't think so." Professor Reid stood before me, his eyes blazing with a ferocity I hadn't seen before. Chest to chest, he smirked and hooked his fingers under my chin. "Our kitten's too pretty to be a thief."

I grasped his fingers and bent them back far enough that he gritted his teeth. Glaring at him through narrowed eyes, I ordered, "Sit your arse down and listen, you chauvinistic pig."

I pointed at the seat I'd vacated and waited until the professor sat down before I seated myself on the coffee table opposite Flynn. Flynn smirked and shook his head, rolling his eyes at the professor.

Professor Reid cleared his throat. "What do you have?"

ELEVEN

Zali

Flynn and I tag-teamed, giving him the rundown and showing him the first diary and the transactions that Flynn had matched. "It continues like that, book after book," I muttered, still pissed at him.

The professor leafed through the diary he was holding, opening at a random page and reading an entry. He frowned, flicked forward a few pages, and read another one. "Your mum was very details oriented." When I nodded, he added, "I can see why you insisted she was brilliant. Her analysis is insightful. I'd love to see the historical stock figures and reports she was working from."

"Can we get them?" Flynn asked.

"Yes. She mentions stock movements in a few entries and talks about quarterly figures in others." He paused and rubbed his stubbled cheek. "We can get historical stock prices. I'm hoping we can get financials too, but tax records only need to be kept for seven years, so maybe not."

"Flynn and I can't double-check all this information in time. I want you to allocate more people to our research," I stated matter-of-factly. I wasn't going to ask, not when he was acting like a fuckwit.

He nodded, his gaze meeting mine. Instead of seeing the cocky bastard that I'd faced off against earlier, his expression was filled with respect. With promise and determination too. "I'll find a way. I'll make it happen," he promised, his tone conciliatory.

"Thank you."

The sliding door opened, and Detective Fraser stepped through. "Afternoon," he greeted smoothly. "Thought I'd check in and say hi."

"Sure, it's a party in here," I deadpanned. "Let's see who else wants to drop in."

"Ryder invited me."

I lifted my eyebrows in surprise at that. *He had? Why?*

Reading my expression, the detective added, "I called Ryder to see where you were. I wanted to check in, and when he mentioned you were docked, I asked if I could swing by. He let me on when I arrived."

Speaking of the devil. Ryder popped his head in from the other end of the room and said, "Lunch will be ready in about twenty. Anyone here have a seafood allergy?"

A chorus of no's sounded, and I rolled my eyes when he disappeared again just as quickly. He was still being quiet and avoiding me, but at least he hadn't told me where to shove the job.

"So, how's it going?" Ezra asked, jamming his hands in his pockets as a furrow appeared in his brow.

"We have a few leads. Zali and Flynn have done some great work."

"That doesn't surprise me," the detective retorted. "Zali's practically a prodigy. She'll get whatever information you want."

"Thank you, detective. That's all for now," I replied tersely. I didn't share details of what I did with people often, and the last thing I needed was for Professor Reid to get more curious than he already was. Flynn came over to my couch and sat on the armrest, squeezing my shoulder and massaging it one-handed. I sighed, a weird mix of happiness and frustration bubbling inside me.

"We have some leads that we're following up. I'll be busy for most of the summer," I added.

Detective Fraser nodded. "No worries, I'll make sure I don't add to that workload."

Conversation was stilted after that, mostly because Professor Reid and Detective Fraser were staring at each other. An intensity I hadn't ever witnessed came over the detective, and that look of lust I'd witnessed on the professor only the day before was back. But this time it was directed at the pretty boy in the room. Flynn fanned himself and leaned down to whisper against my temple, "Damn, the UST between them is hot."

I snorted out a laugh. He was right. Professorhole looked like he wanted to rip the detective's clothes off, and Detective Fraser was trying to push him away and failing. I flicked my gaze down the professor's long torso, trying not to make it obvious that I was checking him out. His hands rested on his thighs, his legs were spread, and I swallowed at the outline of his hard cock. Damn, the man was hung, and he was showing the detective just how happy he was to see him.

My eyes snapped to Detective Fraser's groin, and sure enough, he was packing too. Fitted dress pants did nothing to hide what either man had going on.

"It's ready. I've set the outdoor table so we can eat there," Ryder announced, breaking the spell my two visitors were locked in. It was a good thing I was wearing panties and not just shorts—my G-string was soaked.

I led the others to the top deck that overlooked the marina. People swarmed the dock, but they were moving past my yacht to the superyacht moored on the main pontoon. It was a nice change not to have my Noble Steed be the centre of attention for once.

The table was set with individual place settings accompanied by covered bowls of rice, two different sauces, and an array of seafood and vegetables laid out before the teppan grill Ryder had moved into place.

"Take a seat," I instructed everyone.

Ry went straight to the grill that was now smoking and poured a generous coating of oil onto it. He tossed the vegetables—zucchini and onion—until they were cooked al dente and used the flat spatula to dish a serving up to each of us. Within moments, he had the seafood on and off the grill. Prawns, salmon fillets, and scallops were plated for each of us.

"Are you eating?" I asked.

"Yeah, just about to start cooking it."

I waited until Ry sat down with us before digging into my lunch. It was as gourmet as it got. Ryder had gone grocery shopping that morning, but the first place he'd stopped was at the trawlers to buy up their premium catch.

Sitting back, I watched the banter between the men before me. Flynn and Detective Fraser were talking cricket—I quickly tuned out whatever it was they were droning on about—and Professor Reid was questioning Ryder on his cooking skills and how he'd learnt to manage maintenance for a yacht, cars, a plane—*and who owned a plane?*—and me. Ryder smirked when the professor asked what the highest maintenance item was, and I narrowed my eyes, pointing my chopsticks at him. His hearty laugh brought a smile to my lips. Apparently my '67 Mustang and the Noble Steed were a breeze.

I didn't realize I was smiling until Flynn nudged me and grinned. "This is fun."

"Yeah, it is."

Ryder stood up to clear the dishes, but Detective Fraser stopped him. "Let Tris and I do it."

"No, guests don't clean up. That's what I'm hired for."

"Ryder, stop," he instructed, the detective's tone leaving no room for argument. They stood up, stacked the plates, and disappeared into the galley to fill the dishwasher.

"How about I make some green tea?" I asked.

"I can do it," Ry responded, moving to stand. I touched his hand, and he sat back down, his confused gaze bouncing between Flynn and me.

"You've just cooked lunch. Let me do this." I knew why he was bewildered. I normally didn't offer to help, but I also wanted to make sure the professor and detective weren't using my crockery to kill each other or my galley bench to fuck on. Either way, I didn't want to put Ry in that position again so soon.

I wasn't far off the mark. Walking into the galley, I was met with the professor pinning Detective Fraser up against the bench, his front pressed to the detective's arse. His movements were fluid, his body practically dancing against the detective's. Grinding, hard body against hard body, the professor whispered something in his ear. I couldn't hear the words, but the deep rumble and the whisper of sex in his tone had my cunt clenching. Fuck, the man was potent. No matter who he was with, he had a commanding presence. Detective Fraser's moan was illicit. He arched into his touch, shoving back when the professor gave him a sliver of space.

He whipped around.

Chest to chest, and nose to nose. Their mouths were only a hair's breadth apart.

They were breathing hard. Like magnets drawn together, they moved as one.

Detective Fraser speared his fingers into the professor's hair, gripping him by the nape as Professor Reid's hands found the detective's back. Their mouths brushed together once in a whisper-soft caress.

I didn't know who moaned, but it kickstarted the other into action, deepening their kiss. Tongues duelled, teeth clashed, and I wanted to know their story.

But then it was over.

Detective Fraser stepped back, severing their connection, and held up a hand to stop the professor chasing him.

"No," the detective uttered, his tone a mixture of resignation and determination. His hands against the professor's chest were gentle, the pat seemingly an excuse to touch him rather than push him away.

Leaving the professor wasn't easy for him. The detective's strides were slow, his feet dragging. His expression was shuttered, as if he needed time to shove his emotions back into the box. Pausing before me, he cupped my face with one hand and gently kissed my cheek. He hovered there for a moment, and I breathed him in. I touched his chest, the curve of his hard muscle moulding to my hand. I'd never thought of him as built before, but he had some serious definition under that business shirt. Electricity sizzled through my veins, and the desire to see him without it on while up close and personal with Professor Pushy again was overwhelming.

It was the first time the detective had done that. He'd never shown me any affection before. We'd always just been colleagues, he my boss and me his employee. This change seemed monumental. I tightly clutched the small piece of himself that he gave me.

I leaned into his soft touch, not wanting it to end.

But he pulled away and stalked out of the galley without a word.

Professor Reid prowled closer, his eyes locked on mine. They were ablaze with desire dancing in the depths of his irises. Without hesitation, he tilted my chin up and nuzzled the same place that the detective had before pressing his lips to mine in a demanding kiss. He forced his tongue into my mouth and slid his hand down to my arse, gripping tight and rubbing his hard cock against my belly.

"I won't accept no from you," he murmured against my mouth. "This time I'm going to feast on your pussy."

"Keep dreaming." My rejection sounded a lot harsher than it was. As much as I hated him, I wasn't going to fight him if he wanted to fuck me again.

He dropped his shoulder the same way a rugby player does to charge forward. But he didn't knock me off my feet. Instead, he gripped my thighs and hauled me over his shoulder effortlessly. I squeaked and aimed for his kidneys when I punched his back. "Angel," he barked. "Bedroom."

"Stateroom," I muttered, trying to twist out of his grip.

"I don't give a fuck what it's called, kitten. All I know is that you're going to suck my cock, and I'm going to lick your pussy until you're screaming around Flynn's dick."

My cunt clenched and I bit back a moan. "And if I want you to fuck me instead of Flynn?"

He chuckled darkly. "I could get on board with that. Maybe I'll take both of you. Abuse your holes until you're dripping with my cum."

I stilled, my whole body lighting up like a firework. I needed him to do exactly that. Hard and fast, deep and all-consuming. But *I* wanted it. Not Flynn. It wasn't because I was jealous or didn't want him to experience the same high. I wanted him taken care of for his first time. I wanted it to be good for him, without any hint of pain, because while I loved the bite of a pinch or a slap and the sting of the professor's cock jamming inside my ill-prepared hole, he might not.

"Be gentle with Flynn. Don't hurt him."

The professor stopped at the bottom of the stairs, letting me slide down his hard body until my feet were on the last step. I barely cleared his shoulder with heels on. Without them, I was below his armpit. But he stepped down onto the floor and pulled me tight to him, his face a mask of seriousness. "I like to fuck, kitten. I'll hurt you because you like it." He pressed his erection into my belly, grinding on me. It set off another chain reaction, my nipples hardening and my cunt throbbing, my juices drenching my panties. "Mmm, I can smell how much you want it again. Our little slut."

I was panting like a bitch on heat, desperate for him.

He licked my cheek, gripping my arse in his big hands and lifting me effortlessly. Bulging biceps and six pack abs, and I was jelly. But that dick. Good lord in heaven above. It was instinct that drove me to wrap my legs around his waist, desperation to have his cock inside whatever hole he chose. The man, his personality, I could take or leave. But that body, that cock? I wanted them. And I was a shameless slut about it.

"But I know when to be gentle. And I will be with him. Our angel needs it tender." He paused as I took him in, eyes serious and no hint of sarcasm in his tone. "How experienced is he? I sensed—"

"Fuck me. Now," I ordered through gritted teeth, changing the subject before he could finish his question. It wasn't my place to answer his question, and I'd never breach Flynn's trust like that.

"Right here?"

We were in the loungeroom. But as much as I wanted him to get on with it, I needed to be behind closed doors. I needed Flynn right there with me.

The door to my stateroom opened, and Flynn leaned up against the doorframe. "You coming?"

"No, that's the problem," I complained.

Professor Reid smirked, his eyes containing a promise to fulfill every one of my wicked fantasies, and he stalked to Flynn, leaning down to brush his lips with the barest whisper of a kiss. My man's eyes fluttered closed, and he chased the professor's lips as he pulled back. Walking backward into my stateroom, Professor Reid focussed on me and raised his eyebrows in question. Dashing across the room, I slipped past Flynn into my stateroom and practically skidded to a stop at the professor's feet.

"Lock the door, angel," the professor ordered, his voice a deep rasp. It was the same sex voice he'd spoke in yesterday, the same one with which I'd heard him whisper to

Detective Fraser. I locked gazes with Professor Reid, licking my lips and shifting my weight to get some friction against my needy clit.

Flynn came to stand behind me, his hands caressing my bare belly. He dropped a line of kisses on the side of my neck, the professor's gaze locked on the point he touched. Flynn licked the sensitive spot below my ear, his tongue teasing a line up my sensitive skin before he nipped my lobe. "Want you naked," Flynn moaned. The loose linen of his lounge pants did nothing to prevent his monster erection from pressing into me.

Professor Reid reached for the hem of my crop jumper, edging it up off my body. He dropped it unceremoniously onto the timber floor of my stateroom and growled his approval at my bra. It was white and completely sheer except for the underwire and embroidered lace that ran along the edge of the plunging neckline. It was sexy, showing enough skin through the material to make my guys' mouths water, but at the same time, it teased them with a layer of clothing between us.

My shorts went next, falling straight off my hips as Flynn popped the button and unzipped them. The matching panty set was just as see-through and absolutely soaking wet.

"Leave those on," the professor ordered when I hooked my fingers in the elastic waist of my panties.

"These?" I fingered the scalloped edge of my thigh-high stockings before running my nails up the insides of my thighs. Gooseflesh broke out on my skin, and I moaned at the mere whisper of a breeze against my swollen clit. I knew looked pure and innocent in my underwear. I was anything but.

And I'd be nice and dirty before the afternoon was through.

The professor reached for my bra straps, and Flynn flicked the open the clasp on the back. The soft material fluttered to the floor, leaving me mostly naked and very needy.

"Lean back against me," Flynn whispered, stepping back a little so I had to arch back into him. He cupped my tits, presenting them to the professor.

The other man smirked, gripped my knee, and hitched it over his hip, then bent forward to feast on my nipples with sucks and bites until I was writhing against him. His hard cock rubbing against my clit, his magical mouth, and Flynn's heated breath on my neck as he sucked marks into my skin had me close to combustion.

He put me down. I whimpered, crying out in a plea for them to keep going. I wanted to be filled to the bursting point. To be fucked to within an inch of my life. But he was stalling. Fucking around.

I slid my fingers down, pinching and rubbing my clit until I was on the edge.

"I want to watch you make yourself come one day, Zee, but today is not that day," Flynn growled. "Get your professor naked."

Professor Reid's moan was deep and growly, and the sound stroked my cunt. My juices flowed. My hands shaking from desperation, I unbuttoned his shirt and slid my hands along his olive skin, parting the material when the shirt was open. His chest was decorated with a tattoo, words that I was too preoccupied to read in the design. As I pushed it over his shoulders to his wrists, I saw more ink on his arms. A football, a helmet, a black stallion's head and mane, arrows, and an eagle decorated his fine skin, the colours popping among the dark lines. My mouth was watering. With his six pack abs, pecs that I wanted to bite, and olive skin, I was desperate to lick him.

As if he read my mind, Flynn ordered, "Taste him." I slid my hands up the professor's chest again, flicking my thumbs over his erect nipples, and then I lowered my lips to his chest. Kissing and licking him, I breathed him in, getting high from his spicy scent.

His abs danced as Flynn moved up beside me and sucked on his other nipple. The professor threaded his fingers into my hair, holding me in place. I sucked harder, lashing his skin with my tongue, and slid my hand down lower to work his cock.

But Flynn already had his hand there and was massaging the iron rod. The professor whimpered when I moved my hand to his balls, rolling them through the soft material of his suit pants. "Suck me," he ordered, his voice rough, like he'd swallowed gravel.

Flynn stripped the professor's pants off, the tiny black boxer briefs he wore hiding nothing of his erection. His head was poking from the waistband of his briefs, the glistening tip begging me to suck. "Get on your knees, Zali," he begged.

I fell to the floor, taking his briefs with me. Flynn knelt next to me, and I gripped the professor's dick, angling it between us. I licked him, his salty skin and musk filling my lungs as I breathed him in. Flynn did the same, our tongues touching as we licked and sucked our man.

Fuck, I loved dick. I had two of the most beautiful ones I'd ever seen right in this room with me. With the kind of desperation only an addict understood, I wanted them to fill me up.

I was a slut for them. Wanton and needy.

Rubbing my legs together, I delved deeper, reaching around to get a handful of that meaty arse I'd been admiring since the first time I'd witnessed its glory. Flynn dropped his down face to the professor's balls, licking and sucking on the skin of his sac. "Suck one into your mouth," the professor rasped, his tone urgent.

"Want to eat you up," Flynn rumbled, his fingers slipping into the professor's crack as I sank my nails into his cheek.

Professor Reid cried out, pushing his hips back to meet Flynn's wandering hand, then forward into my mouth.

"Get on the bed, Zee. Hang your head off it so you can suck him."

Oh, hell yeah. I loved my guy's dirty directions. I followed them without question, and the professor was there, bending over me and sucking on my nipples once more. I couldn't reach him with my mouth, but I knew how to jack a man off like a pro.

Flynn nudged his legs wider and gripped his waist, grinding against the professor's arse. "Bend at your waist. I want your balls."

Professor Reid fell forward and canted his arse, licking a path down my belly to the edge of my panties. Sucking straight through the material, he latched onto my clit and flicked his tongue against the sensitive bundle of nerves. I cried out, thrusting my hips and grinding my cunt against his face. He straddled my face, and I cried out when he tore my panties, ripping them apart like tissue paper. He rubbed his stubbed chin against my cunt and I whimpered.

I sucked his dick down to the back of my throat. He punched forward, pushing deeper, past my tonsils. I swallowed around his length before he pulled out almost to his tip. "Oh fuck," he breathed, his voice wobbly.

Opening my eyes, I spied what had him cursing. Flynn had his eyes closed, ecstasy written on his face. Hands on each of the professor's cheeks, he spread him open as he licked stripes from his sac up to his hole. I threaded my fingers through Flynn's, and he opened his eyes, staring down at me with a mouth full of another man's cock.

"Thank you," he whispered, his forehead resting against the professor's butt. "I never could have dreamed of having this without you having the courage to take it first." He bent and kissed my forehead, before shifting his hand, his thumb getting frisky with the professor's pucker as he went back to feasting on him.

"Fuck. Fuck! Too close," the professor gasped, standing up and pulling out of my mouth. He clamped a hand around the base of his cock. There was a note of unhinged desperation in his tone. Flynn dropped to his haunches and pulled his hands away, severing our connection.

"Get me a toy I can fuck our girl with," he instructed Flynn.

He headed to my bedside drawer, pulled it open, and rifled through my lacy underwear. He found my black double-dick vibrator first, plucked it out, and tossed the dual cocks joined at their sacs to the professor. The other man caught it and propped one knee up on the bed, leaning over me to rub the lifelike veins against my cunt. "Remote?"

"In the drawer," I gasped as my legs fell open, and I shamelessly rode the thick dildo pressed against my clit. "It's black too."

Flynn found it, together with the lube, came back over to us, and popped the lid, drizzling slick along the cock that would fill my arse. I groaned when the professor rubbed its tip over my hole, stretching me with each push forward. He knew it was what I wanted, what I craved. I loved the bite of pain that consumed me, then quickly turned to ecstasy the instant the burn subsided. Craving hit me like a ten-tonne wrecking ball. Fuck, that rough touch of his drove me wild. I wanted the dildo, and I wanted it now. My juices flowed, my channel clenching in invitation to the thick black dick at my entrances.

"Swallow my cock to the root, and I'll fuck you until you can't walk or talk," the professor promised, his fingers tracing my lips.

"You gonna let Flynn fuck you?" I asked, challenging him. I wanted to sixty-nine the professor while I watched Flynn's cock sink into the infuriating man.

He paused, his gaze darting from mine to Flynn's. I watched the shock and nervousness cross Flynn's face—before finally settling on desire. It looked good on him. Fucking sexy. He licked his lips, bit down on his plump lower one, and gripped his dick through his pants.

"No one gets my arse. But for you...," the professor whispered, his voice raw.

Flynn's smile turned soft. He moved quickly, stripping off his button-down and shucking his pants. Naked as the day he was born, those beautiful piercings the only decorations adorning his body, his chest heaved. He stepped forward, gripping the professor by the nape, and drew their lips together. He kissed him, the move sensual and sexy as he slipped his tongue into the professor's mouth.

I took over from where the professor left off, rubbing my big black cock against my cunt. I was going to hold the professor to his promise, but until then, there was no reason I couldn't get off.

"Tristan," Flynn whispered, pulling back and kissing a line down his throat. "I promise, I'll make it good for you." He pressed their lips together again, humming as the professor gripped his bicep and groaned into his mouth.

Professor Reid's dick was leaking, pre-cum dripping from his slit. I licked up the salty liquid, moaning as it burst onto my tongue. I drew both their cocks to my lips. Feasting on their heads and rubbing their sensitive tips together, I was rewarded with more pre-cum from each of them.

One of my guys—probably the professor knowing how much of a control-freak he was—flicked the vibrator on, and I moaned long and low. Buzzing filled my veins as it kicked up a notch, my orgasm already on a knife's edge from having been teased for so long. I sucked them as Flynn leaned forward and whispered something to the professor.

When he pulled back, the professor responded, "I'll teach you."

Flynn pulled away before I could get another taste, but Professor Reid was there. He straddled my head, kneeling on either side of my face as he bent his mouth to my cunt and positioned the vibrator. "Lift your knees up, kitten. Spread yourself open for me."

I did, gripping my knees and opening myself up wide.

It was the only warning he gave me before pressing the vibrator against my holes and pushing forward. I cried out, my nails cutting into my shins as I gripped harder and rode the wave of pleasure/pain that threatened to drown me. He paused, retreated a little, and then shoved forward again, hard, until the thick dildo was buried inside me. My insides gripped it like a vice, not wanting to let the burn and impossible fullness go. When the professor's teeth connected with my clit and he bit down, I screamed, my body convulsing as an orgasm as fast and fierce as a summer storm hit me.

"Swallow my dick, Zali," he ordered.

I scrambled, reaching for his fat cock and then sucking him deep. It instantly calmed me like a pacifier given to a baby. But while I quietened, that voice deep inside me flared up, shouting for me to cover myself in dicks. *Fill every hole. Rub on me. Get off on me. Use my body. Cover me in cum. Fill me up until it's leaking from me. Fuck me until I can't stand. Wreck me. Give me so many orgasms that I'm on the edge of consciousness.*

I was a slut for cock, and I was about to get a close-up show of the best porn in existence. The cute twink with the big dick fucking the alpha?

Yes, please, and thank you for coming.

Again and again.

But it was nothing like I'd imagined. Flynn coated his fingers in slick and teased the professor with light touches and teasing licks on his cheeks and the seam where his arse met his leg. The professor's moan and the way he canted his hips, pushing back against Flynn's fingers, was so sexy. The visual, as well as the professor dragging my vibrator along my sensitive walls, working my holes in exquisite torture, was almost all the stimulation I needed. I was riding the knife's edge again. Professor Reid lowered his mouth to my clit and sucked on the nubbin. White-hot blinding ecstasy ripped through me, my holes spasming and sensation washing over me like a tsunami.

I shouted out, choking on the professor's dick as he thrust hard down my throat. It was as if he'd zapped me with an electrical current. My body lit up again, fiercer this time. My vision swam, and I was lightheaded from the lack of oxygen and the ferocity of the orgasm tearing through me.

Professor Reid withdrew his cock from my throat, and I gulped in air, blinking open my eyes once more as I came down from the high. Tears stained my cheeks, I had drool covering my lips, and a sheen of sweat coated my body, but I was in heaven.

I wanted more. I wanted everything. A couple of orgasms weren't enough, not when I had two men here who could make me scream.

Flynn had two fingers inside the professor, pumping slowly and scissoring his digits at the older man's direction. When he added a third, the professor started fucking me with the vibrator again, slowly moving it in and out. He upped the strength of the vibrations, and an aftershock rocketed through me. "That's it, kitten," the professor gasped as Flynn added a fourth finger. "Flynn," he groaned, his tone a mixture of pleading and warning. "Fuck, I obsessed over this the moment I saw you two in my classroom."

"Me too," Flynn growled. He licked a stripe up the professor's sac and pulled back to look me in the eyes. "Wanted you to watch me fuck Zee."

I moaned, remembering the look on Flynn's face when he'd seen the professor.

"Then I wanted to bend you over and slide my cock into your hole. Fuck you until you were screaming my name and I was pumping my cum into your arse," Flynn added.

The professor whimpered, his cock thickening in my mouth. I groaned, thrusting my hips up off the bed, chasing another orgasm. The picture Flynn was painting had me soaring higher and higher.

"Get. Inside. Me," Professor Reid ordered through gritted teeth. "Now."

Flynn pulled his fingers out, and I wished I had a view of the professor's hole all stretched and waiting for Flynn to plunge inside. Video footage would have been just as good. Flynn rubbed his slicked-up his dick against the professor's hole, notching it at the opening. Professor Reid growled and pushed back, impaling himself on the head of Flynn's cock.

Oh fuck, what a sight. Flynn's piercings disappeared as the professor pushed further back, his needy hole swallowing Flynn's cock. Professor Reid might be bottoming, but there was no doubt he was in charge. He rocked his hips, fucking my mouth and taking more of Flynn with every pass.

"Fuck. So tight," Flynn cursed.

"So fucking thick," the professor countered on a groan. His heated breath brushed my cunt. His handling of the vibrator was choppy, and his dick was throbbing in my mouth. Professor Reid was riding the edge of a monster orgasm too. As if chasing the high, he sped up, pushing back harder against Flynn before shoving his dick deep into my throat, making me gag with each pass.

The professor moved that vibrator into just the right place, hitting my G-spot dead-on. My muscles locked, and he hummed against my clit. I detonated, shouting out again as another orgasm swept through me. My cunt tightened in a vice grip before relaxing and letting the professor press the vibrator in harder. With each contraction, he held still, only to fuck me hard and fast when it let up. The whole time, his hips pistoned back and forth, alternating between fucking my face and Flynn's cock. Their sacs hit me in the face, and the grunts, slurps, and skin slapping together filled the room, the soundtrack to our fucking sending me higher.

My orgasm waned, only for the professor to step up his game. I didn't know what he did, but the bite of pain on my clit was magic. I cried out, my body locking tight as the familiar sizzle in my veins hit me again.

The professor shouted out and buried his cock in my throat, each pulse rocking my world. He emptied his load one throb after another, and I wished I could taste him. It was the second time that we'd been together and I hadn't had his cum on my tongue.

I wanted it.

Flynn withdrew to his cockhead before slamming forward again, punching the professor's still pulsing cock deeper. His cry set me off again. Knowing he was pumping his cum deep inside the professor was so fucking sexy.

The professor collapsed half on top of me, his sweat-coated leg resting on my chest as he used my leg as a pillow. I could see his hole, still slightly open and a little red from the pounding he'd taken, Flynn's cum and the lube wetting his rim. His chest heaved, and his cock left a sticky trail down my side as it shifted. My body was sated, the buzz in my veins a high that I didn't want to recede.

"You had enough?" the professor mumbled against my side as Flynn wiped my face with a wet washcloth.

"Mmm," I croaked, unsure whether I could handle another round with them. A nap would be nice. The vibrator clicked off, and he slowly withdrew the thick dildos from my cunt and arse. Cool air washed over my sensitive skin, and I moaned, an ember of desire flicking back to life.

"Sleep first, then I want both of you to DP me."

I sighed, closing my eyes.

TWELVE

Tristan

I slipped out of bed but paused before walking away. Zali and Flynn were fast asleep, Flynn curled around Zali and holding on to her protectively. She deserved that. Underneath the sass was a strong woman who'd been dealt a shitty hand at life. Losing her mother and brother must have been awful. Having me dig up those terrible memories would be worse. But I couldn't back away now. I had something. I was sure of it. My backers were pushing hard. They wanted the podcast published.

I wish I knew who they were.

Meeting Zali had stumped me. I was so determined to see this thing through. Not even a death threat had stopped me, although admittedly, I had hesitated. It was hand-delivered to my front door and nailed into the timber. Given that I lived in an apartment building that had security fobs coded to each floor, it was a wake-up call. But I'd used it as motivation. I was onto something if there was someone who didn't want me to find what I was looking for.

My worlds would quite possibly collide in a spectacular fireball, but now that I'd hopped onto this train, I wasn't getting off. Especially when the two people in front of me were so willing to give me part of themselves.

I brushed a lock of Zali's hair off her face and smiled at Flynn when he blinked his eyes open. I pressed my forefinger to my lips, and he nodded and let his eyes slip closed, falling back into sleep quickly.

I rubbed my forehead. I was in trouble.

Deep, deep shit.

Turning on my heel, I tiptoed over to my discarded clothes and picked them up. After slipping out the door and closing it quietly behind me, I turned and walked straight into Zali's sexy cabin boy.

"That's great," he muttered, shaking his head. His eyes, which were a molten gold, narrowed dangerously, and he pressed his lips into a thin line. He was spoiling for a fight, but I couldn't afford that. Not when I wanted more of the woman and man on the other side of that door.

"Excuse me," I murmured, trying not to incite him to violence. I looked up and down the hallway, searching for another open door that I could slip into. I gestured to the one behind Ryder and added, "I need to get dressed."

He squared his shoulders and balled his hands into fists. "Don't you fucking dare hurt her," he threatened.

I smirked. Apparently, he'd stepped into the role of Zali's big brother in Asher's absence. "I'll do my best."

"Do better." He stepped forward until we were chest to chest. He was a couple of inches taller, but I was wider, and

I'd had plenty of experience brawling. This pretty boy didn't look like he'd seen a day of hardship in his life.

"Or what?" I raised my brow. I was trying to keep the peace, but I also wouldn't stand here and let some little shit threaten me.

He chuckled, but the sound was cold. "Or she'll bury you. You don't need to be scared of me. I'll break your nose, give you a black eye if you hurt her. But Zali? She'll end your career and destroy your life."

"Only that?" I shrugged as nonchalantly as I could manage. I was good at presenting a façade to the world, but the pressure on my chest was making it hard to breathe. Zali was intense. There was something about her that screamed danger. I'd been trying to push her buttons when I told her she was too pretty to steal anything. But I'd believed her. Deep down, something told me that Zali was even more hazardous than the death threat I'd received.

Sighing, I added, "Look, I like both her and Flynn. You might not realize it, but I've got things on the line here too." Zali only needed to report me to the dean. If he found out I'd slept with both her and Flynn after they'd come to my office to talk about the course, he'd fire me on the spot. "Now, if you'll excuse me, I need to put some pants on."

"You planning on leaving?"

I shook my head. My mind was screaming at me to distance myself, but I wasn't ready yet. Not when there was the promise of more time with Zali and Flynn.

"Good." He nodded. "Zali won't mind if you're naked. She's rarely dressed herself."

"And you?"

"I'm just the staff. I blend into the background. I'm not meant to be seen." It was Ryder's turn to shrug. He tilted his head toward the loungeroom. "She'll be impressed if you're doing whatever research you've planned when she and Flynn wake up."

"That's why I'm out here."

A ghost of a smile tilted his lips. "Okay. I've got to run out for a bit. I'll avoid the loungeroom when I come back in."

It was as if he was giving me the green light to pursue something with Zali and Flynn. His approval was meaningless, yet I appreciated his candour.

"Probably a good idea." I smirked when he rolled his eyes, and I dropped my clothes beside the door.

Striding out to the loungeroom naked, I chuckled when Ryder called out, "Thanks, mate. Wanted that eyeful."

♟ ♟ ♟

I'd been reading Flynn's notes and compiling data for an hour, building on the information Flynn had started compiling. Some of the names of companies Zali's mother identified as investment opportunities were familiar. Like ReimagINC, some were infamous victims of the GFC. Others were still around.

I downloaded another set of historical share price records from the stock exchange's site. I'd later compile a timeline that matched up the dates in the diaries with movements in the share price, release of financial data, and if and when investments were made. But to do that, I needed the financials. The regulator's database would give me much of what I was looking for, but given the age of the records, I was going to have to wait for them to be emailed.

Zali had earmarked posts, having shown them to me as she ran through the information. I wanted to read the diaries—they'd be worth their weight in gold for my research—but I couldn't bring myself to overstep Zali's trust in me. Even showing me the diaries in the first place was huge. But she'd wanted me to see them. She'd asked me to read parts of them. I picked up the first diary she'd shown me and held it gingerly, tossing up whether I should read the tabbed entry or not. Finally, I opened it, making sure not to read more than the parts she'd highlighted.

It was a heartbreaking read.

Entry after tabbed entry showed me a glimpse of their perfect little family. They were happy. Zali had been a bright and bubbly little girl who adored her big brother, and Asher was a sweet kid who loved rugby and idolized his dad. Even back then, Zali and Flynn were already joined at the hip. The snippets Rosa shared of Flynn's childhood didn't seem happy. There wasn't any real detail in there, but she'd painted him as a lonely kid whose family seemed to forget he even existed. She said more than once that he needed a bath and a decent meal.

The two of them had followed Asher and Ryder around, gazing at them with stars in their eyes. It was exactly how I'd viewed my older brother once upon a time.

Then there was Monroe, Rosa's husband. She adored him. He worked hard and loved his kids. Rosa dreamed of jetting off to an island with him for a holiday where they could relax. She called it the honeymoon they'd never really had.

They had a dinner on the beach every Friday night, and when she had the time, they'd swim or kayak and explore the rock pools or fish. They were always on the water, something Zali had continued. It was so domestic, an idyllic environment to raise kids in.

Even reading only the tabbed entries, I got a sense of Rosa's personality that my research had never uncovered. I wasn't stupid enough to think that she was some robot, but the descriptions of her highs and lows, her love for her family, and the passion she had for her work made her human, more so than I'd been prepared for.

Zali had already changed me. There was no way I could cast her mother in the light I'd planned on when pitching this podcast. When Zali had defended her mother's honour in my office, it had knocked me sideways. But these diaries added another dimension that I couldn't ignore. Maybe Zali was right. Rosa didn't come across as incompetent or even close to negligent in the way she spoke about those investments. Maybe it was all bad luck.

But that didn't sit right either. My gut told me there was something more. I just wasn't sure what it was. Otherwise, why would someone threaten me? Who was behind all this? Who would try to stop me?

If only the death threat was my main problem.

But it was the lowest on my list of fears. Falling for them was so much more dangerous. I could destroy everything I'd worked for. No, it *would*.

But I was beginning to suspect it'd all be worth it.

I couldn't get the picture of Zali and Flynn out of my head. My hole was still tender where Flynn had fucked me so well, and no one had ever swallowed my cock like Zali had. I fucking loved sex with them.

I'd never bottomed for anyone before Flynn. I loved being stuffed full, loved the feel of a dildo up my arse, but I didn't let anyone get close enough to let it happen. I wasn't some emotionally damaged hero in need of saving. I just liked to keep things simple. If I controlled what happened, hook-ups didn't get messy. They didn't ask to stay the night. They didn't want a repeat. There were only a handful of people I'd had seconds with, and even fewer who I intentionally sought out to go another round with—three to be exact.

My hook-ups were bathroom-stall blow jobs and hotel stays during conferences or weekends away where I'd be gone after a few days anyway. The women wanted a quick fling, and the men understood keeping it simple.

But Flynn.... The man was sweet and so very innocent. He was angelic. I'd fallen under his spell the moment I'd locked eyes with him in class. I should have averted my gaze and never thought about my student bent over and taking my cock. But Zali was sitting right next to him. Her fiery personality had been the perfect complement to her sex-kitten looks.

I was a lost cause.

My plans quickly devolved into figuring out a way to fuck Flynn after I'd made Zali scream my name.

Then Zali had uttered those famous last words. *You gonna let Flynn fuck you?* Memories of fingering myself in my office had roared to the forefront of my mind, and my dick and hole did the decision-making for me. Not that my brain wasn't 100 percent on board too—it was just slower to catch up.

I'd agreed before I could even think up a decent objection. But saying no hadn't even crossed my mind.

I was Flynn's the moment he'd looked at me with those lust-filled eyes while sitting in the front row of my class. I would have let him do almost anything. Then he touched me, and I was lost. He was that good. Getting his dick inside me was like a fast track to heaven. Those piercings rubbed me in all the right ways, hitting my P-spot and sending me into orbit.

Prostate orgasms were few and far between for me—not surprising, given no one got access to my arse. But Flynn was a natural. It didn't matter that he was inexperienced. He knew exactly how to get me there. In what world did forty-three-year-old men have multiple orgasms? Apparently, all it took was a twenty-something-year-old virgin to make it happen.

I shifted on the couch, my dick hardening as I closed my eyes and relived what had gone down. The attraction between us was electric. Zali liked to say how much she hated me, but she loved my dick. And I loved Flynn's. Look at that—we could be a happy little daisy chain.

I didn't want this hook-up to end, but that in itself posed a significant problem. My brain was finally coming back online, and it was telling me I was in way deeper than I should be.

Already.

How was it even possible? Then again, I shouldn't be surprised. The last time I'd been so captivated was when I'd met Ezra. He still owned a piece of me even a decade later.

Thinking about my pretty-boy detective had my dick hardening even more. Watching them together was like a homing beacon to my cock. It almost split my pants open when he'd kissed Zali's cheek. He also watched Flynn with a sense of longing and sadness. He wanted both of them, and I'd seen that same wistfulness in Flynn's gaze. Zali was a harder nut to crack. She was so fiery and obstinate on the surface, but when you got close enough, she melted like butter.

There was something between them, something simmering just below the surface that would be beautiful to watch if it ever boiled over. But that was the thing. Ezra would never act on it—he was a Boy Scout. Sleeping with an employee or a man over a decade younger than him, never mind both, would be out of the question.

"There you are," Zali murmured against my ear, making me jump. I'd had my eyes closed, my feet up on the coffee table, and my laptop still on my thighs. My dick was saluting the world and betraying the thoughts running through my mind.

I sensed Flynn in front of me without even opening my eyes, and a smile tilted my lips up. He lifted my laptop and straddled my thighs, earning him a hum of appreciation. I drew them in, wrapping one arm each around Zali and Flynn and pulling them close. Flynn kept coming, his lips meeting mine in a slow kiss. Filled with passion and a need to get nearer, I dominated the kiss, thrusting my tongue into his mouth and getting high off his heady flavour.

Zali kissed a line up the side of my throat, and I tilted my head, giving her more room to nibble. Between my girl and her wicked mouth, Flynn's kiss, and his pierced monster rubbing against mine in a sexy-as-fuck frot, I was lost. Floating in bliss as my body started to wind up. I couldn't get enough. The sensations ricocheting through me were driven higher by the heady sounds we were making.

Moaning, I wrapped my hand around Flynn's hardening dick and my own and jacked us both.

Flynn broke our filthy kiss to lean back, and I took in the decadent sight before me. Compact muscle, a face that deserved to be on magazine covers, and a fat cock that had a bead of pre-cum leaking from its head, the man was a vision. He was a sight for sore eyes.

"He's gorgeous, isn't he?" Zali whispered. "You want him as much as I do."

"I do," I admitted, swallowing past the lump in my throat. I'd been living in denial. Anyone else, and I would have politely asked them to leave my office, but the combination of Flynn and Zali had me breaking not only my own rules, but those of the university too.

Turning my face, I captured her lips in a drugging kiss. Flynn stroked my chest, his thumbs brushing over my pecs as he flicked my nipples. Like a lightning bolt straight to my dick, sensation shot through me, and I gasped.

Zali pulled back, and I nuzzled her nose with mine. On a whisper, I added, "You too, Zali. You're just as beautiful."

Her eyes were bright, but there was a softness in them. She bit back a smile, her teeth sinking into that plump, perfect lip of hers. "You should use this," Zali murmured, before drizzling lube on our cocks. The cold was a shock to the heat Flynn and I were burning up with.

I spread the cool liquid over us, the slip between our shafts delicious. The vision of our dicks sliding against each other's was porn-worthy. I was leaking like a dripping tap.

She wiggled her eyebrows playfully—I loved this side of her—and with a grin, added, "Get him as hard as you are, professor. I want you both to take me."

Ah, hell. I squeezed my cock tight, slowing my lightning-speed rocket to the edge. I shivered at her words, at the potential and the visual she painted. I shouldn't love how she still insisted on calling me professor.

It reminded me of just how dangerous and illicit this affair was.

And yet... I wanted it.

I needed that reminder.

I wanted Zali to keep telling me over and over what a dirty old man I was for wanting my students as much as I craved her and Flynn.

I loved pushing Zali's buttons. I loved getting her riled up until the only thing to do was shut her up with my dick. I loved flashing that look at Flynn and watching as desire overtook his body, his eyes glazing over and his lips parting on a gasp. I loved watching his dick harden and seeing him transform from a sweet angel into an adventurous man who loved sex.

Zali had accused me of being a chauvinistic pig, but I wasn't. Despite what she thought, I didn't underestimate her. From the moment I'd first seen her, I knew she was special. Not because of her looks, not because her body was made for sex, but because of her confidence. The way she met my gaze head on, analyzing me, was hot as hell. There I was, struggling to tamp down my base desires while she was challenging me to a mental dual.

Then when Flynn had introduced her, and I put a name to her face, I understood just how brilliant she was. Ezra wouldn't have sent her to me unless she was the best he had, not when he'd known how high the stakes were. If there was someone else—anyone else—who could have found data on her mother, he would have had them enrol. He would have protected Zali. But he hadn't. He'd sent her. She was the prodigy he was so proud of, the one who he spoke of with a mix of intimidated awe and longing in his voice despite trying so hard to hide both.

I might be stubborn and demanding, and I might like control, but Zali gave as good as she got. She was more than capable of putting me in my place and shutting down any moves I made. Having her utter those words—*I want you both to take me*—was... I shivered, want curling low in my belly.

I couldn't wait to get inside her again, to feel the tight walls of her channel strangling my cock. The slide of Flynn's cock against my own with only the thin wall of her pussy between us would be everything.

"You want her pussy or her arse?" I asked Flynn, my voice a rasp, rough and deep, pushing her for a reaction once more. She loved it, loved being owned and used, even though she'd never admit it out loud.

"Pussy. She likes my piercings just like you do." He smiled that sexy, shy smile of his. "They're my holes now. I'm claiming them."

"I'm good with that." I grinned, a lightness in my chest buoying me.

It was a foreign feeling, laughing during sex. It was rare that I did, and even though we hadn't laughed during the times we'd already been together, I'd had the time of my life with them. That first time, the shock of how right it had been shook me to my core. I'd panicked, not even able to put off the dean when he'd asked to pop by my office after he'd made a coffee. It was the kick in the arse I'd needed to wrap up my rendezvous, but my head was so messed up that I was rude as hell and abrupt to boot.

But this time I didn't have the same issue. I was going to savour every moment I had.

"Maybe one day you'll get to watch someone else take my hole. Wreck me like I did you," Flynn whispered.

I loved that he knew and understood without me having to tell him what I wanted our dynamic to be. There are perceptions of alpha personalities that scream toxic masculinity. The assumption that I always wanted to top was one of them. I was just as much of a hole slut as Zali. It was true I didn't just let anyone come inside me, but for the right man, I'd spread my legs as quickly as a gymnast does the splits. Just because I was the one getting reamed didn't mean I wasn't still in charge of how it was happening. I was an expert at topping from the bottom, and Flynn seemed to love it.

"Would you like that?" he asked, tearing a groan from deep inside my chest. My dick pulsed in my hand, and a bead of pre-cum pooled at my tip. There was no doubting just how much I liked that, because fuck me, I was about to shoot off like a bottle top, just picturing it.

"You want that?" I asked, my gaze travelling to Zali. I could just imagine what it would be like.

"Mmm," she moaned, shifting her weight from side to side. She was rubbing her legs together, trying to find friction for her pussy.

Flynn licked my throat before thrusting his hips and dragging his dick against mine. "C'mere, Zee," he encouraged.

"Sit on my lap, kitten," I directed. Flynn climbed off and I spread my legs wider, helping our lady to perch between my legs, pointing her cute little butt in my direction. The sight was delicious. Soft round globes with a tiny waist and that beautiful blonde hair cascading in waves down her back. I could feel how her breasts jiggled, the perfect blend of soft and firm. I couldn't keep my hands off them. She was so responsive too. Touch her anywhere, and her juices flowed. It was such a fucking turn-on, knowing she wanted both Flynn and me so badly.

I wanted to possess her, to own that beautiful body so I could turn her inside out. I wanted to make her scream, give her orgasm after orgasm until she wouldn't leave. Not couldn't—*wouldn't.*

My man lubed me up again and reached between us, gripping my dick and positioning it at her hole. Grasping the underside of her legs, I took her weight and eased her down. My dick notched at her hole, and Jesus Christ, the sight was something to behold. Her heat was so tempting, so soft and tight and inviting. I wanted to slam inside her, to bring forth those sobs she'd let go of when I'd first fucked her tight hole. But I desperately wanted to take my time too.

Slowly and gently I lowered her until my cockhead popped through her resistance. So much heat. So tight.

She hissed, her arse already sensitive from the dildo I'd fucked her with. I held still, my muscles vibrating and every instinct in me screaming to push her down hard and fast, basking in her wet heat until I lost it.

Zali moaned, her hole clenching and loosening as she adjusted to the stretch. "Need you to move," she choked out.

I lowered our gorgeous girl, my slick cock sinking inside her like it was coming home. I bottomed out, stretching her hole wide as I impaled her. Zali leaned back against me, panting. Her back arched, and those gorgeous breasts beckoned to me. I wanted to see them bounce as she screamed.

Taking the entirety of her weight in my arms, I lifted her, spreading her legs until she was straddling me, her legs bracketing my own. "Beautiful," Flynn whispered, his eyes fixed on the point where we were connected. I could just imagine it, my balls drawn up tight against my body, my shaft buried deep inside her stretched arse, all pink and slicked up.

Groaning, I ran my hands over her sweet body, mapping her curves with my palms. I slid them up to her breasts, her soft skin like silk under my touch. I flicked my fingers over her pert little nipples, and she shivered, a full body shudder that tightened her channel around my dick. I was cross-eyed with lust, ready to fire off just from getting inside her.

But bloody hell, I was in heaven. This woman was nirvana. Never mind searching for a place in some far-off world—it was right here in her arms.

Her breath hitched as I trailed my hands back down to her hips and flexed my own, pushing deeper into her.

It wasn't enough. I needed Flynn, and so did Zali.

He busied himself coating his length in slick before pressing his dick against her opening. She wiggled on my lap, arching as she tried to get him to push inside her. Zali clenched her pussy, the movement making her arse tighten around me. Fuck me, I was going to lose it before he got inside her at this rate. But Flynn wouldn't be moved. He rubbed against her clit before barely pushing his cockhead inside her and retreating. Zali gasped, her legs spreading further in a blatant invitation to come closer. Her toes were curled, her breathing shallow and her nipples hard as diamonds as Flynn sucked a mark on her throat.

Her whole body quivered as he kept up his slow entry. His movements were unhurried despite the precipice Zali and I were already on. This man was something else, a cinnamon bun outside of the bedroom and a confident tease within.

He tore his vision away from the place we were all joined and looked up at me, our gazes clashing as Zali whimpered while we stretched her. Flynn's eyes held me captive. They were bright, filled with mischievousness as he teased us both.

Finally, fucking finally, he pushed inside far enough that the first of his piercings kissed my cock through the thin barrier between us. I couldn't help my shiver. Holy hell, this was something else. Something wickedly delicious and taboo but so intimate too. Zali was giving us a gift. Her body was a temple I wanted to worship at for as long as she'd have me there. Flynn was a believer like me, his own body praising the rapture that she was bringing us.

Zali moaned, her back arching. I'd learned quickly that she loved friction against both her nipples and her clit, and it didn't matter whether it was a rough touch or the soft swipe of a tongue. Her hands scrambled for purchase, and her breathing was thready, ecstasy ratcheting up and coursing through her, and in turn, us. She was lost to us, her body strung tight.

When Flynn bottomed out, Zali snapped her legs around his waist, her knees bent and heels pressed against Flynn's arse. Her toes curled as Flynn ground down, pushing further inside her. She cried out, and I closed my hands over her hips, snapping mine forward. Flynn slowly withdrew to his cockhead and punched his hips forward before mixing up the tempo and plunging into her depths in long slow thrusts that were more of a grind than a pump. We played her body like a finely tuned instrument, taking all of us to heaven.

"So fucking gorgeous, kitten," I whispered on a hoarse moan as I fingered her nipples. "Seeing you take our cocks together is so fucking hot."

"So full," she gasped leaning her head back on my shoulder.

"So tight," Flynn breathed dropping his mouth to the breast I cupped and presented for him to suck on. "You're incredible. I'm gonna lose my mind in a minute. Gonna come so hard that I'll feel you around me for a week."

"Never want you to stop," she moaned. "Want you both to do this forever."

"Never stopping," I ground out, willing myself not to blow yet. I was right there, on the edge. Ready to go careening over into the abyss and float for a millennium. But hell would freeze over before I allowed myself to come before my beautiful kitten.

I caressed her, kissed her throat, and sucked a bruise into her skin. I wanted to mark her.

Own her.

Possess her.

Cherish her and protect her.

She was ours, and we were hers for as long as she'd have us, risks be damned. I didn't care. I wanted her, I wanted Flynn, and I was making them mine.

Running my fingers through her glorious hair, I wrapped it around my fist and tugged until her head was tilted further and her throat was exposed to me. I licked the shell of her ear, then whispered, "Staying with you forever."

It was probably too much, too soon. I'd laid down my cards for them to see while they were still getting their hands dealt, but Zali and Flynn needed to know what I wanted.

Flynn slowed his thrusts even more, our bodies pressed together in the most intimate of ways. This wasn't fucking. This was something so different.

"Love you," Flynn murmured. "I'm staying forever too." Flynn was no doubt speaking to Zali—he'd probably been in love with her since he was a child—but I was happy living in hope. I closed my eyes and nuzzled Zali's throat again.

Flynn tipped my chin up and kissed me, our lips melding slowly together, our tongues dancing. He wanted me as much as I wanted him, at least for tonight.

We moved together, finding a rhythm that was taking us higher with every thrust.

Zali whimpered, and her channel fluttered around me. She was close. "Come for me, kitten," I encouraged. "Come for us." We kept up our thrusts until her pussy clamped down, locking tight, and she cried out softly. Flynn held her close as she buried her face against the crook of his neck and rode out the high.

I needed to be closer, needed to touch them. I wrapped my lovers in my arms, holding them in an embrace that I never wanted to let go. Tangled there together, Zali still clenching rhythmically around us, I let go, emptying myself into her with a long moan. I was flying, soaring in the warm air currents of the tropics like a bird gliding in the skies. My fingers and toes tingled, my limbs heavy and light at the same time. My head spun, simultaneously high and grounded.

Flynn's choked out cry as his cock bucked deep inside Zali renewed both her and my orgasms, each of us moaning and clutching one another harder.

I floated in a cloud of bliss, touching and caressing the two people who'd turned me inside out. I'd never experienced anything like it before. Not like this. Not slow and sweet and loving. Not with the two people who were very quickly coming to mean so much.

And that was it—two people. I'd never had a relationship, never even wanted one. But I was beginning to realize that it was because I'd never found the right people. Not person.

Everything was riding on the next couple of months—the podcast, my research funding, my career if anyone ever found out about us. I shouldn't risk it. But I had no intention of backing down now.

THIRTEEN

Zali

Coming down from that high was going to take a while, but no one seemed in any hurry to move very far. I hated how I loved that they were sticking around. Professor Reid's arms around me were comforting. He wrapped me up like I meant something to him. He was being all loving and sweet, getting handsy with me but not in an I'm-ready-to-go-again kind of way. It was more that he was caring for me, touching me to let me know he was there and cherished me.

I was jelly-legged and completely unable to stand, but I didn't want to go anywhere either. Flynn had hauled himself up onto the couch, and the prof tipped us sideways, our heads landing on Flynn's lap. Closing my eyes and floating in the bliss that they'd brought to my body was the easiest thing to do.

Sighing happily, I kissed Flynn's leg, and he ran his fingers through my hair. "Love you," he murmured, and for the first time, I wanted to say it back to him. But it wasn't just him I needed to say something to. It was Professor Reid too. Tristan.

Twisting onto my stomach, I looked at Tristan, then up at Flynn. I licked my lips, hesitating. This was big. It was heart-pounding, sweaty palms, churning gut, butterflies doing loop-de-loops in my chest big. My voice was steady, despite the freaking-the-fuck-out moment I was having. "I love you too."

It was as if a weight had lifted off my chest, one I'd been carrying without even knowing about it. I laughed, high on the hit of adrenaline and happy sex hormones that were coursing through me. It wasn't only the sex that had done it though. Admitting to myself and saying the words to Flynn was so freeing. It was warmth and sunshine, ice cream cones on a summer's day, swimming and laughter all wrapped up in three little words.

Feeling something for Tristan other than the need to throttle him had been impossible less than a few hours earlier, but now it was as if the walls were crumbling, and he was letting us see his true nature. He was grumpy and wanted things to go his way, but he was sensual and caring, gentle when he wanted to be. He knew I liked it rough, and when I was in the right frame of mind, I loved the bite of pain during anal when I wasn't prepared properly, but he'd taken it slow with me. He'd been gentle, only giving me as much as I could handle. He'd left it to me to ask for more when I was ready, despite being able to yank me down on his dick and fuck me any way he wanted. His kisses had been druglike, his touches like he was worshiping me.

Flynn and Tristan cherished every part of me, showed me how much they wanted me. Their touches were reverent, like I was worth something more than what they could get from me. They showed me that my body wasn't just there to get them off, and they weren't using my mind to benefit themselves. Between them, I felt loved. Telling them that I was gone for them too was nerve-wracking but fucking amazing.

Grinning like a loon, I lifted on my elbow and leaned into Flynn. His lips met mine in a kiss that was as sweet and slow as it was toe-curling. I didn't want to pull away, but I needed to show Tristan too. Our lips met and Flynn ran his fingers through my hair, nuzzling my temple until I turned back to him, deepening our kiss. When Tristan kissed a line across my cheek, I shifted, capturing his lips again and turning our kiss into a three-way one.

"Do you want a shower, love? Or a bath?" Tristan asked, his gaze warm and his lips tilted up in a soft smile.

"I'd really love a swim," I sighed wistfully. Bloody marinas. They were always so busy and hardly the place I'd dive into the water. "But I don't know I have the energy for it. We could hop into the hot tub instead?"

"I'd love that," he murmured against my lips. "Flynn?"

"Yes, please."

I'd barely sat up when both my guys were helping me off the couch. Tristan carried me up the stairs to the top deck and over to the bow where the hot tub was sunken into the deck. Sheltered by the soaring arcs of the hull that met in a point directly in front of us, he held me as Flynn looked after the cover. I could see the boardwalk from where I was perched in Tristan's arms, and if anyone looked at the right angle, they would definitely be able to see me too.

But it was the first time that I'd only wanted to be naked in front of the two people I was with and not the whole world.

As soon as the three of us were in the water, my muscles melted. Flynn sat at my feet, propping them in his lap and massaging until I was in heaven. Tristan's hands were at my shoulders, loosening the knots there too.

"Massages are my favourite thing in the world," I sighed.

"I prefer ice cream," Flynn deadpanned.

"Kale and coriander for me," Tristan added. I snapped up, falling off his lap with the move. I went under, flailing until I could extract my foot from Flynn's lap and push myself back up. Water streamed down my face, and I coughed up the mouthful I'd taken in.

"What the fuck is wrong with you?" I asked, among coughs, disgusted.

Tristan snorted out a laugh, his smile lighting up his face. The frown and concentration lines disappeared, and he looked relaxed and happy. He was gorgeous.

But he also had taste in his arse.

"I'm kidding. I hate the stuff. It's an abomination. But I'm definitely a savory person. Give me cheese, olives, meats and a rich wine, and I'm in heaven."

"I'll pass on the wine, but the rest is good." Flynn hummed, reaching for my feet once more and digging his thumbs into my arches.

"Don't like wine?" he asked.

"I don't drink at all." Flynn paused, the air heavy with anticipation. Would he tell Tristan the reason? He took a deep breath and explained, "I don't drink because of my parents. I've seen what happens to people when they drink too much."

I wanted to reach for him, to give him the hug he deserved for being so brave and telling Tristan that piece of himself. It was a big deal. He was such a private person. After all the shit we'd gone through as kids and teens with those motherfuckers bullying both of us, telling anyone anything about himself was a huge step. I smiled softly at him instead, mouthing, "I'm proud of you," to him.

"I get that. Parents can be... difficult." Tristan wrapped his arm around my waist and pulled me onto his lap again before running his fingers through my wet hair. He huffed out a laugh, but it sounded sad rather than humorous. "My mum was quiet as a mouse. If you didn't see her, you'd never know she was there. It was as if she'd merge into the walls. My dad made up for it. He was loud. He ran the household with an iron fist. If any of us stepped out of line, we were punished. His belt usually, but he enjoyed a variety of implements. My older brother towed the line. I rebelled. A lot. Then one day he'd had enough of me. Told me not to bother coming back home. I'd broken the rules for the last time."

"How old were you?" I asked softly.

"Oh, already an adult." He shook his head, waving off my concern, but he pulled me tighter against him and dropped a kiss on my temple. "I was bumming it in the granny flat in the back yard. I didn't have a job. I was smoking weed all day every day. I was stoned a lot." He stopped speaking but resumed playing with my hair. It was as if he needed a moment to gather his thoughts before he could continue. "We were such dickheads. I got high with some mates. We stole a car, took it for a joyride, damaged a bunch of other cars and smashed through a fence. The car was totalled, and we were lucky we didn't kill anyone or ourselves."

"Geez," Flynn murmured. "So lucky."

"I was convicted and served six months on top of some time in remand. I'm lucky it was only that—mine was the shortest sentence. The others were in there for a couple of years."

"Do you still speak to them?" I asked. "Your parents, I mean."

"Not really. Mum's birthday and Christmas mostly, but I only speak with her. Haven't talked to my dad in decades. My brother, yes, but he and I are very different, so it's hard."

"Yeah, that's me too," Flynn admitted. "Mine have mental health and addiction issues. They're hoarders, they were neglectful, and, yeah, my house wasn't a fun place to grow up." We were quiet for a moment. Reflective. The conversation had turned heavier than any of us had intended, but I loved the connection we were building.

"How did you end up an academic?" I eventually asked, breaking the silence.

"The rookie copper who gave evidence in my trial also gave me some good advice." Flynn's smile had me shifting so I could see Tristan's face. His own smile was soft, almost wistful. "He told me to clean up my act and use my time productively or I'd never get what I wanted. I'd had no idea until that moment what I wanted, but it was like a light had been switched on. So I did. When I was released, I was partway through a degree. I went to live with my grandparents, finished uni, and dived straight into another degree. By that time I was doing research and tutoring, and it naturally evolved into becoming an academic."

"Wow," Flynn murmured. "Totally not what I expected."

"Yeah, not the typical route, that's for sure," Tristan responded with a small smile.

"What about you, Flynn? Where do you see yourself in a few years?"

"I don't know." He shook his head and gave a small shrug of his shoulders. "I don't know what I want, except to be secure. I don't need much, but enough for the odd brunch would be great." Flynn grinned, and this time his shrug was one of self-deprecation. "I can brunch with the best of them."

"Oooh, favourite brunch food?" Tristan asked, sitting up straighter, as if the fate of the world was resting on the answer to his question.

Flynn laughed, happiness lighting up his face, his blue eyes sparkling. "Anything on the menu as long as it doesn't involve pumpkin. Bad experience as a kid with them." He shuddered and gagged. I remembered the experience he was talking about. It was the most disgusting thing I'd ever heard of. "So yeah, no pumpkin."

"Not even pumpkin scones?" Tristan asked, aghast.

"Nope." He shook his head and shuddered again. "*Anything* but pumpkin. Heck, I'd eat only coriander and kale for a month before I ate a single mouthful of pumpkin."

"That's beetroot for me." Tristan grimaced. "What's your favourite food, Zali?"

"Anything Asian. Ryder cooks the best Japanese and Thai food. Vietnamese and Malaysian—I love it all."

"Is he a chef?"

"No, he's just really good in the kitchen.

"How long has he worked for you?"

"From the moment I started looking for the yacht." I smiled, remembering the day I'd asked him. He was seriously shocked, but he couldn't contain his grin. It was his dream job. "I was sixteen when I told Dad I wanted one, but I didn't get it for two years."

"This one?" Tristan asked.

"No." I shook my head. "This is my second yacht. My first was about half the size."

"And Ry takes you wherever you want to go?"

"He does, but I can pilot it too." Every possible gadget to make moving the yacht around was included in the wheelhouse. There was still a hell of a lot of skill involved in piloting something so big, but Ry had taught me enough that I could manage it. Of course, I didn't actually have a boat licence, but that had never stopped me before.

"He's really good with anything mechanical," Flynn added proudly. "He looked after the restoration of the 'stang."

"Yeah, the mechanic was a dick, and Dad doesn't know anything about cars. Give him cranes and boats and he's good, but cars never interested him. Ry offered, and I jumped at the chance not to have to deal with the mechanic. Ry ended up pulling the restoration and doing half of it himself. Anything he couldn't handle, he gave to his friend who'd just opened his own company. They were so much better."

"How did you come up with Noble Steed?" Tristan segued. "It's not exactly a typical name for a yacht."

I barked out a laugh and shook my head, still grinning. I was doing that a lot. I was enjoying myself. I hadn't been unhappy, but I was lonely. I liked having them in my space, just hanging around shooting the shit. "It started off as a joke. Ry found a huntsman sitting on my car in the marina car park. He shooed it away and bragged, saying he was my brave knight. I asked him where his noble steed was. Then I found the design for my girl online and before they could name her, I told them I wanted her. We performed the naming ceremony in Italy before Ry and his other pilot friend brought her home.

The sun was much lower in the sky, and my skin had turned pruny. "How are you feeling?" Tristan asked.

"So relaxed." I smiled again, leaning into his embrace. "But we all have work to do, so we really should get some of it done."

We eventually made our way back to the stern to sit on the couch. Wrapped only in towels, we curled up together and got to work, Tristan on his laptop once more, downloading reports, and Flynn compiling spreadsheets of information both from our own sources as well as Tristan's. I was finishing my read of the diaries. There were lists of sources that we needed to follow up on, a mountain of things to do, yet I was distracted. I was having trouble focussing. I wanted to put this research to the side and bask in this feeling, this relaxed happiness that had stolen over me.

But something was telling me not to completely let down the walls. Truthfully, I was scared.

I didn't want Tristan to just fuck us over the moment his job was at risk, and it would be if anyone ever found out about us. The uni had no-fraternization rules in place for a reason, and we all had jobs to do. The other students were working on gathering enough information to prove Mum's guilt. It was up to me to prove her innocence. I couldn't take my foot off the gas. I needed evidence, insurmountable, inarguable, rock-solid evidence.

The only way I could do that was to focus.

Steeling my spine, I turned the page and kept reading. Mum's beautiful cursive writing filled the page, her loopy l's, slopey s's, and curly y's and g's making me smile. I remembered her teaching me how to write and how much trouble she'd had getting the letters to look like the alphabet I'd bought home. She was much better at teaching me maths, so we'd focussed on that. Dad had been the one to teach me how to read and write. I'd loved those evenings when he'd sit me down with a book or when Mum and I counted together, then started learning how to add and subtract, how to multiply and what fractions and angles meant.

Shaking out of my trip down memory lane I leaned back and rested my head on Tristan's shoulder, focussing once more on the words before me. There was something different about this entry. Before, Mum's need for a break was a desperate longing. But there was a gritty determination that shone through now. She was almost manic in her need to get away.

Two months. It was two months before she went missing. Two months before she drowned, before she took her final breath in the midst of her first weekend away from work. The tear landing on the page startled me. I wiped it away roughly, sniffing and letting out a soft laugh at myself. Shaking my head, I huffed and went back to reading.

"Hey, Zee, what's wrong?" Flynn asked me, his hand coming up to cup my face.

"Nothing. I'm just being stupid."

"Don't do that," Tristan scolded gently. "We want to be here for you. Let us try."

"This entry was written two months before Mum died. She was desperate to go on a holiday. The one she finally went on killed her. Fucking irony."

Tristan shifted on the couch, wrapping his arms around me and pulling me close. He dropped a kiss on my temple and squeezed me tight, draping his body over mine. Flynn leaned in close, taking my hand in his and threading our fingers together.

It was the catalyst. Like a levy opening, the tears flowed, and I couldn't stop them. It was like losing Mum and Ash all over again. I was drowning in a sea of grief because this time I knew the horror of what the reality facing me would be like. Unlike when I was younger, I knew that tomorrow when I woke up, this wouldn't all be a bad dream I could forget about. I knew that they'd still be gone, and I'd see the haunting devastation in Dad's eyes the next time I saw him. I knew I still had Mum's name to clear and that this podcast, while bringing me closer to her, had the potential to destroy her reputation.

I hated being vulnerable.

We sat there quietly until the breeze shifted from that of warm afternoon to cool early evening. I was wrung out and exhausted, my muscles aching and my head pounding. I wanted to go to bed and curl up, warm and safe between my men.

When I shivered in my still-wet towel, Tristan murmured, "Let's get you inside, kitten."

Two hours later, I was full after a dinner of tomato soup and grilled cheese sandwiches. But instead of being fast asleep, I was standing at the security gate to the mooring. I hadn't wanted either of them to go, but both of them had engagements first thing in the morning.

It was probably a good thing anyway. I needed time. I needed to process everything. I wanted to be on the water, taking a few days to myself, just me and the currents. I was tempted to send Ry with them and navigate the Noble Steed myself to my spot at Jumpinpin and drop anchor, but the likelihood of his saying yes was Buckley's and none.

The yacht was his baby as much as it was mine. Bend her, and I'd be having an awkward conversation with him. Run her aground or punch a hole in her hull, and I'd never hear the end of it.

"Will you be okay?" Tristan asked, leaning against the railing. He looked casual, standing far enough away from me that a passerby wouldn't think we were anything more than acquaintances. But I could see in the tense set of his jaw that he wasn't happy. "I hate this. I want to touch you," he confessed.

"Me too. But next time I see you, I won't be moored here. We'll have more privacy, and you'll be able to."

Flynn leaned in, wrapped me up tight, and pressed a lingering kiss to my lips. "I'll see you tomorrow yeah?"

"You will. But after that I'm going to need a few days. I need to get out of here." I gestured to the busy marina, the nearby restaurants filled with people.

He paused, assessing me. It was obvious he didn't like my answer, but he knew I needed it. "Okay. Drive safe tomorrow, and I'll see you in class."

We said our goodbyes, and I watched as they walked toward the restaurants lining the marina. Flynn paused at the top of the stairs, turning and waving before he ducked his head and strode after Tristan.

I was onboard again after a moment, and the familiar comfort of my space surrounded me. "Ry," I called. "I'm off to bed."

"Okay, 'night." His response came from the other side of the yacht, but I could hear footsteps.

When he turned the corner, I asked, "Can you get us out of here tomorrow evening? I need to go to class, but after that, I want a few days at Jumpinpin." It was my favourite spot, the place I escaped to. I needed the peace and quiet and to be away from so many prying eyes. It was like being in a fishbowl here at the marina, and I was sick of being on display for other people's amusement.

"Sure. I'll make sure we're ready to go the moment you get back." He paused, then hesitated to add, "I'm here if you ever need to talk or want a shoulder to cry on, Zali. I'll give you all the space you need, but you don't have to be alone when you're going through this."

My throat closed up, and my eyes stung. I couldn't get any words out, so I nodded, crossing my arms over my chest, relieved that I could hide in my oversized jumper. He saw right through me, coming over to wrap his arms around me and hold me tight. I sank into his embrace, needing him more than anything in that moment. "You're a bad-arse motherfucker who I'm in awe of every day. But it's okay to be vulnerable too. I'll never judge you for needing a hug, and I'll never hesitate to give you one when you do. Got it, boss?"

I huffed out a laugh and nodded, the warmth in his tone making my eyes water and my nose run.

"Good, now off to bed." He slapped my butt playfully. "I'll bring you a glass of water."

FOURTEEN

Flynn

I lay in bed, staring at the ceiling, sleep eluding me for the fourth night in a row. This apartment was my safe place. It was my home and my refuge from all the shitty things I'd lived with growing up.

Those diaries had thrown me back fifteen years into an unhappy childhood where my only escape was to Zee's house. I hadn't known it wasn't normal to have rats living in your house until I'd seen Zee's. I hadn't known that playing on piles of piss-soaked newspaper and soiled clothes wasn't normal, that a kitchen full of cracked plastic fast food containers with rotting food inside and dirty dishes piled on whatever surface that could be found wasn't the norm.

Mum and Dad had started collecting junk when Dad got laid off. They were always planning on selling it, but then it got too hard to find what they were looking for. The collections grew and grew. By the time the piles had reached window height, they were attached to the security that having so much stuff gave them. It was a way they could escape the poverty they found themselves in, but they never acted on it. They never did anything except collect more junk.

Stuff got broken, but they never threw it out. It got ruined, but they never tossed it. By the time the rats and mice moved in, they were both drunks and so far beyond a healthy mental state that they didn't even know what to do with either the mess or the rats.

I should have been taken away long before I moved out. Monroe reported my living situation over and over to child services, but nothing ever happened. Nothing ever changed.

Until Zee moved me out. My apartment was her first big purchase, before her car, before she even got her dad a place. It became my sanctuary. Everything had its place, everything was clean, and it was secure. Safe. I was protected from them.

I loved my parents, but our relationship hadn't been easy. I was cheated out of a childhood. I'd shouldered responsibilities that no five- or six-year-old should have had to bear. I'd hidden how bad it was from people I now knew were only trying to help because I didn't want my parents to get in trouble.

They repay that loyalty with demands for me to take care of them. The security guard who is as loyal to Zee as they came—thanks to Queen helping him and in return asking him to look after Zee and me—the security-coded lift and a deadbolt programmed to only a handful of people's fingerprints, were just an inconvenience to them. In their twisted minds, I was rich because my home was clean.

Nothing was expected of my sisters and brother, but they all turned out just like Mum and Dad.

But despite how difficult my relationship with them is, I still have them. Zee doesn't. She lost two-thirds of her family in one go. The woman she wanted to be like never came home to her. The brother she adored went out for the weekend and failed to return. Reading her mum's words so many years later had to be hard.

She was exhausted when we'd left her. Ry told me she was already in bed before Tristan and I had even reached his car. She'd slept through to lunchtime the next day, then come to class. The discussion about planning the podcast hadn't been easy. But our time afterward…. I flushed at the memory, heat crawling over my skin.

We'd talked some since then, but not a lot. We'd texted too. I missed my friend. I missed my girl. I wanted her back. I wanted to be there to support her, and so did Tristan.

He had to be careful that no one saw us together. It had been hard not being able to greet him the way I'd wanted to in class. Then yesterday, we'd met at the coffee shop, going through our results so far, building a picture of the companies Rosa had picked to invest in. The only saving grace for the half a day's torture was that we had to sit close on the tiny table, pressed together from shoulder to knee as we shared our results on a laptop.

Now, today was the day. I was seeing Zee as soon as I could get over to the marina and take out the runabout.

At least it would be the day, once the sun rose, but time was crawling at a snail's pace and I couldn't even sleep it away.

Twiddling my thumbs wouldn't get me anywhere though, so I threw on some sweats and searched through my fridge for almond milk that was still within its use-by date. One hot chocolate later, and I was sitting on my balcony with my laptop as I sorted through spreadsheets of raw data, compiling graphs to analyze the timelines of decisions made by Zee's mum.

When I next looked up, the pinpricks of light in the pitch-black sky had given way to a grey dawn, and I was ready for food.

The vibration of my phone made me jump. Who was calling me at this time of morning? It was barely even 5:00 a.m.

"Hey, Ry," I answered, my brow furrowed and fear swirling around in my gut. Why was he calling? "Is Zee okay?"

He hesitated, and that only made my unease spike higher. "Flynn... I... I don't think so."

"What the heck, man? Why didn't you call me sooner? What's going on—"

"I just went past her cabin to check on her like I do every morning. Her bed hasn't been slept in. Again—"

"What?" I shrieked. But then it occurred to me that I'd spoken with Zee twice since she'd left class a few days earlier, and she hadn't told me anything. This time my voice was quieter, confusion colouring my tone. "Why didn't you stop her?"

He huffed out a laugh, but it held no humour. "We are talking about Zali, aren't we? Short of carrying her into bed and tying her there, what could I have done?"

"You could have called me sooner," I grumbled, the fight leeching out of me. He was right. My girl was too damn stubborn for her own good, and there was no way either one of us could have stopped her. Tristan, on the other hand, might have, but he also wasn't our babysitter.

"Has she eaten?"

"She ate breakfast with me the day before yesterday. Since then she's eaten in her office, but she's only picked at everything I've given her." He sighed, his voice weighed down with concern. "Flynn, she's still wearing the day before yesterday's clothes, and she hasn't been in the water since we got here." The clothes were a warning light. The lack of swimming was the emergency siren. But maybe there was a simple explanation. Possibly?

"What's the water like?" My voice wobbled, and I swallowed back the lump in my throat.

Ry blew out a rough breath. I could hear the seagulls in the distance. If I closed my eyes, I could picture the spot where they were anchored. On a sunny day, the water was the most surreal cyan, so clear that you could spot different-coloured shells on the sandy sea floor.

"There's no one here. It's perfect. The water is pristine. Any other day and I'd be dragging her out of the water, but she's drawn the blinds and locked herself indoors."

I swallowed hard, trying to figure out a plan of attack. I was heading to them anyway. I'd have to catch a rideshare—public transport didn't go to the upscale marina where the runabout was docked this early—but it was doable. "Okay, um, give me an hour. I'm on my way."

"Are you bringing the professor?"

"I'll call Tristan now. I don't know if he has classes or meetings." I'd been in twice-daily contact with Tristan since I'd last seen him. He wasn't Professor Reid to me anymore. Something had changed between us. At first it was living out this naughty fantasy between us. The risk of getting caught heightened the thrill of sleeping with a sexy older man. He was forbidden fruit, and I was feasting on those apples. But now I was terrified for him. If he lost something as important to him as his career because of me, I'd never forgive myself.

But Zee needed us, and I knew he'd want to be there for her if he could.

Ry was quiet, but the silence wasn't as heavy. "Okay. Should I call her dad or Ezra?"

I hesitated. "I honestly don't know. My gut tells me that worrying Monroe might not be the best idea. Ezra might be a different story, but I'm not ready for his interference yet— not when he put her in this mess."

The sight that greeted me when I knocked on the door had my head spinning, and not in a good way. Balled up pieces of paper littered the floor, and Zee's snack was untouched on the coffee table, a fly buzzing around the miniature charcuterie board.

Her back was to me, but I recognized her shirt as the one she was wearing during our video call the day before yesterday. Zee's hair was thrown up in a messy bun atop her head, and her leggings were ratty old ones with a hole in the thigh. This wasn't Zee—not by a long shot.

Tristan stepped up beside me and looked around the room. His questioning gaze ping-ponged between Zee and me, and I winced. "Let's try to get her to talk," he whispered.

I nodded; I could do this. She needed me to do it. Tristan squeezed my waist and wandered over to the wall, studying what she'd pinned there. It looked like a family tree with a bubble at the top and branches coming down from it, but within each bubble, there was much more detail than simply a name. I couldn't read it from across the room—the font she'd printed it in was tiny and handwritten notes were scrawled across a few. Next to it was what looked like a timeline horizontally spanning the width of half a dozen A1 pieces of paper with dates highlighted. One toward the end had extensive notes written under it, and a stack of papers clipped together sitting on the floor.

I stuffed my hands in my pockets, feigning casual as I greeted her, "Hey, beautiful. I brought Tristan. Thought we might go for a swim."

She held her hand up, silencing me. "Can't. I'm in the middle of this."

"What are you working on, Zali?" Tristan asked, tilting his head toward the wall.

"It's my research all mapped out—what I've found so far." Whatever she'd found, it was out of control. Even if Ry hadn't warned me she'd been working non-stop for days, it would have been obvious from The Wall.

"I think you need a break…," I started. Zee spun in her chair and glared at me, my words trailing off at her acidic look. "Or not," I squeaked.

"Don't tell me what to do, Flynn," she warned. Her eyes were like flint, cold and hard, but the dark circles below them betrayed just what she was doing to herself to make this much progress.

"He's worried about you, kitten. We both are." Tristan leaned his butt against her desk and eased her yellow glasses off her face. "So is Ryder. We just want to know you're okay."

"I'm fine. There, you can go."

Tristan laughed, but the sound held no humour. It wasn't walls that fell into place when he slipped into this persona, but a mask of sorts. The man was warm and affectionate with the people he let into his circle. I'd slipped in there a few nights ago, as had Zee, but the Tristan before me now was on the defensive, pushing Zee.

"Little girl, I tell you when we'll come or go, and right now, I'm not going anywhere."

"Fuck off, arsehole." She shoved away from him with her foot, her chair wheels spinning as she moved across the timber floor.

"There's my kitten." He smirked and lifted his chin, daring her to react.

"You think you know me so well? You've fucked me a couple of times. So, what? I'm an open book now?" Zee stood and faced off with him, her arms crossed and her eyes narrowed defiantly. She was in bare feet, and the height difference between them was comical. She really did look like a kitten who thought she was a lion. I knew her well enough that I didn't make that mistake, but Tristan had a knack for getting her to react.

He raised an eyebrow, looking entirely unimpressed. "Enlighten me then. You've probably been running around in circles anyway. What information could you have possibly found that I haven't already?"

Man, he was baiting her, but it was working. Zee's eyes were ablaze, her hands balled into fists, and every muscle in her body primed to attack.

"Or we could get naked and go for a swim," I suggested, my voice sounding like a child's next to Tristan's deep baritone.

"Fine. You want details? Sit the fuck down and listen." Her glare at Tristan softened somewhat when she directed it at me, but she was on edge.

I swallowed, waiting for her to speak. What bomb was she going to drop on us?

"After you both left the other night, I got to thinking. Professor, you were building a timeline with dates in the diaries, investment records, share prices, that sort of thing. You were going to match it up with events during the GFC.

I decided to look at it from the regulator's perspective. What did they say about ReimagINC, and what was the liquidator's opinion?"

She pointed at the midpoint of the timeline and picked up a printed report from the floor below it, then dropped it onto her desk. The pages, one after another, were tabbed with coloured flags. "Long story short, the liquidator—and based on the liquidator's report, the regulator—both determined that the company's collapse happened because of deposits being made into high-profile US organizations that were almost bankrupted during the GFC. They agreed with your conclusion that negligence was a factor. I'm waiting for yours and Flynn's data before coming to any conclusion about that."

Tristan gestured to the wall. "So, what's the rest of this information?"

"This part—" She pointed at the left-hand side. "—is additional background information on all the companies Mum was investing in—directors, shareholders, related entities, that sort of thing. I just need to incorporate the financial data that you've both been gathering, but there are a few organizations of note that we need to investigate further."

"In what way?" I asked, puzzled.

"One has loose ties with one of the world's richest families. A director is a related through marriage to them. They're old money and as dirty as they come. I don't have any proof that the company or its director is in any way affiliated with the family, but I've come across these people in my online dealings before. They're ruthless and should not be crossed."

I stumbled over to the white leather couch that faced the porthole and sank into it. I was gonna be sick. I swallowed the bile and rested my head in my palms, rubbing my eyes with the heels of my hands and breathing through my nose. I willed the churning in my gut to ease.

Something unnamed was coursing through my veins. A dark terror that this was far worse than I could ever have imagined hovered above me like fog. Investigating the reasons why people lost money through corporate negligence was one thing. But this was so far beyond that. I wanted to help. I wanted to ride in on a white horse and help save Zali's mother's reputation. I was only too happy to do that. But crime families? I didn't want that. I didn't want to be looking over my shoulder or, worse, worried about Zee failing to look over hers. She didn't have a self-preservationist bone in her body. I trusted Ryder to keep her safe, but he wasn't a professional bodyguard. This might be a step too far even for him.

But what choice did I have? What choice did any of us have? If Zee was onto something, she'd follow it through, consequences be damned.

And I'd follow her, not because I was a sheep. But because she was the love of my life, and turning my back when she needed me was unacceptable. Walking away while she faced any kind of danger was incomprehensible. I wouldn't abandon her, not now, not ever.

"Organized crime?" Tristan inquired.

I flicked my gaze to him and watched as he swallowed before rubbing his forehead. His skin had turned pallid, a sweat breaking out on his brow.

"What about the rest?" he asked slowly, his green eyes wary and his lips pursed unhappily. He pointed at what looked like a complex family tree with a multitude of names and numbers in each box. Some branches ended at the first level, while others went on with extra limbs underneath.

Zee traced a line along the top row of boxes. "The first level are all the investors you found who deposited funds with ReimagINC. The second and third levels are the ones who lost money and their descendants, respectively."

"How did you get this information? These look like tax file numbers and bank accounts." Tristan stepped closer and trailed his fingers over some of the butcher's paper tacked to the wall.

I closed my eyes again, not wanting to even be here as this went down. It was make or break time. Once the truth was out there, there was no going back. Tristan would either walk away, tell us he wanted nothing to do with us anymore, or he'd shrug it off as no big deal. I wasn't naïve enough to think it'd be the latter.

Zee's voice came out slow and clear. She wasn't dumbing down the information, just making sure there was no misunderstanding. "The liquidator had records of all ReimagINC's creditors. I matched up the financial records to verify who were investors. Some people had died by the time the liquidators filed their report, so for those, details of the estate were already known. For the rest, I did a few searches and came up with the data I needed."

"What searches? How did you get bank accounts and tax file numbers?"

"You just need to know where to look." There was a pregnant pause, and I groaned, wishing she'd just give him the answers he clearly wanted.

I dared steal a glance at them. They were facing off against each other, Tristan standing with his legs shoulder width apart, his back straight and his eyes locked on Zee's. My girl was leaning against the wall, both her ankles and arms crossed. Zee wasn't intimidated by Tristan's size or the way he filled the entire room.

"Zali, I need you to be straight with me. Where did you get this information from?" Tristan growled, his tone short on patience.

She checked them off on her fingers as she spoke. "The liquidator, births, deaths and marriage registries, the courts, a couple of different banks, and the tax office."

"How?" he asked, surprise colouring his tone. His brow was furrowed, his palms turned up in question. "How do you get around privacy laws? You need warrants for that kind of thing, and on what possible grounds would one be issued?"

Her smile was patronizing. "Security measures, laws, and those kinds of boundaries are more—" She pursed her lips and looked up in thought. "—guidelines, perhaps? After all, I'm known as Queen for a reason."

"I'm sorry, what?" Tristan asked, his gaze snapping to mine before moving back to hers. "Who are you? I thought you were a cyber investigator."

"That's the title I have when I'm working for Detective Fraser. But I don't do that full-time; it's only when I want to take on a case. The rest of the time, I work for myself." Zee checked her fingernails, wiping them on her shirt as if she was buffing them. She looked completely unfazed by Tristan's shock, but I could see the move for what it was—an act.

Tristan opened his mouth, then closed it again, clearly speechless.

Zee laughed coldly. "Did you think I was joking when I said I stole my money?"

"You're a hacker? For real? Queen's your avatar?"

"Look my online alias up, professor." She patted his chest and gestured to her chair. "Now, if you'll excuse me, I have work to do. Make yourselves at home in the lounge-room or on deck. Or you can leave. I won't stop you."

FIFTEEN

Tristan

Flynn hesitated, waiting for Zali to add something more, but she'd already dismissed us. I wanted to shake her, to knock some sense into that stupidly brilliant head of hers. But she was as stubborn as she was beautiful and determined to ignore both of us.

Her words rattled around in my head, gaining speed. I was barely holding on. Everything was spiralling out of control, like the mine cart in an *Indiana Jones* movie. Any moment now, I was going to come off the tracks and go careening headfirst into a disaster of epic proportions. Maybe I already had.

Turns out, karma could be a bitch.

My chest was tight, my breathing choppy. This wasn't supposed to happen. I'd been out of control before, and look where it landed me—jail. But this? This far and away eclipsed that night of stupidity and irresponsibility.

I'd changed after that night, after the time I'd spent in hell, and I would never go back. Not now. Not ever.

Right now, I had to get out of here. I had to think, to figure out a way to extract myself from this fucking nightmare. I didn't want a single part of whatever hornet's nest she was disturbing with her digging. Zali could figure that shit out on her own.

Storming out of the office, I shouldered past Flynn and headed up to the main deck. The sooner I got off this yacht, the better. But I didn't have a clue how to sail—can you even sail a boat without sails?—the boat we'd come here on. I paced, trying to calm my breathing.

Jesus, what had she done? As lead researcher, I was responsible. Any breaches of ethics or illegal acts my assistants undertook were on my back. How could I possibly justify this to the dean? Never mind worrying about losing my job for sleeping with my students. I could list off half a dozen laws that had been broken here. This was way beyond getting slapped on the wrist for breaching a condition of employment. This was illegal.

The sea breeze, the morning sun, and rippling of the current against the hull should have been calming, but all they did was serve as a reminder that I was trapped here until Flynn was ready to leave.

Flynn knew, he had to know, what she was. How could he be okay with Zali putting herself at risk like that? Did she have any idea of the kind of people she could encounter online? She'd said it herself that there were people—organizations—who shouldn't be crossed. She wasn't some white-coat hacker who helped people with their security systems and protecting their Wi-Fi passwords. She trespassed and stole data, and by the sounds of it, money too. Information like bank account numbers would go for a pretty penny on the dark web. Did she sell them? Is that how she'd made her fortune?

What the fuck had I gotten myself into?

Catching the feels was one thing. But falling for her could jeopardize everything I'd worked for.

I was screwed, so screwed.

Because it wasn't just Zali I was falling for. It was her angelic boyfriend too.

With shaking hands, I googled Queen's hacking exploits and groaned out loud. Fucking hell. She was infamous, pegged as being responsible for one high-profile attack after another. The one thing they all had in common, though, was that she left no trace. No one could definitively link anything back to Queen, but her calling card—cleaning her targets out of every cent—was everywhere.

"Fuck me," I muttered. Now what the fuck was I going to do?

I dialled Ezra's number. He was literally the only person on the planet that I could talk to about this. But did he know what Zali did outside of his work? Surely he wasn't as naïve as me. Pacing, I waited, cursing when I was prompted to record a message.

"Call me back," I snapped, my voice a low growl as I lashed out. He'd done this. He'd been the one to assign Zali to my class. Why hadn't he let it go? I hung my head and blew out a breath, trying to keep my calm. I knew exactly why he'd had Zali sign up. "Why the fuck didn't you tell me who Queen is? What the fuck have you got me involved in?"

"Hang. Up. The. Phone," Ryder snarled from behind me. I spun around to see Ryder with a smudge of flour on his cheekbone and standing with his hands, covered in the remnants of dough, balled into fists. His hazel eyes were a molten gold that looked as lethal as the vibes the man was exuding.

I ended the call and slipped the phone into my pocket. "She's—"

"Zali, nothing." His voice was like a whip crack, sharp and brooking no dissent. "You'd better think very carefully about what you're doing right now. I threatened to break your nose. I told you Zali was the risk here, but I lied. I'll fucking kill you if you hurt her."

"She's put everything on the line that I've worked for. She's risking everything," I bellowed.

His laugh was cold. "Really? Is that the lie you're telling yourself?" Shaking his head, he added, "You smart dudes are too fucking dumb for your own good. Fucking a student is enough to get a teacher fired. Everyone knows that. Fucking two of them will make it indefensible. You think that Zali put you at risk? You've done a pretty good job of it yourself, professor."

I threw my hands up in the air. "This is jail time we're talking about." My thumb hit my chest. "My fucking freedom. Time that I could spend behind bars. Again. Don't you get it? She's a fucking criminal. She's going to get caught, and we're all going down with her."

I closed my eyes, my hands shaking, an equal mix of anger and terror coursing through my veins. I was back there. Back in that tiny concrete block cell.

Back sharing a cell with Jordan "Carnage" Rowe, the gang enforcer.

My breath caught. My heart raced.

Pain rolled through me, phantom memories that still haunted me.

I'd cowered in the corner like a scared little rabbit. It's what he'd called me, taunted me with over and over.

Humiliation washed over me. Despair and a self-hatred so deep and so engrained that I would never be free of it.

Little rabbit was the old name. Pisspot became the new one.

I caught the sob in my throat as it threatened to escape, and my knees wobbled, nearly buckling.

That night, and the nightmare weeks that followed, would be burned in my memory until the day I died.

His hand around my throat.

His foul breath in my face, spittle flying as another punch landed.

My ribs punishing me for the half breath I'd stolen when he eased his hold.

A knee to my nuts.

My lungs screaming for oxygen.

My vision blurring.

Darkening.

Waking up.

Unable to open my bruised eyes.

Wet.

Piss soaked.

Cum soaked.

My throat raw. Burning.

I still wasn't sure if it was because I'd been orally raped while I was out, or from his hold on me. It hadn't mattered.

My injuries saved me. I was in the hospital wing for a week under observation. It'd taken that long for me to stop pissing blood. He was gone when I got put back in my cell, and I waited on tenterhooks for the other shoe to drop. For him to walk back into the cell and end me. Every second of every day dragged, lasting eons.

I hobbled out that gate a free man a couple of weeks later and swore I would never go back. Never in a million years. Never in a million millennia.

"She's the love of my life," Flynn murmured from behind me, snapping me out of my nightmare. I flexed my hands, wiping my sweaty palms on my pants. "Your opinion of Zee might have changed, but she's still the same person as before."

I cleared my throat, hoping against hope that my voice was steady. I didn't want to give away any more pieces of myself, not when I needed to preserve the already-cracked foundations of the walls I'd hastily built. It had been easy to let them in. I should have clued in to the fact that they were too good to be true. I should have listened to the warning bells going off the first time I stepped onto the yacht. I should have said no to Ez when he told me I needed his investigator in my class.

Shoulda, coulda, woulda. But I hadn't. Now I was fucking kicking myself.

"Except now I know a key fact about her, one that I'm not prepared to have anything to do with." I flicked my gaze to Ryder. He stood as still as a statute, but the death glare he was shooting me hadn't softened. His hands were still clenched, his muscles rigid. He was like an attack dog readying to strike. I was the intruder trespassing on his property.

My phone vibrated in my pocket with a call coming in. I pulled it out and answered before Ryder could object.

"You found out," Ezra fished.

"Apparently," I deadpanned. "She's out. I don't want her in my class. I don't want her involved with the podcast." The heaviness in my chest was making it hard to breathe. Speaking was almost impossible, but I forced the words out.

"You realize she's not going to back down. You try to take her out of this, and she'll just bury the whole thing." Ezra's words sounded flippant, but his tone was deadly serious.

I shook my head, grinding my teeth together, determined not to back down. I didn't break Ryder's stare as my gut churned at the reality that faced me. "I don't care. I'm not going back there. Not for her to feel better about herself. Not for anything or anyone. I won't condone illegal activities in the name of something I'm heading up."

"I get that, mate."

"But?" I snapped.

"But nothing. You've made your position clear. I'll let Zali know she's off the project and anything she does going forward is on her own back."

"You do that." I flicked my gaze to my phone, about to end the call, but Ezra's quiet question stopped me.

"What's she found?"

I sighed, my shoulders dropping with the weight of responsibility that now faced me. "Nearly all of the investors or their next of kin. Bank account details, everything. I have no idea what she's planning on doing with that information."

"Refunding the money they invested plus interest," Flynn explained, catching me off-guard. My eyes snapped back up to Ryder's, but he didn't seem surprised. If anything, pride shone back at me. "Zee might not do things conventionally, and she doesn't give a shit about what laws say, but she has the biggest heart of anyone I know."

"Oh," I uttered, unable to form anything more coherent.

"Did he just say pay it back? That's millions of dollars," Ezra exclaimed, awe and shock in his voice. "Put me on speaker." I did, and he repeated his question.

Flynn nodded. "Yes to both." He sighed and added, "I trust Zee."

"Maybe you shouldn't."

His shrug was one of those what-can-you-do? Ones, and his smile was more of a twist of his lips than humorous. I wanted to reach for him, to wrap him in my arms and protect this beautiful angel from any harm coming to him. I wanted to protect him from getting his heart broken and from any danger he was voluntarily stepping into by even being friends with Zali. "Possibly."

Ezra's disembodied voice came through the phone, startling me. I'd zoned out, forgetting he was even there. "The information she has, Flynn…. She couldn't have gotten it legally."

"I know," he answered quietly, his gaze never leaving mine. "Detective, she needs access to the Reserve Bank's archives. Do you have access?"

"No," he responded, confusion lacing his tone. "Why would I? And what does she need it for?"

Flynn sighed. "I don't know. She told me to ask you but wouldn't give me any information."

"I'll make a call and see what I can do. But it's doubtful, Flynn."

I ended the call in the ensuing pause, the tension ratcheting up between the three of us standing on the main deck. I had to warn him. I had to try. Flynn wouldn't survive if he was put in jail. He would be destroyed, his mind and body mutilated beyond repair. I'd been there. I'd seen what could happen.

"Don't do this, Flynn. Don't help her," I begged. "She's going to ruin your life."

"I won't abandon her." Flynn pursed his lips, his eyes lacking their spark. His shoulders were slumped and his shrug resigned. "But I understand your choice."

That one sentence was the final nail in the coffin for our relationship. It was over. Done for. A line had been drawn. I couldn't cross back, and he wouldn't join me. He'd made his choice. It was one I'd never had any doubt that he'd make—Zali would always be his first and greatest love. But even that knowledge didn't prepare me for the soul-wrenching pain hearing those words would wreak.

I rubbed my chest, trying to ease the grief shattering my heart. "I guess this is it, then," I wheezed, unable to look at him. My gaze landed on the runabout tied to the yacht.

"Ry, can you take us back to the marina, please?" Zali called out from the deck below. "I've just been called to an urgent meeting in Sydney this afternoon."

"Sure. Let me make a phone call to get the jet ready for us, then we can go." Ryder's eyes were hard when he turned back to me. "Looks like you're getting your wish, professor."

Sixteen

Zali

'd been an idiot for thinking that Professor Reid—he was no longer Tristan—would have reacted in any other way. How else would he have dealt with the news that I'd been busy breaking the law to research content for his podcast? He was responsible for my actions in a university context, but it would never come back to him. I wouldn't let it. But he'd never know that. It was reasonable for him to think that if it ever came to it, I'd sell him out to get myself out of trouble.

He didn't know me well enough not to jump to the worst conclusion. But fuck me, I wished I'd been wrong.

Why did his leaving have to be so fucking painful?

I'd been living a fucking lie, thinking that this cute little menage we had going on could survive. Smoking-hot sex with two men whom I'd fallen hard for wasn't enough when one of them was horrified by me. I'd barely gotten the words out telling him to leave before he was racing out the door.

Flynn had stayed with me. He'd asked me what I needed and what he could do for me. He was so damn selfless, but that was exactly why I should cut him off the same way Professor Reid had cut me out.

I didn't want to hurt him, but I feared I was going to do a whole lot worse.

My heart clenched hard, my breaths shallowing out as the heartbreak cut me deeper, plunging, twisting, and tearing at my bleeding flesh. Tears formed in my eyes, but I batted them away angrily. Zali Stephens did not cry over men. Fuck that.

No, I wouldn't. I'd hold my head up high and get through this like anything else. I wouldn't be brought to my knees by dick, no matter how good it was, or who the person attached to it was. I'd go back to hating him. Loathing the sight of his spectacular pale green eyes and that perfectly sculpted jaw. Those lips I was desperate to kiss one last time.

Sitting here with my thumb up my arse wouldn't do me any good. I needed to do something, and that meant finishing what I'd started. Stripping off as I walked out of my office, I was naked by the time I reached my shower. The water heated quickly, going from chilled to scalding in seconds. I didn't linger under the stream, though, no matter how relaxing the heat was on my exhausted muscles.

I washed myself, scrubbing my body clean. My mind wandered as I did. There was no doubt I'd miss the sex—who wouldn't?—but it wasn't just about that. The words he'd whispered while buried deep inside me had meant something. They'd knocked down my walls and worked their way into my heart. They'd filled me up and left me on a high that I'd never wanted to come down from.

They were taunting me now. Words like "never stopping" and "staying forever" were big fat fucking meaningless lies now.

He was something else. The first time he'd fucked me, it was hard and dirty. He took my arse like he owned it. He'd made me cry out in pain and soar with ecstasy at the same time. Even his kicking us out of his office had been hot in its own way—a reminder that our affair was one that needed to stay secret.

He'd relentlessly fucked my throat, making me scream while taking Flynn's dick like a pro. That mouth, those hands, and his dick were magic. It was unfortunate that no one except porn stars listed fucking as a talent on their CVs because he deserved a gold star. Hell, he deserved public recognition for how amazing a fuck he was.

But apart from that, he was smart and stubborn. He knew what he wanted and how to get it. He didn't stand for mediocre. He also gave as good as he got. He loved to push and to provoke a reaction from me, usually shutting me up with his dick. Which I was totally fine with. It was rare that someone had me hooked so quickly and easily and kept me on my toes, challenging me every time I saw them.

Then he'd called me *love*.

He'd held me while I cried.

He'd been gentle and loving, and I'd gone and fallen for him. But it was over now. He'd made it pretty fucking clear that he was scandalized by who I was.

But it was my fault. I had to take responsibility for being me. I'd told him that I'd stolen my fortune, but he hadn't believed me. I should have been more upfront with him. I hadn't mostly out of a sense of self-preservation—I didn't exactly go announcing to the world that I was Queen. But with the benefit of hindsight, I realized I should have at least shown him the basic respect of disclosing to him how I'd find the information we were after.

My history wasn't pretty. I'd done some very illegal things in my not-so-distant past. It was a mix of talent, skill, and sheer dumb luck that I hadn't fucked up and been arrested or hunted down by a target. But it was what I did, who I was. Queen was as much a part of me as Zali was.

It seemed strange to think of myself as two different people, but that was my reality. I kept those personas separate out of necessity. If I didn't, I could put the people I loved at risk. My targets weren't always lawyers who did the dirty on their kids or politicians who took bribes. They were the worst of society—they stole children and sold them into sex slavery, they got kids hooked on drugs, they stole identities and destroyed lives. They weren't good people. One day, eventually, one of them would outsmart me. I had to give myself the best chance to keep my family— Dad, Flynn, Ryder, and even Ezra—out of the firing line, because if there was one way they could destroy me, that was it.

Should I just throw in the towel? One day I would have played with fire one too many times. I'd get burnt. Was being Queen worth it? If I said, "Fuck it," and quit tomorrow, would I miss it? Could I hop on the straight-and-narrow path if it meant keeping Professor Reid?

I didn't have an answer for that, which was perhaps answer enough. It was by far the hardest thing to acknowledge. I didn't know if I was ready to hang my keyboard up. Didn't I deserve a man who could accept all of me, warts and all?

On-screen, his criminal record stared me in the face. I understood exactly why he didn't want anything to do with me. The medical records attached to his stay in detention were horrifying. The injuries he sustained were enough for him to never want to risk going back in.

I got it—I did. But I was no longer doing this as part of a university assignment that I'd been talked into doing. I was finding the information because I needed to. Professor Reid had told me over and over that he had to publish something; his backers were insisting on getting the truth out there. So I had to have something—for myself just as much as Mum and Dad. If Mum had somehow screwed up, and I had a terrible feeling that she had, then I needed to be the one to fix things for her. Why? Because I could. To do that, though, I needed information. I could satisfy my professor's requirements for this class at the same time and ensure that the podcast wouldn't totally destroy Dad.

Mum should be able to rest in peace. She didn't deserve to have her reputation destroyed. What good would it do?

It wasn't like anyone would get their money back. Professor Reid would get his podcast, he'd write up a report on how changes to whatever laws could stop people from being incompetent in the future, and we'd be left picking up the pieces. Again. Dad would be left grieving his wife all over again. He would have to go through the pain and humiliation of having his dead wife's name dragged through the mud. He'd be guilty by association once more. I remembered strangers walking through our house, searching in drawers and taking notebooks and computers from Mum's desk. I remembered Dad crying and begging them not to break things—trinkets that were important to Mum and Asher—and not to disturb Asher's room. He didn't deserve to relive all that again.

And I would do what it took to protect him from going through that again.

No matter the price.

There was no way I would back down, not even if it meant losing one of the people I cared about most. I couldn't control Professor Reid's opinion of me. All I could do was protect the people closest to me from getting hurt. If it meant that I would take the brunt of that pain, so be it.

I knew what needed to be done.

After turning off the shower, I wrapped the towel around my hair and strutted out to the stern deck.

"Ry, can you take us back to the marina, please?" I called out. "I've just been called to an urgent meeting in Sydney this afternoon."

"Sure. Let me make a phone call to get the jet ready for us, then we can go," he responded immediately.

I knew I'd made the right decision when I picked out what served for corporate in my world—black glasses, white button-down shirt, skin-tight black leather pants, and my black alligator-skin Manolo Blahniks. Slipping into them was like donning armour. Finishing the look with my hair pulled back in a tight bun and red lipstick was the icing on the cake.

Head held high, I went back to my office to make sure I could execute my plan.

S E V E N T E E N

Ryder

I watched the flex in his arse as the professor stepped off the yacht onto the dock. He had a nice one.

What fucking rabbit hole had I fallen into? It really was some *Alice in Wonderland* shit. Since when did I check out another bloke's arse? Seriously, though, when? Because it had been happening far too often. First him, then Flynn—although in fairness, it wasn't Flynn's tight little arse I'd been checking out, it had been his cock—and then Detective Fraser's.

Focus, Ry. Focus.

It didn't matter what kind of butt the professor had. It didn't matter that I'd seen it flex as he'd wandered naked down the hallway. It didn't matter that I knew it was smooth and plump with no tan lines. It was the perfect handful for someone to latch onto when he was pumping inside of them. I couldn't help but wonder what he'd looked like fucking Zali and Flynn.

The cum gutters also didn't matter, despite how they made a perfect V lighting the way to his cock. They were like a strip of lights framing a runway, guiding a lover to their destination.

What did matter was that I needed to get rid of him. Security would escort him off the marina if he was caught skulking around, looking any kind of suspicious. But it was my job to keep Zali safe.

And I took that job seriously.

Good riddance to him anyway. I didn't need him breaking Zali's heart, never mind messing up my nights. Flynn was the one interested in getting railed by the bloke, not me.

Despite what my recurring dreams said.

If I told myself enough times that he was a bloke and I should be repulsed by him, maybe I'd forget waking up with a raging boner and coming as soon as I wrapped my hand around my dick. Maybe I'd forget the way he wrestled control away from me, binding my hands and kicking open my legs before sinking into me. Maybe I'd forget the way he wrapped his hands around my throat and pinned me down, taking what he wanted.

Maybe they were things I'd remember I wanted to do to Zali. Not that I'd ever forgotten. I fantasized about that woman every damn day. I wasn't the one who got to sink inside her tight little pussy, but she needed me in other ways. She was mine to take care of. Mine to protect and look after.

Nothing would ever happen with another man, never mind two. I wasn't bi or pan. I didn't want any guys. Good old straight for me, thanks very much. Traditional sausage in bread. I loved women, loved being with them. Loved everything about them.

So why couldn't I get Tristan and Flynn out of my head?

Ezra either?

I growled at my stupidity. Ezra was a whole other story. I'd admired him for years. But it was completely innocent. It was the way that every other man checks out another bloke's progress. He managed to keep his muscles perfectly sculpted. It took mad dedication to his craft to look that good all the time. The man was objectively gorgeous too. His hair was that silky-smooth caramel colour that you had to remind yourself not to touch. There was never a strand out of place, but it wasn't because of a ton of product in it. He had this effortless style too—businessman but not stuffy. His navy-blue suits and crisp white button-downs always looked fresh even when he was finishing up his day. I'd seen him in casual clothes too. Ripped jeans as soft as butter that moulded over his thick thighs and a fitted black Henley.

He was the go-to man women drooled over, like a standard us mere mortals could only hope to one day achieve. He was the man I'd wanted to be.

Except now I was wondering whether I needed to add a "with" to the end of that sentence.

I shook out of the rabbit hole of mindfucks I'd fallen into and watched as the Professor paused at the top of the stairs, turning back to gaze at our group. His shoulders dropped, and his lips turned down sullenly. I couldn't see his eyes behind the dark sunnies he wore, but I could imagine that the playful spark those pale greens had glittered with when I'd met him in the corridor would now be missing.

He exited the security gate, and as it banged closed, the lock clicking into place, a weight lifted off my shoulders. He was gone. Out of Zali's life and out of mine.

I jogged ahead, going for the Range Rover parked in the space we had reserved.

I pulled up to the curb, Zali and Flynn hopped in, and I did another double-take. My lady looked like a fucking boss. Hot as hell in skin-tight black leather and a white shirt that was somehow tailor-made to show off every curve and be professional at the same time. Even Flynn, who was always suave in his linen pants and button-down shirts, paled beside her. In that getup, she looked badarse, and he looked like a work-experience kid following her around like a puppy.

"You didn't tell me what you'd need when we got to Sydney. I've organized a car, but that's it. Did you want to stay overnight?"

"No, I only need to be there for a few hours."

"Where are we going?" Flynn asked.

"You're not coming," she responded, her tone leaving no room for discussion. "We're dropping you off before we leave."

Flynn laughed, but it held no humour. It was the first time I'd seen him stand up to Zali like that. Usually he was like a Labrador puppy, always smiling and always trying to please. "You aren't in any kind of mindset to be there by yourself—"

"I'll be there," I supplied helpfully, a little pissed at Flynn's complete disregard of me. I'd half joked with the professor, saying that I was the staff and it was my job to blend into the walls, but that wasn't the relationship I had with Zali. I was as much her protector as her cook.

"No, you won't. You're staying with the car." Zali was determined to exclude both Flynn and me, which only made me more determined not to let her go alone. I couldn't help but question why this meeting had come up today of all days. I met Flynn's gaze in the rear-view mirror and could see that potent mix of puppy-dog regret and gritty determination in his eyes. I nodded, accepting his silent apology, and tilted my lips up in a proud smile. Finally, our baby boy was growing up.

"Don't bother arguing, Zee," Flynn stated. "We're both coming. We aren't leaving you, and we're not accepting no for an answer."

Zali huffed and added "Or what?"

I didn't even have time to open my mouth and issue the threat to her. I'd never carried it out before, but damn, I was itching to. Flynn was already putting it out there. "Or you'll get a spanking, little girl. Ry will bend you over his knee and make your arse red."

Flynn's words were so unexpected, so left of field, that I choked on my own breath. Damn, the man had done a complete one-eighty in terms of his shy, sweet, and innocent demeanour that I was used to seeing.

"At least make it a threat I'll dislike." Zali's eyes held a challenge, daring me to do it.

I wanted to. Man, did I ever. But giving her what she wanted when she acted out was only asking for her to do it again. If that meant putting herself in danger, I wouldn't stand for it.

Flynn smirked, and I bit back a chuckle, meeting Zali's gaze with a raised eyebrow and a wolfish grin. If she wanted a spanking any other time, I'd gladly give her one.

"Be a good girl, and I just might," I muttered under my breath. My voice didn't hold any of the bark it normally did. Instead, it was reverent, like a prayer.

She deserved worshippers too. I'd hoped it would work out with the professor—he lit up something in both Zali and Flynn—but it was better that he was gone now rather than after she'd had time to fall in love with him. Flynn was a given; he'd been crazy about her for the longest time. Even as a toddler, he was head over heels.

I didn't blame him one bit. Fuck me, she was gorgeous. The curve of her tits and the sweetheart shape of her butt, her bare pussy that I'd now seen being used by one of her men—it was hot as hell. I wanted to pull over and feast on her too. But there was a line, and I wouldn't cross it.

Not yet, anyway. Not until I knew she was ready.

Zali shivered, my words penetrating the lusty haze she'd slipped under with my promise. Maybe she was closer to ready than I'd thought.

It didn't take long to get Zali's jet into the air. I was just settling in, the take-off complete, when Flynn slid into the copilot's chair next to me. "Thought you'd be with Zali," I noted.

"She sent me up here. She wanted to keep working." He gave me a ghost of a smile, the small tilt of his lips troubled. "I'm worried about her."

"Me too," I confessed. "She's feeling the pressure."

Flynn was quiet for a time as we watched the clouds shoot past below us. "Why aren't you with Zee?"

I barked out an unexpected laugh. He was throwing me for loops today, but my response was automatic, one I'd rehearsed over and over again. "She's my boss."

Flynn huffed out a laugh himself. "I call bullshit. Try another excuse."

My hands tightened around the yoke. "She's not ready for me, Flynn. When I take her, there won't be anything casual about us. I'll expect everything from her."

He eyed me seriously for a moment, and the weight of his disapproval hit me hard. "Fair warning, if you equate serious with monogamous, you're shit out of luck. You won't drive me away. Unless you can accept that she'll be with other people too, don't bother. She's poly. She isn't wired for just one man."

The truth of his words settled in my gut, smoothing out the ragged edges to my desires. One day I would make her mine. I'd kept a tight lid on the desire to possess her, mostly out of fear—if I let it out, if I gave it an inch, the need to claim her would override all sense. Once I owned her, no one except me would touch her.

But if she had other men... men who I liked, then maybe it wouldn't be that way. If she had men who were strong enough to stand up to me and temper my desires, then maybe I could get a handle on that green-eyed monster lurking just below the surface of my skin. Maybe no one except us would touch her.

The idea of seeing her with another man or men should have made me wild. In some ways, it did. But not with Flynn, and I wasn't quite sure why. Watching her with him was enlightening. I couldn't get it out of my head.

My mind and body had been at war with each other that day. My head had told me to close the door and give them some privacy. My body screamed at me to spank her for showing off, then plunge my cock inside her pussy alongside Flynn's. The desire to get up close and personal with her slick heat as well as his piercings was overwhelming.

After I'd watched them—and imagined what they'd be like with the professor—I'd jacked off more times than I could count. Watching them fuck had gotten me going. But the way he held her, the soft kisses he'd dropped on her shoulder and throat, the way she trusted him completely to take her where she needed to be was what I kept coming back to.

I wanted that for her, and even if I didn't want to share her, I would if it meant giving her that.

There would be haters, people who wouldn't understand. My mum would question it, my brother would roll his eyes, but he wouldn't say anything. He'd only called out her behaviour to my face once. He still had the crooked nose from where I'd shattered it as a reminder to keep his trap shut.

There was something to be said for Zali's utter disregard for societal pressure. She didn't give a fuck about what anyone thought of her. She was in your face and always did things her way. If you didn't like it, you could fuck off.

It was the same with sex. She clearly loved having an audience, and I'd loved watching her. I hadn't touched her, but I'd still been a part of it. They were putting on a show for me, and my only regret was the door being closed when the professor had been there. I'd wanted to watch again.

His deep, gravelly moans were like electrical charges to my skin. Every time I'd heard him, my hairs had stood on end. I'd stood outside their door, listening to Zali gagging and Flynn and the professor moaning. I'd wanted to see what position they were in. Were they spit-roasting her? Did she have both of them in her mouth?

Jealousy had bubbled up inside me, the need to tear the door off its hinges and fuck her until she was screaming like a rising tide I couldn't hold back. I'd come the first time with my fist wrapped around my cock right there outside her door. The second time was inside my own quarters a few cabins away from hers.

With the door open and my eyes closed, I pictured her mouth around my dick instead of my hand, and as I had played with my hole, I imagined the professor's cock at my entrance.

Like a fucking masochist, I'd gone back to check on them a couple of hours later, listening at the door like a creeper. I'd nearly been busted, too, when Tristan walked out of the stateroom, holding his clothes in front of his groin.

He'd eyed me off like a juicy steak, and my cock had bucked hard, leaving me reeling. The fantasy was one thing, but seeing him right there, naked and able to answer the question that was on repeat in my head was confronting.

"I take it you don't have an answer for that," Flynn mumbled. Answer? What were we talking about again?

Oh, *oh*.

"I won't try to push you away, Flynn. I can't guarantee it with any of her other men, but I'll bear your thoughts in mind." It was the best promise I could make because my answer would depend on who she was with. If it was the wrong dude, all bets would be off.

Flynn's next question was quiet, hesitant. A mixture of uncertainty and unease radiated off him. "What other men do you think she has? Apart from Tristan."

I couldn't help but reach over and reassure him with a squeeze of his shoulder. "None as far as I know. I certainly haven't heard her talking to anyone or seen her with anyone, but you have to know that there's something there with Detective Fraser."

Flynn's sigh was dreamy, love hearts in his eyes as he blinked and smiled wistfully. Yeah, that something definitely extended to him too. They were circling around one another, none of them making a move, but wanting to, nevertheless. I'd even seen that same spark between the professor and the detective, but it was coated in a layer of stubborn denial.

"Yeah, between the four of us, we have the potential for a whole poly love fest." His soft chuckle held a note of longing.

I flicked my gaze to him and took him in. The kid looked like a cherub—not that he was that much younger than I was, not even two years—but he seemed so innocent. It wasn't naïveté. It was more an open acceptance of everything. He was untouched by cynicism and greed. He radiated joy and light, painting everyone with his special brand of magical happiness. No wonder he wanted lovers he could share with Zali—he had so much love to give that it could easily extend to a group.

"Putting aside your issues, is there another reason why you haven't made a move?" he asked, clearly curious.

I barked out a laugh. "My issues?"

"Well, yeah. Everything you said about not wanting casual and expecting everything from her are 'you' problems, not 'her' problems. Is it you who's not ready?"

It was a good thing the radio crackled to life just then, because I needed time to sort through my thoughts. It was Sydney Airport's tower checking in and giving me approach directions. "Received. Thank you, Kingsford Smith tower." I repeated the directions they'd given me and began the jet's descent.

After a time, I finally responded, "You're right, I do have a few things to work through myself. The whole relationship dynamic between you and the professor, for one."

"Why, because Tristan and I were together?" His voice held a note of challenge, calling me out on what he thought was homophobic behaviour.

It wasn't. I just needed to work out how I was going to stop myself from demanding the same from them.

Between lowering the landing gear, raising the flaps, checking my approach one final time, and speaking to the tower, I deflected before asking, "So, it's completely off between you two as well?"

He nodded, his shoulders dropping. "I like him, but if he doesn't want to be with Zee, too, I won't keep seeing him. I don't want it to work like that."

I checked the airspeed indicator and pulled back slightly on the yoke to slow her just a touch, readying to set down. We were only a few metres above the runway. Slowly easing off the jet's speed again, I flicked my gaze down to check on the gauges and reduced our altitude a touch more, repeating the process until the wheels touched down against the tarmac.

"Fair enough," I added after I'd slowed the plane's speed to a taxi and checked in with the tower again. I stopped directly outside the hangars, where Zali's baby would now be ready for our return flight.

Flynn interrupted Zali while I unlocked the cabin door and lowered the stairs. She was all business, straightening her shirt in no nonsense, sharp movements and double-checking the contents of her satchel before she followed us out. She didn't linger, marching straight for the Audi I'd arranged and tapping her foot impatiently when I had to re-trieve the keys from the hangar.

She huffed, yanking the door open the moment I got it unlocked. My gut sank, and that protective streak roared to life inside me. "Where am I taking us?" I asked from the driver's seat, my tone full of false peppiness.

She rattled off the address, reiterating, "I'll head inside alone. You can both wait outside for me."

There was barely a second's delay between Flynn and me both retorting, "No."

Zali groaned and rubbed her temples. She was out of patience. "Guys, I don't have time for this. I need you to get me there faster than we're moving now." She waved her hand as if to flick me away, and I gritted my teeth. This woman would make my head explode out of sheer frustra-tion one day. "Actually moving would be a good start." Zali's raised eyebrow challenged me as if she were the one giving the orders around here.

I squeezed the leather steering wheel until it creaked and laughed off her retort. Through gritted teeth, I de-manded, "Answer me one thing. Are you doing something dangerous? Be straight with me." I gestured to Flynn over my shoulder. "With us."

"We're not waiting for you outside, regardless of what you say," Flynn warned.

"No, okay? It's as dangerous as walking into any building is. It's more dangerous to drive over the speed limit. Which you'll be doing if you don't get this car moving in zero point five seconds flat."

She sighed and added, "It's not your job to protect me, Ry."

She was dead wrong there.

Zali

Ry pulled up at the front entrance of the address I'd given him and into the loading zone usually used by couriers. The building was shrouded in scaffolding, the sandstone undergoing repair work and the interior getting a major overhaul too. The only thing untouched was the server room, the place where I needed to be.

Undetected.

My heart was beating at a frenetic pace, and I was sweating up a storm in my leather pants. They were hot, literally and figuratively. But I was hoping that they worked to my advantage. As a general rule, construction workers were happier to see a woman in a suit than a man—men usually meant supervisors coming to check on them—especially if said woman looked fuckable. And I looked fuckable.

I pulled myself back into the moment, slowing my breathing and checking out where we were parked. The busy street wasn't ideal, but at least the construction workers surrounding the place were all entering and exiting along the back. Staff, on the other hand, would enter in the front doors where security was usually set up.

Not that there was any. Would you believe that they disengaged all the building's security systems when the builders were on site? The building's HVAC system was turned off and its fire prevention system was suspended. It made sense with all the dust, but they should have moved the server room out while the renovations were taking place. It was actually hilarious how little thought had been put into what would happen if there was a physical attack on the building. Their incompetence was my good luck.

Right, I could do this. Pulling my shoulders back, straightening my spine, and forcing the fear down, I stepped out of the car.

Pausing, I blew out a breath and made sure I was steady on my feet. My Manolos were high even for me, but they were a necessary part of my uniform. Lifting my chin, I didn't bother checking to see whether Ry and Flynn were following. I had no doubt they'd be hot on my tail, but this boss lady wasn't waiting for them.

After all, I had an emergency with the servers I needed to deal with.

I marched through the front doors like I owned the place. I did have a high rise or two in my portfolio, so who knew, I might. Looking around, I assessed the lobby as I would if it were my own project. High ceilings and open windows would let the light in. There were two separate entrances into the heart of the building, delineating the public and more private areas. I nodded appreciatively and picked my way between toolboxes, stacks of gyprock, and buckets of glue over to the bank of elevators.

I really hoped I could pull this off. If Ryder, or more likely Flynn, gave off any kind of vibe that alerted the sole security guard wandering the site to the fact that I lacked credentials, I'd never get the information I wanted. I'd also likely get arrested.

The dude in a set of coveralls open to his chest with a thatch of hair peeking through frightened the shit out of me. I jumped, stumbling on a piece of plastic strapping. He whirled around, removing his earbud. It explained why he hadn't heard the click of my heels before.

Shooting him a seductive smile and taking my time to look him up and down, I stepped over to the lifts and pressed the button to summon the carriage. I resisted the urge to check my hair or adjust my shirt. Act confident, be confident.

"You right there, li'l darlin'? Access is restricted to this building."

"Yes, thank you. I head up IT. We got an alert on the server room, so I'm training my staff—" I gestured over my shoulder to Flynn and Ryder who were striding after me. "—how to check that the cooling system is still working optimally."

"No worries. Go on up. I'll call the foreman if you want."

"No need." I licked my lips slowly, my tongue running over the blood-red lipstick I'd applied. "But write down your number for me so I can grab it on the way out."

"Abso-fuckin-lutely."

His grin lit up the room, and I touched my chest, then squeezed my elbows together, before biting down on my lip. Flynn tensed, and Ryder shot him a glare, but neither dimmed the man's happy.

The doors opened, and Flynn held them while Ry waited for me to make a move.

I looked the tradie up and down again before playing with my imaginary necklace, opening the collar of my shirt a little more. "We'll be back in about twenty minutes."

"See you then, darlin'."

The lift doors closed behind us, and they rounded on me the minute they did. Eyes hard, Ryder snarled at me. I rolled my eyes, laughing at him. So growly.

I smoothed Flynn's frown with my thumb and dropped a kiss on the corner of his lips, my tongue sneaking out and teasing at the seam. "I'll make it up to you later," I assured him. I patted Ry's chest and added, "Relax. Purely fake it until you make it."

"He needs to think we're allowed to be here," Ry concluded quickly.

"Something like that," I hedged. I hadn't told them exactly what I'd be doing in the building. I didn't want to implicate them, but now that they were too damn stubborn to stay in the car, I could use their help.

"Spit it out, Zali. What are we doing?" Ry demanded.

"There's something in the research that doesn't add up. It was public knowledge that the investments Mum had targeted were on shaky ground. Why would she throw money at them when there were obvious red flags? It doesn't make sense, and it's certainly not a good investment strategy. Something else was going on behind the scenes. I need access to confirm where the payments went."

"You think there was a discrepancy with what was reported?" Flynn asked, his brows hiked up high and his eyes wide.

"The liquidators didn't look beyond the company's financial data. They didn't perform an audit. They were so stretched with bankruptcies and liquidations by that stage in the GFC that they were just reviewing the accounts. They saw a payment had been made to a company and assumed it actually went there. The only thing they looked further into were related party transactions that they could claw back."

"So, what makes you think it's problematic?"

"Seeing that family's involvement has made me rethink everything."

"I'm clueless. What are you getting at?" Ry asked.

The lift pinged, and the doors slid open silently. Flynn stuck his head out and checked the hall before succinctly surmising my thoughts. He spoke in a hushed tone as we stepped out. "You think that it was recorded as going somewhere but went to a different place? But if they were only an investment target, how does that help them?"

Getting into the server room was usually the hardest thing to do—heightened security existed at every stage. But I had a back door in—a spreadsheet recording who had access to the server room and their PIN in a password-protected Excel spreadsheet wasn't the smartest. Making the password "PASSWORD" was dumber. But at least these were only backup servers for archived data. I hoped that the servers with current financial data had better security.

The architect's plans had everything noted—both the level and the location of the server room door. It was like placing a giant flashing neon sign above it with an honesty box for keys and expecting that hackers wouldn't jump at the challenge.

We stepped our way through the hallway littered with construction equipment, and in a whisper, I answered, "What I didn't tell you earlier is that they were also investors, and big ones. I don't know if or how it changes things, but I need to find out."

We were wasting precious seconds that we didn't have.

The entrance to the server room was on the south side of the building. It would stay cooler in Sydney's brutal summers, meaning that the standalone air-conditioning systems didn't need to work as hard to cool it, even though there were no external windows to the room. Being elevated also meant that there was no risk of flooding the room or the utilities units servicing it.

I typed in the PIN I'd memorized on the electronic keypad and shook my head when the lock disengaged. "Unbelievable," I muttered. "Get in here with me."

I slipped the cables out of my satchel and passed them to Flynn while I grasped my laptop. "Get the shelf for me?" I gestured to the steel cabinet in front of me that had shelves built in at chest height. I handed the bag off to Ryder and set everything down before plugging into the system. It only took a moment to connect in and a few more to get access to the server. I really needed to speak with them about security.

"What are you looking for?" Ry asked in a whisper over my shoulder.

"Transaction records—account names and numbers."

"We're in a bank?" he asked, horror in his tone.

"Not quite," I hedged, wincing a little at the white lie. Technically we weren't in a bank. Kind of. "I need to match the records up with the financials, like I said. The banks only keep the data for a few years. After that, it's destroyed. But because the GFC was so significant, financially speaking, the Reserve Bank ordered that the banks archive complete records of the years leading up to it and during the recovery phase for research purposes. The data is stored here."

"We're in the Reserve Bank?" he hissed.

I huffed out a laugh that I didn't feel. He was making me jumpy when I was already on edge. Flynn had been right—I wasn't really in an emotional state to be working this job.

"No, just the museum. Relax, I can't steal anything."

"Except data, Zee, which is exactly what you're doing."

"We need to go," Ry ordered, grabbing a hold of my arm. "Now."

I shook him off and narrowed my eyes at him, stomping my foot for good measure. "No. I'm not debating this, Ry. I'm not leaving until I have the information I need."

Turning back to the computer, I brought up the search function for the archives. I input the bank and started on the dates, but Ry wasn't finished his tirade.

"You're going to get us arrested, Zali." He wasn't panicked, but that didn't surprise me one bit when it came to Ry. He was intense but also uber laid back, and he thrived on challenges. Learn how to rebuild my Mustang? Done. Pilot a yacht? He'd excelled. Fly a plane? No problems. No, Ry was pissed. Like I'd personally offended him. Well, fuck that.

"So leave. I told you both to wait in the car, but you insisted on being heroes. You could have been having a beer up the street if you'd listened."

"And let you come here by yourself?"

"No one would have even known I was here," I snapped. Now was not the time for him to go all cave man on me. "But if we don't hurry up, they *will* find us."

"Except for the guy you chatted up."

"Oh, grow up." I was done with this conversation, done with his moronic attitude. If he wanted to stake a claim, fine, but he'd better get his dick out, because no one was going to presume to tell me what I could do without following it up by a good fucking. I'd ignore their demands regardless, but at least I'd get the spectacular orgasm out of it.

"Zee, please," Flynn begged, his voice high and sharp. Unlike Ry, he was panicking.

"Shut up and let me work," I snapped far more testily than I'd intended. "Or get out." I pointed at the door and waited, glaring at them to disagree. We didn't have time for me to deal with overprotectiveness, jealousy, or freakouts.

Flynn stubbornly shook his head, the man I knew and loved staring right back at me. "I'm not leaving you."

My gaze softened at him, and I cupped his face, sliding my thumb along his cheek.

Ry grumbled, "Leaving isn't an option, Zali. It's not how this works."

"Yes. It is." I executed the search on the database, and once the results started popping up, I began the download. The databases were huge, but I'd narrowed the scope so much that I hoped it would be quick. Still…. "Leave now. That way, if I get caught, you won't be implicated. At least you won't lose anything."

"How can you think I wouldn't have already lost everything?" Flynn asked. He grasped my hand, holding it between both of his. He brought it to his lips and kissed my knuckles slowly, and it chipped away at my annoyance. "If anything happens to you, everything on this planet that I love is snatched away from me. I'm not leaving without you."

I tilted my head and smiled, love hearts no doubt in my eyes. That was by far the sweetest thing anyone had ever said to me.

I grabbed his face, bringing his lips to mine in a fierce kiss. I thrust my tongue into his mouth, teasing him as our teeth clashed together. He tasted of raspberry lollies, sweet and addictive. Pressing my body against his, I wanted to get lost in him. But I couldn't. I pulled back, breathless, and murmured, "I love you too."

My laptop pinged, and I pulled away, leaving Flynn staring at me in a daze. His pupils were blown, and his lips still wet where I'd nibbled on them. His beautiful cock was tenting his pants, and although I longed to sit on that bad boy, I had other things I needed to do. Getting Flynn naked would have to wait.

"Right, download is done. One more thing, then we leave." I inserted the USB stick directly into the server and managed the upload from my computer. In less than a minute, we were ready to go.

I blew out a breath and got moving, packing up my things.

"Do you need to clean your fingerprints?" Ry asked, looking over his shoulder and scoping out the place before we left.

I shook my head. This wasn't some *James Bond* movie. No need for that.

NINETEEN

Flynn

From the moment she'd stepped out of the car, Zee was this perfectly poised bad-arse. She was always a force of nature, but now she was on a mission, intent on getting the information she wanted. It was a total turn-on as well as being slightly terrifying.

It was a good thing that I knew her like the back of my hand, because right now, if she were anyone else, I'd be as intimidated as heck by her.

As it was, I was still freaking out.

We were inside a government building, the Reserve Bank of all places, holding onto data that could get us hit with some serious jail time if we got busted. I had images of the *Blues Brothers* car chase and the police shootout from *Point Break* running through my head. I'd never done any-thing this insane or exciting before. But the fear was real too. How were we going to get out of here without getting arrested?

"You ready?" Zee asked us, zipping up the computer case she was holding. With her head held high and a serene smile, she added, "We go out exactly the same way we came."

"What if the tradie wants to talk?" I asked, biting back my worry. I wasn't jealous—Zee could flirt with as many men as she wanted. I knew she'd come home to me—but I was scared that he'd distract her enough that we'd get found out. Even a single extra second spent in the building was a second too long for my liking.

Now I knew where Ryder got his fiercely protective streak from. I wanted to protect Zee, even if it meant protecting her from herself.

She grasped my hands in hers, squeezing them tight. "You go on ahead, and I'll follow." Turning to Ry, she added, "I'm trusting you to get Flynn out. As soon as you can, park in front of the door, and I'll use you as an excuse to leave."

That wasn't what I'd meant, but before I could clarify, Ry asked, "And if someone asks us why we're here?"

"Leave that up to me." With one hand clasping Ry's forearm and the other on my cheek, she dragged my mouth to hers and kissed me hard and fast, cutting off my comments.

Ry pushed open the door, and Zee stepped out with me close on her tail, making sure no-one caught up to us in the corridor. We made it halfway before we heard voices coming from the direction we needed to go.

I swallowed hard, my heart rate ticking up a notch.

I hadn't realized I'd stopped walking until Zee grasped my hand and pulled me toward the door Ry was holding open. He closed it silently, the lock only making a soft snick as he engaged it. With a finger to her lips, Zee gestured to the floor.

My legs were jelly when I sank down, relieved that I didn't have to coordinate holding myself up and walking anymore. I could do this. Fear was my friend. It would keep me on my toes.

If I told myself that rubbish over and over again, I might actually believe it.

The three of us shuffled away from the door, crouching down under the line of windows looking into the corridor. The room was stripped bare of furniture and window coverings, the walls freshly painted and ready for flooring to be laid. It didn't give us much cover, but at least if we stayed under the windows, we were unlikely to be seen.

I turned my gaze to Zee and couldn't believe my life. How had I landed myself here? She'd always been my best friend, but now she was so much more. I hated that she was putting herself at so much risk, because even though I was scared out of my mind about getting caught, she was the one I was truly worried about.

I couldn't let anything happen to her.

"Hey," Zee soothed, on her knees in front of me, cupping my face as her brow furrowed in concern. "What's wrong?"

"We need to get out of here, Zee."

"I'll protect you. We'll get out of here. Nothing is going to happen. I promise."

I shook my head. Again, not what I was worried about. Well, it was, but that wasn't all I feared. "You can't make that promise, and anyway, I'm more worried about you."

She smiled, the expression warm and filled with affection. I was sure my grin matched hers. "You don't need to protect me, Flynn. I'm perfectly capable of looking after myself."

"I know, and I love you for it. But I want to protect you. So does Ry." I held her hands in mine, trying to take the sting from my words. It wouldn't work, but I had to at least try. "This? This is insane. We're hiding in a federal building after robbing it."

"You trust me, right? I'll get us out of here."

I nodded and closed my eyes, hoping against hope that she was right. Begging the universe to let her be right.

Being arrested, I could handle. Heck, even jail time would eventually come to an end. But there were some things people couldn't come back from. Like death. We weren't armed, but what if the guards were? What if they saw us and started shooting?

I'd never forgive myself if I let anything bad happen to her. Neither would Ry. And if either Ryder or I were hurt, or worse, it would destroy Zee.

Zee inhaled slowly, held the deep breath for a moment, then slowly exhaled. I couldn't help but follow along, copying her moves and soaking up her calm. My hands stayed wrapped around hers, our grip on each other gentle but strong at the same time.

Meeting her gaze once more, I sank into those deep blue eyes. Usually, they were filled with a spark of something uniquely Zee—a little bit of mischief, a little bit of daring—but now they were dull. Whether it was fear or the unacknowledged pain of this afternoon's breakup, I'd likely never know. But her confidence never wavered, nor did the rock-solid belief that we'd be okay. It was comforting, even though I knew that we only had so much control over what would happen in the next few minutes.

"Nothing is going to happen," she reiterated. I think it was for her own sake too.

I looked over at Ry, but his expression was unreadable. He was wearing his usual frown, his lips a straight line. He looked like he should have been an action hero, the guy who saves the world when it's falling to pieces. He would have looked at home with a gun in his hand and his finger on the trigger, ready to bob up and fire off at the people standing in our way.

Instead, he raised himself up to take a quick peek over the window in both directions. "Coast is clear," he whispered. "Let's get out of here."

Ry went first, unlocking and opening the door, then creeping out into the corridor. Zee and I were hot on his tail. For the first time, hope swelled inside me. We could do this. We could get out of here without anyone knowing we had ever even been there. All we had to do was get to the lifts. Once we rode one down, we'd be able to walk straight out the front door.

Simple steps.

Silently we moved, stopping a few times to listen for voices. This level was relatively quiet, but there were people hanging around.

The steel doors of the lift, together with the call button, were only a few short metres away. In the middle of the corridor, there was nowhere to hide if someone rounded the corner. This was it. This was the test. If we could get onto the lift after the ding without anyone seeing us, we'd be almost there.

Zee pushed the button, and I held my breath, waiting for the chime to sound. It was likely that none of the tradies on site would even register it had dinged.

Ry and I flanked Zee, each of our heads on a swivel, checking the progress of the countdown and looking over our shoulders for surprises. We couldn't do much. We weren't armed, and we didn't have anything we could throw at them. But hell would freeze over before I'd go down without a fight if it meant keeping Zee safe.

The lift chimed, and the doors slid open. The carriage wasn't empty. An older man, the foreman if the label on his hard hat was to be believed, stood there, his phone in hand.

His gaze locked with Zee's.

Eyes narrowed. Lips turned down in a frown.

He lifted his hand, pointing at us.

Stepped forward.

I acted on instinct, moving closer to Zee, my hand out as I pressed her back and shielded her. Ry was right there, too, stepping forward as he gripped my arm and shoved me back.

"Oi, stop right there," a man to our right yelled.

His words snapped the foreman into action. He lunged forward and shouted, "That's them."

Time slowed, split seconds turning to hours.

I shifted myself bodily in front of Zee and grasped her hand. I needed to get her out of here. Danger was on two sides of us, a wall blocking our third. The only way we could go was left. I tugged her hand, but Zee hesitated, her feet glued to the floor.

Ry dodged the foreman's charge. He stepped to the side, shielding us both with his big body.

Running footsteps to my right. I risked a glance sideways.

It was a security guard.

He was unholstering his gun.

We needed gone right that second.

There was no time to dash into the lifts. The foreman would be on us within a second.

Left, and hopefully, to the fire escape.

I yanked on Zee's hand. "Move," I demanded, my heart in my throat. There was no way I was leaving Ry there, but the desire to keep Zee safe and get her away from the dude with a gun was overwhelming.

"Ry, gun," I screeched, pushing Zee away from him.

Quick as lightning, Ry reacted. He grabbed the foreman's vest, using his forward momentum to push him off balance.

His foot shot out, sweeping at the man's ankle. It connected with a dull thud.

The foreman's eyes widened, surprise registering on his slack jaw. His foot stopped, but his body kept moving forward. Arms cartwheeling, he overbalanced.

Ryder shoved him toward the wall.

Without a second's delay, Ryder dashed after us. For a man who was so tall, he was incredibly agile, catching up to us in only a few strides.

"Faster," he hissed, grasping Zee's elbow, the two of us sticking close to her.

"Freeze, or I'll shoot," the guard yelled, his heavy footfalls sounding behind us.

"Fucking shoot already," the foremen growled.

Zee sprinted forward, her stilettos not slowing her down in the slightest. But Ry was no longer beside me. He'd paused, bending to pick something up.

"Hurry up," I demanded.

A shot rang out, the bang louder than any noise I'd ever experienced. Instinct had me covering my head with my arms and crouching down as I ran, but Ry was still not beside me. Where the hell was he? I spun around, looking for him.

A clanging noise and a curse, then Ryder was next to me, running again. We rounded the corner, and my heart sang in relief. Zee was holding the door to the fire escape stairs open for us.

Our salvation.

We stumbled through, and I whirled around, going for the door. The security guard rounded the corner, gun raised again.

"Get down," I screamed. With all the force I possessed, I shoved at the door, slamming it shut.

The same bangs, this time four in a row, reverberated in the small space. Even through the steel of the door, they were loud enough to set my ears ringing. I blinked and shook my head, trying to clear the instant headache.

Vibrations rippled through the door, the steel absorbing the force of each of the bullets. My hands shook, the tremor travelling up my arms.

My heart leaped into my throat.

I couldn't get enough air. My gasps were fast and shallow.

Adrenaline shot through me, the hairs on the back of my neck standing on end.

My legs nearly gave out. I hunched over, propping myself up against the door.

That had been too close.

Way too close.

This was beyond the pale now. We weren't just in danger of being arrested, we were running for our lives.

Ry wedged a steel rod under the handle of the door. "It won't hold long. We need to go," he urged. "Are you hurt?"

"No, just freaking out." I sucked in a breath and held it, trying to calm down again. "But I'll be okay."

Zee was a few steps ahead of us as we sprinted down the stairs. I couldn't believe she could do it. She'd break an ankle if she twisted her foot in those heels, but she was running as if they were sneakers and she an Olympic athlete.

Flight, landing, flight, landing, over and over again until we reached the ground floor lobby.

"No," I called out, breathless, when Zee grasped the handle. "Go down one more level. There's always a separate fire stair in the basement that exits onto the street."

Zee went down one more level. We shot out, still at a run. The door banged, echoing through the basement car park. I winced. Shit—we shouldn't have announced our arrival to everyone in here.

But it was silent.

White vans and utes with company logos plastered on their sides surrounded us, blocking our view but also giving us some cover. No one was in them.

We crept between the parked cars, moving as quickly and quietly as we could. It wouldn't be long before the security guard found us.

"There." Ry pointed, the green exit sign illuminating the concrete walls like a rescue beacon.

Relief swamped me, but I held my breath. This wasn't over by a long shot. We still had to get to the car, then out of here.

Legs carrying us as fast as we could run, we hit the stairs. But we were stealthier when we reached the top, easing the door open and using the wall of the building as shelter until we got nearer to the Audi.

Ry already had the doors unlocked as we made the short dash to it.

Police sirens sounded in the distance. Workers spilled out onto the street, some unimpressed and others unperturbed by the distraction.

"Hey, that's them," one shouted as I yanked open the car door. I pushed Zee in, using myself to shield her.

I didn't even have the door closed behind me when Ry revved the engine hard and hit the accelerator.

The car shot backward, launching out of the loading zone and onto the street. I gripped Ry's seat, holding on while I scrambled to shut the door.

Screeching tyres. Horns blared.

I closed my eyes, waiting for the inevitable smash.

TWENTY

Tristan

I closed the door to my office and leaned against it. Exhaling, I thudded my head against the timber and grasped the handle for balance. My head was still spinning with the events of that morning.

Ryder had docked the yacht at the marina, and I'd moved like a zombie, my legs carrying me to my car and my vehicle practically driving itself to my office.

What the fuck had just happened?

One minute, I'd been planning a day of research and reviewing more assessments that had been submitted. The next, I was on the phone with a panicked Flynn asking me to go with him to see Zali. I hadn't hesitated. I'd dropped everything, dumping my plans, bowing out of meetings, and rearranging my schedule so I could be there.

Nothing had been more important to me than getting to her. I should have been scared by the hold that the two of them had over me, but I hadn't given myself time to think. I'd reacted, going with my gut.

And a little with my heart.

In some ways I was glad I'd gone. In others.... Well, I wished I'd stayed ignorant of certain facts.

It was the second time I'd been on Zali's yacht. The sheer opulence of it took my breath away the same as it had the first time. Knowing its price blew my mind. I'd wondered how a twenty-something who didn't come from money had afforded it. I didn't think I'd underestimated her capabilities, but I sure as hell had underestimated just how rich those capabilities had made her.

That should have been my first clue. Cyber investigators were glorified research assistants. But hackers? White coats got paid decent money, but I didn't think that's what she did. I'd brushed off her claims that she'd stolen the money, not wanting to hear it as an admission. But after seeing her progress, I realized that she was telling me the truth in a blasé kind of way, testing me to see if I believed her.

Yet, when I stepped into that room, I didn't see a criminal mastermind. I didn't see someone who could and did destroy lives for their own gain, something she'd admitted doing before. I saw a young woman—the same one I was falling for—who was hurting.

I saw her vulnerable and pushed to the brink. I saw her trying her best given really shitty circumstances. She was mature beyond her years in the way she approached research and analyzed information. But none of that mattered when she was sitting cross-legged on her desk chair in leggings a ratty tee with her hair up in a messy bun. I'd wanted to wrap her up in my arms. I'd wanted to pull her onto my lap and stroke that silken hair, kissing her and touching her until she became pliant in my arms. I'd wanted to curl up with her and Flynn and forget the outside world while she slept.

I'd wanted to walk away from all my responsibilities to shield her from hers.

She had more at stake in this whole arrangement than any of us. It was personal to her on a level I couldn't comprehend, and the stress from it shone through like a beacon.

The progress she'd made was phenomenal, but I wasn't surprised. She'd spent more time than every other student combined had dedicated—and probably would dedicate—to the entire project. The outcome was the mind map of a genius. It outshone every other assignment I'd seen. Although that wasn't difficult. The other students had put together something a whole lot more typical—a written piece or an oral presentation in third person that was detached and devoid of emotion—and ultimately not all that helpful for the podcast.

Zali's time and intelligence had generated some seriously impressive results. She was incredible, a force to be reckoned with. She'd dug up more information on her mother's company in days than I'd managed in two years of research. She'd narrowed down leads and blown open other ideas, making connections between people and organizations that I didn't even know existed. The project was jumping forward in leaps and bounds thanks to her. She'd run ownership checks on each of the investors and many of the target investments and had progressed into double-checking information disclosed in financial reports in an attempt to create a money trail.

It had never even occurred to me to do that. I'd accepted the financials at face value, the same way that the liquidators had.

But as impressed as I was, a disquiet had also settled over me.

Brushing off her comment that she'd stolen the money for her yacht had been a faux pas on my part. I hadn't wanted to believe it, not when—as crass as it was to admit—I could get my dick wet. But what kind of cyber investigator could come up with that kind of information so quickly? I could no longer ignore questions of where she was getting the data from and how was she getting it. Especially when I knew much of the information was protected by privacy laws and unavailable even to legitimate researchers.

The wall of data, as beautiful as it was to see, was also a flashing neon hazard light. It had me backtracking, needing to get myself out of there.

My head screamed at me to run, to get as far away as possible from her.

What she did for a living had finally hit home. The pieces clicked into place. The rose-coloured glasses came off. I saw her in a different light, one that I was terrified of.

I hadn't quite believed Flynn when he'd said she could bury me, another faux pas on my part. I'd blown off Ryder, too, the third in a growing list of shitty decisions on my part. Naïvely, I had thought that revenge porn or a phone call to my boss would be it. But my worst-case scenarios, my foolish thoughts of what she could do were child's play compared to the league she was in.

I'd had no idea what she was capable of.

She'd shown me a glimpse.

I'd run.

Not my finest hour.

My phone buzzed, reminding me of the department meeting I'd blown off in favour of more… enjoyable pursuits. That wasn't a possibility now. I sighed. I'd already been seen in the hallway. Not showing up now would be asking for a voluntary work-intensive role to be added to my schedule.

I logged on but left my camera turned off. I didn't need there to be video evidence of my lack of fucks right then. My mind was so consumed with what was going on that I'd be useless in the meeting anyway.

Sagging into my chair, I leaned back, steepling my fingers, and tried to ignore the memories of what had gone down in my office only a couple of short weeks earlier.

Maybe being in the meeting would be good for me. Maybe I could get my mind off the cluster fuck I'd dived headfirst into.

But I couldn't concentrate. I was only half listening at best, scrolling through photos on my phone. My smile was wistful. Flynn had taken it up to the hot tub and had been snapping photos—hard, irrefutable evidence that I was sleeping with not one but two students. Stupid, but I'd been so high on happy hormones that I just didn't care. I'd been so far gone that for every one that Flynn took of Zali and me or Flynn and me, there were two of Zali and Flynn together, courtesy of me.

It was the one of Flynn and Zali together that I got stuck on. Flynn was standing on the seat, the long lines of his naked body on display. He was bent over, lifting Zali and kissing her. Her back was arched, her arms wrapped around his neck, the whole top half of her rising out of the water. Those gorgeous breasts of hers were front and centre. After taking the photo, I'd dropped my phone, wrapped Zali's legs around my waist, and kissed every part of her I could reach. It hadn't been sexual, more playful than anything, but that snippet of intimacy was burned into my brain.

I replayed every moment of that afternoon over and over. From the conversation to the kissing, all the way to Flynn sinking inside me, and then Zali welcoming me into her body with Flynn alongside. Zali underneath me, then on me. Flynn pressing into me. The taste of her. Heated breath against sweat-soaked skin. The slide of bodies moving together, the smell of sex in the air. The moans and whimpers, groans and whispered curses, praise and shouts of ecstasy all forming the soundtrack to our afternoon of orgasms. It was a turn-on beyond anything I'd ever imagined. I'd never thought it possible to click on so many levels with two people. But click we had, and we'd come even harder.

I flicked my gaze to the table—the same one I'd been studiously ignoring since getting off in my office to memories of that day more times than I could count. I pictured Zali, splayed out and wanting on it, her hands gripping the edge as I lifted her leg and opened her up for my cock. Flynn sitting on the chair next to us, his pierced perfection held in his tight fist as he stroked.

No matter how much I shouldn't want her—want them—I did.

My cock throbbed. I was like a fucking flagpole. My balls were tight, my body priming to fuck—

"Tristan, you there?" the disembodied voice of my head of department asked, snapping me out of my wicked thoughts.

Shit. I scrambled to turn on the mic, wracking my brain for the topic of conversation. I'd zoned out that badly, I wasn't even sure where we were up to in the agenda.

"Yes, sorry. I'm having sound trouble. I'm only hearing every second word, but I think I've fixed it. Loose connection on my speaker."

"Call IT support when we're done," he chastised. "Are you following the discussion around assessment?"

"I was trying to, but it was difficult," I admitted. That was the truest statement—the only statement—I'd made during the meeting.

Professor Redden repeated the gist of what had been said, and I added my two cents, realizing that they were asking me for my expert opinion on student-led assessment design.

I tried to focus, but my cock was getting crushed in the confines of my pants. I squeezed it, trying to calm the fucker down, but the attention just made the need worse. I bit back a groan, unzipping my pants in a futile attempt to relieve the pressure. The blessed relief only lasted for a moment because as soon as my dick wasn't bound up, the throb started in earnest. I slipped my hand inside my underwear and grasped my balls, easing them away from my body.

How long would this torturous meeting last? I needed an orgasm. I needed to come.

But after an hour of mindless chatter, we were only one third of the way through the agenda.

Fuck, at this rate I'd be lucky to stay conscious for another hour with the lack of blood in my brain.

With my eyes fixed on that table and memories assaulting me, I shoved my pants and underwear down to my knees, giving myself access to every part of myself that I wanted to play with. I wrapped my hand around my cock and squeezed, drawing my fist down my shaft and back up. Pre-cum pooled at the slit, and I brushed my thumb over my sensitive head, sending licks of arousal straight to my balls. Using pre-cum as lubricant for my next stroke, I bit back a moan and set a steady pace.

My mind blanked out as I relived those moments of plunging inside our woman. The tight clasp of her pussy, the combination of her juices and Flynn's cum coating me as I fucked her. The grip of her arse as I sank into its depths, the drag on my cock before I let loose and coated her in my spunk, using it as lube until I'd softened enough that I needed to add a finger to keep fucking her.

I saw stars, a rushing sensation travelling through me as I worked my dick. Long slow strokes, teasing twists of my fist, and flicks of my thumb against my engorged balls had me steadily climbing to a precipice I couldn't wait to jump off.

The phantom sensation of Flynn's cock in my arse, of that thick shaft stretching me tight and those piercings rubbing me in all the right places, drove me higher. My cinnamon roll had admitted to being an anal virgin, but it hadn't mattered. Get the man naked, and he transformed into this assertive take-no-prisoners man that I melted into a puddle of goo for, spreading my legs like a cheap hooker and letting him have his way with me.

I needed that same stretch now. The same burn.

I didn't have any toys in my office care of my no-fucking-on-the-desk rule, but I did have lube. Sliding my desk drawer open, I fished around until I found it and slicked both hands up.

My whimper was loud in the quiet of the office save for the talking in the meeting. Wiggling my pants further down my legs, I spread wide, slouching down and coating my hole with slick. Pressing a fingertip in, I teased my sensitive rim of muscle, not giving in just yet to the desire to fill myself to bursting point.

I gripped my dick again and hissed as the easy glide intensified the ecstasy curling low in my belly. I squeezed my eyes closed and pressed two fingers inside my hole, pushing as deep as I could. Concentrating on the stretch and burn, the press against my P-spot and the glide of my fist up and down my rock-solid length, I didn't bother censoring my noises.

A groan, long and low, left my mouth as I shuddered. I was so close to the edge, so close to nirvana.

My movements had turned choppy, my breath coming in short gasps as I pumped my fingers in and out of my arse and twisted my wrist, brushing my palm over the sensitive head of my dick. I was hard, so hard, and leaking every-where. My balls were drawn up high and tight against my body. Brushing my pinky finger over them sent a shudder of sensation through me, my hole tightening around my fin-gers and strangling them.

I pictured my balls firing off, the swell of sensation and its release through my dick as I neared the edge. One more press on my prostate, my grip tightening on my cock, and I cried out, jerking hard as I painted my hand with cum. Pulse after pulse shot from me as I floated in ecstasy. My fingers and toes tingled, my legs heavy after having had them tense for so long. My breaths heaved, and I slumped back, melting into my chair.

Silence surrounded me, the only noise in the office my heavy breathing. Then, "Tristan? You okay?"

"Ah," I choked out a cough. "Yes," I squeaked.

"Sounded like—"

"Sex noises—" Barry helpfully supplied.

A chorus of "Barry!" crackled through the speaker, some of my colleagues scandalized and the others laughing.

"What?" he asked unashamedly. "Sounded like sex noises."

"No." I snapped before forcing out a chuckle that sounded as awkward as it was. Who the fuck forgets to turn off their mic then jacks off in the middle of a staff meeting with the whole department listening? But my cover up lie came easily enough. It was one I'd used before. On Flynn and Zali. I closed my eyes, desperate not to relive the moment—getting hard again while I still had cum all over me and my fingers in my arse wasn't exactly ideal when I couldn't mute the damn mic before I needed to jack off again. "Not sex noises. I twisted in my seat and pinched a muscle in my back. I've been stretching to try to loosen it up."

"Yes, well. Let's try to keep focussed," Professor Redden scolded in his prim-and-proper voice.

I went back to ignoring them as I wiped my hands with some tissues before muting my mic, cleaning up as best I could without actually leaving my office. I groaned and rested my head against my crossed arms on the desk. I was in trouble.

I wanted them, but what was I supposed to do? How could I risk everything? Zali was dangerous. She wasn't an employee of the federal police when she was working on my assignment. She wasn't performing investigative work in that role. She didn't have the protection—as limited as it was where there was no warrant in place—that the police did. That meant neither did I.

She was breaking laws left, right, and centre, not seeming to blink an eye when she did.

Zali's danger came from her power to destroy me. A wave of those magical fingers on her keyboard, the download of a file or the slip into a secure server, and *bam*—everything I'd worked for would be up in smoke.

But it wasn't just my career. It was my freedom.

I could live with walking away from my job. I could find something else to do easily enough. I wasn't one of those academics who'd be a lifer. I had no intention of still being there when I was sixty or seventy.

But ending up in jail again was a hard limit. Do not pass go, do not collect two hundred dollars. I'd dragged myself out of my childhood—where I might as well have been in jail—and landed square in a crowd of kids who were just as intent on breaking free of their oppressive parents' hold. They were military brats too.

Being abandoned by the father who'd loved controlling every aspect of my life to that point in time had left me reeling. He'd tossed me away when I'd needed him most. I was apparently a delinquent that he couldn't change.

It had shocked me into getting myself a free court-appointed lawyer and trying to make up for the shit ton of regret.

Serving time hadn't been the idea. But doing so had put me on another path, one I reminded myself of every day.

I had become a statistic of youth crime then. I absolutely wasn't going to become a white-collar criminal now.

Zali and Flynn had to go. I needed them out of my class and out of my life.

That's all there was to it.

So why did it hurt so much to turn my back and walk away?

I sighed unhappily, the high from only moments ago well and truly fizzled out. Why did I remember Zali's lips turned up in a shy smile as I'd carried her to the hot tub as she'd cuddled into me? Why did I picture Flynn with his warm eyes and fingers in my hair as we talked after we'd made love? And damnit, we had made love.

Fuck. I'd done it. I'd gone and fallen in love with them.

CHAPTER 21

Zali

The sirens grew louder. Flynn curled his hand around my nape, forcing my head down into his lap. I bit back my taunt, knowing he was on the edge. The last thing I wanted to do was fight with him over me making a stupid joke.

"Hold on," Ry ordered. Handbrake on and turning the wheel to the right, we took the corner sideways in a perfect drift. But where I was expecting him to speed up again, to zigzag through traffic on a mad rush to the airport, Ry slowed down, not even overtaking the slow-as-fuck bus in front of us.

Police cars careened past us only a few seconds later, and I swallowed hard.

That was close—too fucking close, if I was being honest.

I closed my eyes, thanking my lucky stars that we'd managed to get out of there without even a graze. Bloody security guard needed his head read. He could have killed one of us. It was a museum, for fuck's sake, not an actual bank.

It wasn't like we were holding anyone up, waving guns around ourselves. What a dickhead.

Flynn's grip on my neck eased, and he loosened my bun before running his fingers through my ponytail. He couldn't disguise the shake in his hands or the wobble in his voice when he asked Ry how far away the airport was.

"Only about ten minutes. We'll be in the air within the hour."

"Why not straight away?" I asked curiously, sitting up. There had never been any delays previously.

"Put your seatbelt on." Flynn reached over and grasped the belt, pulling it across my body and clicking it into place.

Ryder shot me a look over his shoulder. It was dark, a warning not to argue with him. "Because I need to file a flight plan and get permission to take off. Sydney airport is crowded airspace."

"Oh." I swallowed, looking between them. Ry looked murderous, anger rolling off him in waves. I was surprised I couldn't hear him grinding his teeth, given the tight set of his jaw. He was tense, his muscles coiled and ready to strike.

Flynn, on the other hand, was pale, his lips drawn into a frown and his eyes a dark flint rather than their normally vibrant blue. He'd let go of me, clasping his hands in his lap and turning away from me when I tried to smile my reassurance.

I'd put them in danger. This was why I'd wanted to go inside by myself. If I'd insisted on it, if I'd put my foot down and dropped Flynn off before even coming to Sydney, this would never have happened. I could have sent Ryder away for a coffee after having him drop me off down the street, and then I could have walked to the building. He would never have even known about this. Instead, I'd relented. I'd let them be all protective and sweet.

But I didn't need protecting, especially if it meant them getting hurt.

I was perfectly capable of doing this myself. Gripping the handle of my laptop bag tighter, I steeled my spine. I would do this myself. The data I was holding had the power to exonerate my mother. It was priceless.

My lips curled up in a cold smile. My professorhole wouldn't know what hit him.

Ryder closed and locked the plane door as I flopped into the closest of the comfortable armchairs. I was riding a high, knowing I held the key to destroying this pathetic excuse of a podcast in my hands. I'd prove the professor wrong. I'd show him that he was barking up the wrong fucking tree. Then, once I'd done that, maybe he wouldn't be such a little bitch and he'd fuck me again.

Bastard. He shouldn't have left.

"Stand up," Ry ordered, his voice hard.

"Excuse me?" I blinked, my eyes wide in surprise.

"Stand up, Zali. Don't push me." His voice was a growl, menacing and leaving no room for dissent.

I huffed out a disbelieving laugh. Who did he think he was dealing with? But I was in the mood to humour him—he had, after all, just driven the getaway vehicle. I stood up, holding my arms out with my palms up. "And what, pray tell, do you need me standing for?"

"This," he uttered as he gripped the waist of my leather pants, tugging the button open and unzipping them.

I laughed, excitement curling low in my belly at the heat in his eyes. Maybe this time Ryder and I would give Flynn a show. My cunt throbbed, the thought of getting off after the excitement of the afternoon as tempting as a hit to an addict. "Mmm...." I flicked open the buttons on my shirt as Ryder roughly tugged my leather pants and panties down.

The look in Flynn's eyes—desire heating them with a heady mix of anger and adrenaline—was an aphrodisiac. His lips were pressed into a hard line, and his hands were balled into fists. If he unleashed, he'd be rough as fuck with me.

Boy, was I down for it.

Ryder breathed deep. "You're fucking gagging for it, aren't you?"

"You gonna fuck me?" I taunted, lifting my chin up as I let my shirt slide to the floor. I unclasped my bra and tossed it aside, standing nearly naked in front of him. I had one hand on my hip, the other plucking my nipple, waiting for him to make a move.

His responding laugh was cold, and a tendril of fear snaked down my spine, the resulting throb in my cunt sending a gush of wetness through me as he said, "No."

Moving lightning fast, he grasped my wrists and pressed them together, his fingers easily encircling them. He reached out for Flynn, and my boyfriend complied without question, handing him my bra. They were on the same wavelength, and it was hot as fuck.

He bound my wrists, wrapping my bra around them tightly enough to stop me from being able to break free. I tested the give and found very little. "If your hands start to turn blue, I want to know. Otherwise, you only speak as I direct. Got it?"

"Yes." His eyes narrowed and I smiled sweetly at him. "Don't think I'll make this easy on you, Ry."

"You have no idea what you're getting yourself into, baby girl." He pointed at the table bolted to the wall that acted as the dining room for the plane. "Bend over that. Hold onto the edge."

I complied, spreading my legs as far as I could and presenting him with my cunt.

"Good girl."

I bit back my smile.

"Do you know what you did wrong today, baby girl? Do you know why I'm going to punish you?"

"Let me guess—"

The smack that landed against my exposed cunt stole my breath. This wasn't like the smack the professor had given me. This was so much harder. "Try again."

"I...."

"Yes." He rubbed my stinging skin, spreading my juices over my thighs, his thumb pressing against my hole. My clit throbbed, the pain already morphing to a heated tingle.

I squeezed my eyes closed, knowing I was provoking him. "I did insist on you both staying in the car."

The whack that followed had tears springing to my eyes, the breath whooshing from my lungs when the third one landed in exactly the same spot. He was right—this was a punishment. There was nothing pleasant about it at all.

"Wrong answer, baby girl."

I curled my fingers over the edge of the table, holding tighter. "I put you both at risk."

That soothing rub started up again, Ryder brushing my cunt with the backs of his fingers. "You did. And?"

He paused, waiting for my answer. But my mind was blank. "I stole the data?"

Fingers barely touching my clit, he asked, "Was that a question, or an answer to mine?"

"I... I don't know." My shoulders dropped and I let the table take my full body weight as I tilted my hips, all but begging him to play.

"I think you need to be taught a lesson, baby girl. Flynn?"

"Agreed."

I whipped around to face him, wide-eyed with my mouth open. I was sure he'd be able to see the shock on my face. The smirk he shot me was pure sex.

"We don't care about the data. But what else would make Flynn and me angry, baby girl?" He ran the backs of his fingers down my legs, my body jerking as he came close to my cunt, but he skated past without touching. I shook my head, completely puzzled. "Think about it, and while you do, count."

"Oh fuck," I breathed, every muscle in me locking tight.

The smack that landed left my skin singing and my cunt howling. His calloused fingers and palm connected right where the crease of my arse met my leg, directly at my cunt. "One," I mumbled.

"Nice and clear," Flynn corrected.

I lifted my face, staring at him. "One," I ground out through gritted teeth.

Smack after smack connected with my legs and arse, each one hard and unforgiving. But something was building inside me too. My juices leaked down my legs, my cunt hot and needy. I wanted to be filled. Fucked until I couldn't stand.

My nipples pebbled and my cunt clenched. I hated being so empty.

"Seven," I moaned.

"Three more, baby girl. You got an answer for me yet?"

I shook my head, defiant until the end.

Two more smacks cracked against my skin, the noise filling the plane. I gasped in a breath, clenching my cunt as the fire on my skin morphed to a burn that fanned the flames inside me hotter.

"You ready for your final smack, baby girl?" Ryder leaned down, running his tongue up my spine. I sucked in a breath as he nuzzled my ear with his nose before whispering, "What's more important to Flynn and me than anything else in the world?"

Flynn raised an eyebrow as if the answer should be obvious. When my brows furrowed, he mouthed, "You," to me. His gaze flicked up before he gave Ry a small shrug, pressing his lips together in a reluctant smile.

"Me?" I asked, confused.

"Yes, you. We're angry because you put yourself in danger. We could have lost you."

"Wait." I propped myself up on my elbows, my gaze flicking between the two of them. "You're angrier because I could have been hurt than because you could have been?"

The final smack caught me by surprise. I didn't have my body braced, and my boobs almost smacked me in the face from the force of it.

"Lovely," Ryder murmured, his voice rough as he fingered the sensitive skin on my arse. The gentle touch took me higher, my cunt lips all but begging to be spread and filled. "Is that so hard to believe, baby girl? Your man loves you."

"And you?" I stood up, needing to see his reaction when he answered.

But I was disappointed. His gaze, which had been so heated only a moment ago, shuttered. His eyes snapped to Flynn's, and he gestured with a tilt of his chin.

"Sit on Flynn's dick and get that orgasm you deserve. You took my punishment well, baby girl."

"It won't happen again," I warned.

"Of course not, boss." He dipped his head in obvious deference and strode toward the cockpit, tossing over his shoulder, "We're taking off in five."

My jaw hit the ground. What the fuck had just happened? I turned to Flynn, ready to blow my top, when I saw him. He had that fallen-angel look about him, his eyes glazed with lust and his lips red where he'd been nibbling on them. His cock was tenting his linen pants, and my mouth watered at the sight.

"On your knees, Zee. Suck me so I can fuck you nice and deep."

A gush of wetness ran down my legs, and I shifted my weight from foot to foot, trying to get some much needed friction on my cunt. The smacks had sent all the blood rushing there, my skin sizzling.

I didn't give a fuck that he saw me so needy. If anything, my whimper seemed to spur him into action. He helped me down, and when I was situated exactly where he wanted me, he dropped his pants and boxer briefs, painting my lips with the pre-cum beading at his beautiful head.

Fuck, I loved his dick.

"Next time you think about putting yourself in danger, you'll reconsider, won't you," he ordered. I nodded, extending my tongue so his glans brushed it when he ran his cock across my lips again. "Next time, we'll work as a team, won't we. We'll plan it properly. We'll make sure none of us get shot at, but especially not you."

"Yes," I moaned, needing him like I needed oxygen in my lungs.

"Suck me, Zee. I want your pretty pussy sinking onto my cock as we're taking off."

I dove down onto him, taking his cock as deep as I could. He stretched my jaw wide, and my tongue traced each of those piercings that sent both Professor Fuckface and I into orbit. Wrapping one hand around the base of his dick, I jacked him, using my free hand to roll his balls, tugging on the tight skin of his sac and slipping my finger back to play with his guiche piercing at the back of his balls.

His salty flavour flooded my tongue, and I moaned at the taste of his essence.

The plane started taxying to the runway, and I sucked him deeper, trying not to get my teeth caught on his piercings.

"That's enough, Zee," he uttered through gritted teeth. His voice was gravelly, his abs dancing as I slowly pulled off his dick.

Flynn helped me up before dropping to his knees, slipping off my heels, and yanking off my pants. He pulled himself up into the nearest seat and patted his lap. "Straddle me and sit on my dick," he ordered. "Grip the headrest and ride me."

I did exactly that, straddling him and balancing myself using the seat back. He directed his cock to my entrance, and I sank down onto him, my swollen cunt tight around his girth. I was soaked, my juices wetting my legs, and the slip eased him inside.

I moaned, pausing to revel in the stretch. He was so thick, so long and hard. I arched my back, pressing my tits in his face, and I ground down, taking him until he hit my G-spot.

Ry turned the plane, lining up with the runway before announcing over the loudspeaker, "Ladies and gentlemen, please have your tray tables stowed and your seat backs in an upright position. We'll be taking off momentarily."

He accelerated, quickly gaining speed. The G-forces generated when the plane began to lift drove Flynn's cock deeper, and I leaned into the weight of it until he was fully seated and I was writhing on him. I never wanted this moment to end. I wanted to be filled like this forever, never empty again.

My arse clenched, the phantom memory of Tristan's cock inside me haunting even my waking hours.

With his hands on my hips, Flynn pushed me down, impaling himself even deeper. I cried out, stretched to the brink.

Flynn brought his hands up to my tits, cupping them while he sucked and licked me. Each flick of his tongue, each bite of his teeth was like mainlining ecstasy. Sensation shot from my nipples to my clit, taking the scenic route through every nerve ending in my body.

I rolled my hips, needing him to move. My cunt throbbing, I pushed up on my knees, lifting myself until only the head of his cock was inside me. I slammed down again, moaning with the move.

Yes, fuck yes. This was exactly what I needed. I took control, setting the pace to a hard, deep fuck. With every pass, he connected with my G-spot, his piercings kissing the sensitive walls of my cunt and driving me higher.

I wanted to come, needed it, but I couldn't get the right angle to hit my clit. My frustrated growl had Flynn pausing. "Please," I gasped.

He looked at me with wide eyes and whispered, "Promise me."

"Anything, just touch me," I begged.

He trailed his fingers down my belly and pressed his thumb into my clit. But it was too gentle to do anything. "You won't do anything stupid alone. We can't protect you unless you give us a chance, Zee."

The raw vulnerability in his gaze, the fear, stole my breath. I leaned in and kissed him with a soft brush of lips before pressing our foreheads together. "I promise."

"Love you, Zee. I can't live without you."

"Love you too."

We started moving again then, deep grinds and long slow thrusts. Flynn pinched my clit, rolling it between his fingers until I was on the edge. Between breath-stealing kisses, each moan that erupted from my chest was an incoherent litany of praise for him. Jesus, fuck, I was gonna come.

The walls of my cunt contracted so hard, I was sure I'd strangled his cock. He gave a choked-out cry, his movements stuttering. A wave of tingles erupted over my skin, raising gooseflesh in its wake. Ecstasy exploded in my bloodstream, shooting through my veins, and my clit throbbed, sensation drowning me until I saw stars, and my vision went dark around the edges.

Flynn shouted, his cock growing impossibly harder in me. Heat flooded my core, and like afterburners on a rocket, it thrust me ever higher until I was floating weightlessly in orbit. Each pulse of his cum painting my walls was like a branding iron, an ownership mark that only we knew about.

He kept moving, gentling as he softened. His nips and licks turned soft, urging me closer so he could feast on my lips. He kissed me again, this time with a sigh of happiness, his tongue meeting mine in a slow dance that whispered sweet promises of forever.

He tugged my wrists between us and untied me, rubbing the skin where it had turned red.

His touches were tender, his kisses gentle.

Even if the professor had walked out, even if Ryder never took that leap and fucked me like I'd invited him to, I knew I'd always have Flynn. I just hoped I was enough for him.

He kissed my neck, sucking softly on the sensitive patch of skin just below my ear. "We're beginning to descend," he murmured, his arms squeezing me tighter in his embrace.

"Mmm," I mumbled.

"We should get dressed."

"Mmm." We sat there a few moments longer until Ryder dropped altitude again. We'd been in the air for forty-odd minutes. The airport was only minutes away. "We should."

He eased my bra up my arms and clipped it on before helping me stand up. "Bend over the table again. I'll help you get your pants on.

I waited, throwing a look over my shoulder at what was taking so long. Flynn was zipping up his pants, his grin cheeky as he watched his cum run down my legs.

Finally, he turned his attention to me, wiping my legs with my panties before stuffing the silk into his pocket. Lifting my feet, he eased my leather pants on, tugging them up until they were at my arse. He bit me then, sucking a mark just below the still-tingling skin where my smacks had been delivered. "Your butt is such a beautiful pink. I'll put some lotion on you when we get home."

Home. Together. I liked the sound of that.

TWENTY-TWO

Ezra

"Hi, Patricia, thanks for taking my call," I said, balancing the phone on my shoulder while I flipped the page on my notepad looking for the information Flynn had asked me for. Zali wanted access to the Reserve Bank's archives. She didn't give him any other information, so I was largely running blind. But I knew she would have already found anything publicly available—it was the data behind firewalls that she would be after.

"Not a problem, detective. What is it that I can help you with?"

"You're the director of the Reserve Bank's archive, right?" I asked, hoping I'd finally reached the right person.

"No, but I am the director of the library. The archive falls under my purview, so six of one half a dozen of the other, I suppose," she responded, her tone friendly even though she was schooling me on the ins and outs of her job.

"Okay, great. Thanks for clarifying."

I rubbed my forehead and pressed my thumb and forefinger against the bridge of my nose. I was struggling, absolutely torn between my obligations to my job and the need to be there for the people I cared about more than anyone. Knowing the turmoil that each one of them were no doubt facing was killing me.

Tris was on the edge. He'd been pushed beyond his limits this morning. I hated that I played a part in it, but introducing him to Zali and Flynn was a necessity. I didn't expect their chemistry to be so explosive and I wouldn't have guessed in a million years that he'd fall for them. But the way he looked at Zali and Flynn said it all. It was as if they'd hung the moon and stars in the sky and he was their greatest fan. And now he was facing a choice—take a risk that had very real consequences or lose the two people who'd slipped under his defences and captured his heart.

Regret was a bitch. I'd lived with it for so long. I wasn't even sure what it was like to be free from it. But Tris was different. He went after what he wanted. He didn't give up. The thing was that either choice had the potential to haunt him. I didn't want Tris to live with the same regret I did, but I didn't know how to protect him from it.

Especially because I was struggling with the same choices.

Tris wasn't the only one I was worried about. Flynn was besotted by him. Just like Zali, I'd watched him grow up turning from a timid little thing into a quiet young man who was still hesitant about his place in the world. But I was now watching him come into himself. He was a good man with a precious heart who deserved a lifetime of happiness. Even that would be a drop in the ocean against the shitty hand he'd been dealt as a kid. But I could see Tris and Zali giving it to him. He'd been standing straighter and smiling wider since Tris had come into their world and shaken up the rut Flynn and Zali had found themselves in. He was like a butterfly spreading its wings and realizing for the first time just how beautiful the world was with him in it. He hadn't lost a single iota of his charm either. His shy smiles still made my breath catch and my arms ache with how empty they were.

Zali had let her walls down too and the sight was spectacular. It was funny—she and Tris were so alike. Stubborn, fiercely determined, independent as hell, and bold and brash. But she'd shown me a softer side of herself that both Flynn and Tris brought out. It wasn't until I'd watched her with them at lunch that it occurred to me. I don't think I'd ever seen her truly relaxed and happy before, not like she'd been that day.

God, I wanted that. I wanted to see her smile every day, to look at me with love shining in her eyes like she does to Flynn and Tris. I wanted to be someone who could wrap my arms around her and kiss her.

Every day that passed, the temptation to give in, to say "fuck it" and jump in the deep end grew. I wish I could do it. But I was trapped.

Anything more between us was an impossibility, because I faced a choice too. One that there was no going back from.

She was worth it. So was Flynn. They were worth making that choice a million times over. But I wouldn't be the only one affected, and I couldn't be that selfish, not when they'd already paid too high a price for love.

I was destined to sit on the sidelines, watching and trying to keep her out of trouble so she could be happy, and Flynn could be loved.

But that delicate, gossamer-fine thread of happiness and love could never last without some hard truths being spoken. Zali needed to be forthright some time. She couldn't keep her truth from Tris, nor should she. He deserved to know what he was getting himself into, because it was more than just the podcast, or even his freedom, at risk. Being a part of Zali's, and in turn Queen's, inner circle meant accepting an inherent level of danger.

I protected all of them the best I could. I had the same level of digital resources applied to Zali, Flynn, Ry and Zali's dad as some of Australia's highest profile targets. It was significantly more than my bosses would deem necessary if they ever found out about them. But I needed to do it. Monitoring chatter on the dark web about Queen and those closest to her was about the only thing I could do short of a security detail. But none of it was foolproof.

One day I might fail. I could lose her. I could lose Flynn, or her dad or Ry. If Tris wanted in permanently, he needed to know that he could become a target too.

Zali lived among the many gradations of grey in the black and white world Tris had carefully cultivated around him. In his mind, like much of the community's, legal was good and illegal was bad. But it wasn't that simple. Zali navigated the spaces between right and wrong according to her own moral compass. She regularly stepped off the divide between the two, delving into the darkness or coming up into the light. Flynn understood. He saw the person underneath. He knew that she would come back to him in the light. But Tris didn't know that. He'd only scratched the surface and in doing so, had seen the thing that scared him the most—someone so alike him, but who thrived in those grey areas, who could sink into darkness and not be consumed by it.

I rubbed my chest, the ache in my heart worse than the one in my head. I wanted to be there for them. I wanted to help broker a peace treaty, one that would see Zali, Flynn and Tristan safe and happy.

I wanted to say fuck it all and go to them.

But I was stuck here in the office, catching up on paperwork that was already overdue.

"Detective?" Patricia asked, dragging my thoughts back to the here and now.

"Yes, sorry. I was ringing to enquire about access to the Reserve Bank's archive and what information is available," I explained.

"There is a large amount of data that's publicly available. You can search statistics and the like for much of the last one hundred years direct from the Reserve Bank's website," she replied. "Is there anything in particular you're after? Perhaps I can execute some searches for you and send through the results. I'm happy to help the AFP in any way I can, detective."

A helpful person was always good, but I doubted that the results of the librarian's search was what Zali was seeking access to.

"What about someone gaining full access? As in all the raw data instead of just the statistics?" I feigned casual, but I already knew the answer before I'd even asked the question. That kind of data was protected. Very few people would have access to the raw data, and it certainly wouldn't be made available upon request. A warrant, perhaps, but anything less would be like barking up a tree.

"Heavens, no," she gasped, her shock and censure evident in her tone. "The data set includes extremely personal information. It is protected by both privacy laws and the highest digital security protocols. Not even library staff have access to the data set. It's absolutely off-limits for everyone except a select few." She paused before adding, "I'm surprised you're even asking for this kind of data, detective. It's something I would expect that an officer of the law to know is protected."

"Yes, I was hoping it would be," I hedged with an awkward laugh, trying to think up an excuse on the fly. "But given the cyber-attacks on high profile organizations of late, my team—the High Tech Unit—is investigating possible weaknesses in banking data across the sector. As you rightly pointed out, even archived data contains personal information that can be misused." I blinked, surprised at myself. That explanation wasn't half bad given the jumble of thoughts running through my mind. The detritus in my head looked like my mind had been hit by a cyclone.

"Oh," she responded, surprised. All traces of disapproval were gone. "In that case, perhaps you should be speaking with our head of IT security rather than me. Frank will be able to run you through the protocols we have in place."

"If you could provide me with his email address, that would be helpful. Thank you."

I wrapped up the call and rubbed my eyes, groaning at the pounding behind them before I tried, and failed, to put a dent in my workload.

* * * * *

The phone rang and I was torn between being grateful for the interruption and frustrated by it. Heaving out a sigh, I lifted the handset off the cradle and answered, "Detective Fraser."

"Detective, this is Patricia from the Reserve Bank Library. We've had an incident."

T WENTY-THREE

Zali

We landed smoothly, but I was still only half dressed. I adjusted my pants, slipped into my shoes, and did up a button on my shirt. I was ready for a swim as soon as we could get the yacht out of its mooring. I needed to clear my head before I dived into this data. It would be slow going, and I had days of work ahead of me.

The last few days had taken their toll. I'd pushed myself hard, and I didn't like the person I became when I did that.

Ry taxied the plane to our normal hanger, but something was off. He stopped outside, not taking it inside like he normally did. "Ah, Zali, you'd better get up here," he announced through the speaker.

I looked at Flynn. His brows were drawn together, his lips in a frown. Unbuckling my seatbelt without another word, I strode to the cockpit and leaned over Ry's shoulder where he was seated in the pilot's chair. Before me was a sight I never expected to see. Four federal police cars were spread out in the hangar, their lights flashing, and officers and detectives either in the driver's seats or outside the car with hands on their guns.

The only one I recognized, standing front and centre, was Detective Fraser.

Another two blocked the shortcut to the runways.

"I can spin around, take off again, but that's fuckin' dangerous, Zali—"

"Or, you can park my plane in the hangar, and I'll get out and speak to the good detective."

"Zee, no—" Flynn started.

I turned to him and cupped his face, kissing him softly. "Let me handle this, Flynn." Reaching for Ryder, I squeezed his shoulder. "I need you both to trust me. Please."

"Remember what you promised."

"I will, and I promise you, I won't do anything stupid." My gaze bounced between them, trying to reassure them that I was serious. "But you need to promise me something too," I added.

"Anything."

"Give them your names and your addresses. That's it. Nothing else. Answer "No comment" to every other question they ask you. I'll get us a lawyer."

I got an immediate nod from Ryder, who moved the plane into the hanger and powered down the engines.

Flynn's acknowledgement took a lot longer. His shoulders slumped, and he blew out a breath. "Okay," he said quietly before walking away. He didn't look at me again, didn't acknowledge me as I went to stand beside him.

I reached out for him, trying to take his hand in mine.

He pulled away, slipping his hands into his pockets and looking away from me, out the window.

My heart cracked in my chest, and I blinked back tears. I tried to hide how much that move hurt, my expression stony.

I slipped the USB into my pocket, grasped the handle of my laptop bag harder, and blew out a calming breath. Mind racing, my heart thudding in my chest and knocking against my ribcage, my adrenaline was spiking again after crashing hard.

My hands shook.

I closed my eyes and focussed on breathing. I concentrated on faking a calm façade despite the storm raging inside me.

Ry asked, "Ready?" with his hands on the lock for the plane door.

"Do it," I instructed, the wobble in my voice evident. I cleared my throat, pulled my shoulders back, and lifted my chin defiantly.

This was not the time for doubt. It wasn't the time for fear or even the semblance of it. I had a job to do, one that was more important than any other I'd done before. I needed to protect Flynn and Ry. I needed to salvage whatever part of our relationship I could.

I channelled Queen, sinking into her persona.

I pictured myself naked, owning the hangar. All eyes locked on me as I walked across it. Their stares, their desires wrapping around me, spurring me on. They wanted to touch. They wanted to take. They wanted me.

A calm descended over me. My mind cleared. My heart rate slowed. My breathing evened out.

I was ready.

Pausing at the top of the stairs, I looked out over my domain and raised an eyebrow, my lips quirking up in a half smile. All these people were here for me.

Strutting down the stairs, I added an extra swish to my hips. My Manolos clicked on the concrete as I approached the man walking toward me. "Detective Fraser, nice to see you and the welcoming crew. What can I do for you today?" My voice rang out clearly in the hangar, my cocky confidence surprising a couple of the officers, sweet summer children that they were.

"Zali," he gasped, his voice cracking. He cupped my face in his hands, not even trying to hide the shake in them. His eyes were filled with worry, his normally golden skin pale and his chocolate-brown eyes dull. He looked me over, taking in every inch of my face before flicking his gaze to the men behind me. He was searching for something and sagged with relief when he apparently didn't find it.

"What's going on, Ezra?" I asked, looking up at him and trying to read what was happening. His behaviour, his anxiousness, was completely at odds with the welcome party that had been arranged for us.

He leaned in, pressing his lips to mine in a chaste kiss. His moan deep in his chest spurred me on, and I stepped closer, opening to him when he licked at my lip. His arms banded around my body, pulling me against a wall of muscle. Short-circuiting my brain, his tongue touched mine, and he tangled his hand in my hair, keeping me in place as he kissed me with a desperation I'd never imagined from him. Mr Cool, Calm, and Professional was nowhere to be found in that moment.

"Detective," a woman barked. "That's enough." Her voice was short and sharp, and like a whip cracking, it startled Ezra.

My hands curled around the lapels of his jacket. I didn't let him get far when he pulled away. His eyes were glassy when he blinked them open, regret filling them. "I'm sorry."

"What for?"

"This." He snapped a handcuff around my wrist and stepped back, breaking my hold on him. "Zali Rose Stephens, you're under arrest."

I stood stock-still, my brain going offline as he shifted to walk around behind me and gently pull my arms back. He locked the cuff around my other wrist, and like coming up from underwater, the scene around me snapped back into focus, the sounds of a scuffle filling my ears.

Shouts sounded. Urgent, angry words. Someone screaming like a wild animal.

Guns were drawn.

"Get down, now!" was yelled.

"Leave her alone," Flynn screamed.

I spun around, and my world shattered. Flynn was lying facedown on the concrete floor, an officer's knee pinning his shoulders down as another wrestled a set of cuffs onto his wrists. With his hands bound, he stopped fighting, going lax in their arms.

Tears sprang to my eyes, my heart breaking into a million pieces.

Not my Flynn.

The officer lifted his knee, and he touched Flynn's shoulder, saying something too low for me to hear. Flynn kicked his foot out, slamming it against the concrete. He roared in frustration.

The commotion in the opposite direction caught my eye. Ryder was between two huge officers. They had him off the ground.

He kicked out.

Tried to break free of their grip.

Shouted.

Still wrestling them even while pinned, he kicked out again, aiming for a knee.

The officer's leg buckled, his knee hitting the ground. A shout of pain.

Ry whirled around with his fist cocked as the other officer reached for something at his belt.

"Ry," I screamed in warning.

Another officer stepped closer, her gun raised. "Freeze." She aimed squarely at his chest. Point-blank range.

"Ryder, no!" I screeched, lurching forward as I tried to get to him. I'd take that bullet myself before I let him get hurt. "Please, stop. Don't hurt him."

Detective Fraser caught me in his arms, hugging me from behind and stopping me in my tracks. I fought him, trying to get loose. Desperate, I twisted and turned, slamming my head back.

But he held me tighter.

"Please, stop them," I begged, my voice hitching as a sob tore from my throat. Tears streamed down my face, my shattered heart stomped on and left broken and bleeding on the floor.

"They're doing their jobs, Zali." His voice was even, radiating a ghostly calm.

"Ryder, please don't fight them," I cried. But my voice was broken, my words no louder than a whisper. "Please."

I couldn't look. I couldn't watch them kill him. I turned, burying my face in Ezra's chest. "Please stop him."

"Ry," Ezra barked. "Stop."

A thud and an oomph.

"Fuck you," he spat breathlessly, but the commotion settled.

I risked a glance over my shoulder.

Ry was face first on the concrete in the same position as Flynn. His hands were cuffed behind his back, two officers' guns now trained on him.

"Get them into the cars," the same woman who'd yelled at Ezra called out. "Any resistance from this one"—she pointed at Ryder—"and you're authorized to use necessary force to restrain him again." She turned her attention to me and added, "She's with me. Fraser, make sure there are three interview rooms set up."

"Yes, inspector." He squeezed my side before escorting me to a black SUV.

He didn't meet my gaze when he buckled me in. I opened my mouth to speak, but he shook his head, silencing me.

He slammed the door closed, sealing me in a bubble of silence. They then loaded Flynn into the sedan parked next to the car I was in. I willed him to look at me, begged him to turn and face me. But he never once looked up. Never once looked over.

Through the window, Ry's glare cut like glass. His narrowed eyes bored into mine, his lips pulled back in a snarl. Anger radiated off him in waves as two officers practically dragged him to the final SUV.

Message received loud and clear. From both of them.

I clenched my jaw, shook my head, and blew out a breath. If that was how they wanted it, fine. They could walk away. They could shut me out and hate me for all I cared. I'd be fine.

Just fuckin' dandy.

The passenger door opened, and the inspector slipped in while her colleague moved around the front to get into the driver's side. "You're in deep shit, missy."

I laughed, the sound as cold as my dead soul. *Bitch, that's what you think. I'm fucking Queen.*

Haven't had enough of Zali and her men?
Download the bonus chapter:
https://dl.bookfunnel.com/8st23nd78m

The series continues with Bosshole. Order it now at: https://books2read.com/QueensBosshole

He's my boss. I'm his biggest challenge.

I'm a hacker. He's a police detective. Controlling me was never an option—I'm not the good girl he thinks I am. But working for the police has its advantages. It distracts them while I reap the rewards from my skills and live the billionaire lifestyle—yachts, planes, shoes, and men.

Until my bosshole arrests me.

But gathering evidence to exonerate my late mother was worth the risk.

My bosshole has a lot to answer for, especially the kiss that rocked my world.

Now, I can't get them out of my head—my bosshole, my professorhole, and my best friend. I crave them, desperate to be consumed by the fire they ignite in me. I yearn to watch them together.

They're all my fantasies come to life.

It *will* happen too.

If I can prove my innocence.

If I can stop my best friends from being jailed.

I am Queen. I *will* prevail.

♥♥♥♥♥

Billionaire Boss Girl is a contemporary why choose/polyamorous series. There is no need for the leading lady (or her men) to choose in order to find their HEA.

Bosshole is book TWO of THREE in this slow build, high heat new adult romantic suspense series.

Order Bosshole now at:
https://books2read.com/QueensBosshole

I appreciate your help in spreading the word, including telling a friend. Reviews help readers find books! Please leave a review on your fave review site.

About Ann Grech

By day Ann Grech used to live in the corporate world and could be found sitting behind a desk typing away at reports and papers or lecturing to a room full of students. She graduated with a PhD in 2016 and is now an over-qualified nerd. But the grind got old, and the voices got louder. She still has the librarian look nailed, but she's a little freer to be herself now.

She's never entirely fit in and loves escaping into a book—whether it's reading or writing one. But she's found her tribe and loves her book world family. She dislikes cooking, but loves eating, can't figure out technology, but is addicted to it, and her guilty pleasure is Byron Bay Cookies. Oh and shoes. And lingerie. And maybe handbags too. Well, if we're being honest, we'd probably have to add her library too given the state of her credit card every month (what can she say, she's a bookworm at heart)!

In 2019 she was an Award-Winning Finalist in the Fiction: LGBTQ category of the 2019 Best Book Awards sponsored by American Book Fest for her story In Safe Arms.

She also publishes her raunchier short stories under her pen name, Olive Hiscock.

Ann loves chatting to people online, so if you'd like to keep up with what she's got going on:

Join her newsletter (you'll get two free books!):
https://landing.mailerlite.com/webforms/landing/d8m4r2

Follow her on Instagram:
@anngrechauthor

Follow her on TikTok:
@authoranngrech

Like her on Facebook:
https://www.facebook.com/pages/Ann-Grech/458420227655212

Join her reader group:
https://www.facebook.com/groups/1871698189780535/

Follow her on Goodreads:
https://www.goodreads.com/author/show/7536397.Ann_Grech

Follow her on BookBub:
https://www.bookbub.com/authors/ann-grech

Follow her on Amazon:
https://www.amazon.com/~/e/B00IJPO3EM

Visit her website for her current booklist:
http://www.anngrech.com/

She'd love to hear from you directly, too. Please feel free to e-mail her at ann@anngrech.com or check out her website for updates.

ANN GRECH'S BOOKS

BILLIONAIRE BOSS GIRL

Professorhole (why choose/Polyamorous – MMMMF)
Bosshole (why choose/Polyamorous – MMMMF)
Alphahole (why choose/Polyamorous – MMMMF)

RULE OF THREE

Three Hearts (MMF) (Also available in audio)
Yes, Captain (MM)
Triple Beat (MMF)
Threepeat (MMF)
Third Time's A Charm (MMF)
Triple Threat (MMF)

PEARCE STATION DUET

Outback Treasure I (MM)
Outback Treasure II (MM)

SPINOFF FROM PEARCE STATION

Three of Us (MMF)

UNEXPECTED

Whiteout (MM)

White Noise (MM)
Whitewash (MM)

MY TRUTH

All He Needs (MMM)
In Safe Arms (MM)

STANDALONES

Home For Christmas (MM)
The Gift (FMMM - free for newsletter subscribers)
Take Two (MM – free for newsletter subscribers)

M/F TITLES

One night in Daytona
Ink'd

GERMAN TRANSLATIONS

Outback Treasure I
Outback Treasure II